# Finding Somewhere to Belong

## Seaside Wolf Pack Book 1

C.C. Masters

# DEDICATION

Dedicated to everyone who has supported me along this journey!

Special thanks goes out to the Seaside Wolf Pack for always keeping me inspired and motivated.

# Chapter 1

The morning my life changed forever, there was no warning, no omen, and no signs of the dark events on the horizon. I woke up to a bright, sunny bedroom and two puppies happily licking my face to get me to wake up. I groaned and wiped off my now sticky cheeks with the back of my hand. The pups were ready to get out of bed, and that meant I was, too, whether I liked it or not.

I rolled out of bed and landed on my feet. My two wards for the weekend wagged their little tails, eager for me to lift them off the bed so that they could run free. Luckily for me, they were too small to jump off themselves. Otherwise, I could see them getting into trouble during the night. I was too soft-hearted to lock them in their kennel and listen to them cry themselves to sleep at night.

I stretched out my back and followed them as they ran ahead of me to the kitchen. I couldn't help but grin as I watched the two puppies slipping, sliding, and scrambling to be the first one to the door. Their excitement was infectious, and it was impossible to be grumpy when those two little guys were so joyful at the simple fact that the sun had come up for another day.

When I opened the back patio door, they gleefully bounded out into the fenced-in backyard, ready to explore. I, however, wasn't prepared for my day to start just yet - coffee was needed. I made my first cup like a zombie and brought it out to the patio so I could watch the puppies. I gradually started to come to life as the scent of coffee drifted up to me, and I wrapped my hands around the mug, blowing gently on the top so I could get it cool enough to drink.

Kelsey was coming back into town later tonight. I needed to tidy up her house and bathe her puppies before being relieved of my house-sitting duties. I honestly looked forward to the weekends she went out of town, whether it be for business or her man of the month. She had an awesome house two blocks from the beach, two adorable little Shih Tzu puppies going on eight months old, and a fenced-in backyard to provide plenty of entertainment for them.

I inhaled the delicious aroma as I brought my mug up for the first sip of the day. I also had lunch planned with Evelyn today after she got back from church. This morning I wanted to take the pups for a walk on the beach to tire them out. That way, I'd be able to escape the house later this afternoon while they napped.

Barking caught my attention, and I looked up to see the pups had chased something up a tree and were intent on getting it to come back down. Since they were finished doing their business for the morning, I decided to call them back in and give the creature they were chasing a break.

I leaned out the door and glanced around to see if anyone was within hearing range, then winced before I shouted, "Tigger! Eeyore! Breakfast time!" Yes, Kelsey had named her pups Tigger and Eeyore, which is why I referred to them most of the time as "the puppies" or "the pups." It could be worse; she could have gone with Piglet.

Eeyore could be as serious as his namesake sometimes, but he was very smart and would stop and think before jumping into anything new. He had a pure black coat and dark eyes that added to his somber appearance. Tigger, on the other hand, was always happily bouncing from place to place and had a white and gold coat. He wasn't as cautious as Eeyore, and I had to watch him more closely to prevent him from getting in trouble.

The morning flew by, and by noon I had the house cleaned, and the puppies fed, walked, bathed, and tired out. They settled down in their kennel for a nap, and I picked up the baked mac and cheese I was bringing as my contribution to our weekly Sunday lunch.

Evelyn lived about five minutes away from Kelsey, which is another reason I didn't mind house-sitting for her. If I weren't staying at Kelsey's, it would have been at least a forty-five-minute drive from home to Seaside for me. loved the idea of living at the beach, but it was more practical to live close to my job instead. I also saved money, and I saved a bundle by living across the tunnel in Port Idris. Seaside was an expensive place to live because of its proximity to the beach and tourist areas.

I think Evelyn was pleased with my decision as well. She didn't bring it up often, or ever. But I knew she was still worried about her past coming back to haunt her, even though her dark past was almost forty years ago. She had sat me down for a serious discussion about it only once in the sixteen years that I'd known her. I thought about the last time we had "the talk" back when I was about to graduate high school and head out into the world.

*I knocked on the door and let myself in as usual. "Evelyn, I'm here!" I called out.*

*Her voice floated out to me. "In the sitting room, dear." She didn't have a living room, she had a "sitting room" or "parlor" and would frown at me if I dared to suggest it was a living room.*

*I slunk down the hall and to the right. Today hadn't been a good day for my uncle, and he was in rare form. After one of his episodes, I had a difficult time standing up straight or meeting anyone's eyes, preferring to lurk in the shadows unseen.*

*Evelyn's warm smile greeted me, but I could tell she had a serious look in her eye. She sat on the sofa in front of a coffee table covered in pictures and waved me forward. I hesitated in the doorway, and she gave a sad sigh when she took in my current state.*

*She knew better than to try to hug me, as we had been through this more than a few times before. I preferred to pretend nothing had happened, and she was resigned to the fact that she could do absolutely nothing about it. Her very life depended on her staying unnoticed and anonymous. Making accusations against a well-liked and respected police officer would drag her out in the public eye and catch the attention of some dangerous people.*

*She patted the sofa next to her, and I gingerly sat down on the edge of the seat and leaned forward to see what she was doing with the pictures. I'd never seen any photos of her family before, and she rarely mentioned her daughter. I looked up at her and saw her gazing sadly down at the photos in front of her.*

*She picked one up of a sad-looking girl who was about my age. "This was me," she said softly. "I printed these out at the local library. Did you know that they have high school yearbooks on the Internet now?"*

*"Hmmm." I had the feeling that if I stayed quiet and didn't interrupt, she might continue. Evelyn never spoke in detail about her past, and I'd never seen her in a sharing mood like this before.*

*Evelyn picked up the photos one by one. Some looked more recent, maybe from the eighties or nineties? They were professional photos of different high school clubs, but all of them had one girl in common. I'm guessing that was her daughter. She didn't say anything as she gazed at the pictures with a sense of nostalgia, and it was killing me not to ask any questions.*

*I finally blurted out, "Are these of your family? That's great that you were able to find those-"*

*She cut me off immediately with a sharp look in her eye. "It's not great, it's dangerous." She swept all the photos up into her arms and stalked over to the fireplace. "I wanted to show you these to warn you. You might think that you're safe in hiding, but you're not. You're never truly safe...." Evelyn's voice trailed off, and she leaned against the fireplace. Her exhaustion came on just as quickly as the burst of energy that had originally carried her over there. She tiredly tossed her stack of photos into the unlit fireplace.*

*"I like to think that I left it all behind me," she started, then paused. She turned and headed back towards the sofa, taking a seat and leaning back. "This is just one reminder that anyone can come for me at any time. If the wolves find me, they CANNOT know about you. They will take you, and your life now will seem pleasant in comparison."*

*A chill ran through me at the look in her eyes. "There's no way anyone could recognize you from those pictures, Evelyn. You look so different now-"*

*"The pack would know," she told me adamantly. "They always know more than you could possibly imagine." I was doubtful that high school photos of Evelyn and her daughter could lead anyone to Seaside, where she was hiding under a different identity. Still, I knew better than to mention it to Evelyn when she was in one of her paranoid moods.*

*"I haven't mentioned this before because I didn't want to scare you more than I have to." Evelyn paused and appeared to be considering her words carefully. "Female wolves are becoming rare and are considered valuable by most packs. Human females have a difficult time conceiving and carrying wolves. A human female rarely gives birth to a healthy baby that was fathered by a male wolf. It's even rarer that the baby has the abilities of a full-blooded wolf. Most of those children never turn." She took a deep breath. "I didn't." Shock hit me like a punch to the stomach. Evelyn was half-wolf?*

*She continued, oblivious to my shock. "Males are put out of the pack if they aren't able to shift, but females are kept to produce the next generation. My pack thought that they could gradually breed the human part back out of the line. My daughter would have been seventy-*

*five percent wolf, and her daughter even more. The pack didn't consider bearing children to be optional, even though the risk of death was high for females who had even a small amount of human blood. And they make examples out of those who try to run to keep the rest in line...*"

I was horrified, and a wave of nausea hit me. This is what must have kept Evelyn in hiding all these years. I swallowed nervously, not wanting to ask but still wanting to know. "Your daughter?" I said softly.

"Yes, she only made it five months along," she replied with tears in her eyes. She grasped both of my hands in a shockingly strong grip. "You have to promise me that if anyone suspicious comes around asking questions, or if anything happens to me – you run. You don't look back, you don't try to help, you just run."

I couldn't meet her eyes, trying to form words to communicate the fear, sadness, and compassion that I felt for her and what she must have gone through. She gave my hands another squeeze. "Promise me!"

I'd never heard Evelyn raise her voice to me before. I was shocked enough to look up into her eyes to see desperation there. "I made it through what happened to me, I made it through what happened to my daughter, but I can't..." Her voice broke, and a tear slowly started down her cheek.

"The only way I can go to my end peacefully is to know that you'll be safe. Don't make an old lady give up her peaceful afterlife to haunt you." A small grin quirked the corner of her mouth up as she tried to inject some humor and lighten the mood.

My throat closed as I tried to speak. I couldn't imagine a world without Evelyn in it. She has been a constant, steady presence in my life since she found me at ten years old. I was covered in dirt, naked in her garden, and completely confused about what was happening to me. I'd just changed back to human after my first experience as a wolf. She had guided and supported me through so much the last eight years that I couldn't imagine my life without her.

Almost as if following my thoughts, she added, "I've already lived a fulfilling life. You're just starting yours."

All of the emotions swirling around inside of me were just too much for my teenage self to handle. I buried my face in my hands and *broke down into sobs. Evelyn gently patted my hand. "Know that anything I do is always in your best interest."*

*My wracking sobs slowly calmed into hiccups. I wiped my eyes and looked up at her. "I..."*

*"I know this is too much to put on you right now, but there's never a good time to have a discussion like that." She got to her feet and gestured for me to do the same.*

*"Let's get you cleaned up. I need help making sugar cookies for my bible study."*

*The discussion was over, and we never spoke of it again. But there were times when she would get a sad look in her eye when commenting on how I was growing up into a young lady, and I could tell she was thinking of her daughter.*

Evelyn was a sweet older woman who I met during my difficult and confusing transition. She wasn't a wolf herself, but she had grown up as human intertwined in a wolf pack - and not in a good way. She had recognized me for what I was and guided me in getting control over the shifts and my wolf.

It was a challenging process. Evelyn's experience with the change had been limited to watching a few other wolves come of age and transition; she had never experienced any of it herself. But she had done her best to impart all of the wisdom and knowledge she had obtained over the years. And as I got older, I realized just how lucky I was to have had her in my life.

From the way Evelyn's pack had treated her, I wouldn't have been surprised if she'd wanted nothing to do with another wolf for as long as she lived. It showed what a kind soul that she had that she was willing to help a confused, potentially dangerous lone wolf like me.

What about my pack? I've never had one. I was adopted as a baby to a couple who had no idea what I was. When I was eight, they were killed in a car crash, and I was sent to live with my adopted uncle and his family. I don't have any memories of my life before I moved in with my uncle, and I don't remember my parents at all.

My uncle wasn't pleased to be saddled with another kid. He already had three of his own and barely tolerated them. But he was a police officer who wanted to move up in the ranks and become a pillar of the community, so throwing me out into the streets wasn't an option for him. However, being forced to feed, house, and clothe me made him resentful and me a frequent target for his anger.

In public, he always put on a smile and spoke about how glad he was to have me in their lives. He would make it a point to tell people that I was the adopted daughter of his sister-in-law. That way they'd be impressed and tell him what a great and charitable man he was for taking me in.

Out of the public eye, it was a completely different story. I don't like to dwell on the past, but one of the happiest days of my life was getting out of that house. The only bright spots of my childhood were when I would run over to Evelyn's house. No one even noticed if I disappeared for a few hours if my chores were done. Evelyn was always happy to see me, and I think she thought of me as the granddaughter that had never been born. I'd always considered her to be my grandmother, even though I'd never told her that.

I shook myself out of my nostalgia, picked up my bag, and maneuvered to scoop up the mac and cheese on my way to the door. I headed out to the car, and after some more finagling, I managed to make it into the car without dropping the food.

It was a short drive, so I had the windows down. The cool breeze blew through my hair, but I didn't mind the cold, and I enjoyed the scent of the ocean. As I drove down the road, I could see small slices of the ocean between the houses as I coasted past. How nice would it be to just walk out to the beach any time you wanted? I briefly fantasized about morning walks on the beach and late-night dips in the ocean beneath the stars. I did get a small taste of that every month or so when I would house-sit for Kelsey, but it wasn't enough.

As I got closer to Evelyn's house, I saw the flash of police lights. I had a brief thought about her neighbor, Mrs. Peterson, who had several children that tended to be accident-prone. I'd been called upon to patch them up or evaluate if they needed a trip to the emergency room quite a few times over the past couple of years. I hoped all of them were okay...

It wasn't until I pulled up across from Evelyn's house that I realized the cars weren't just on the street, but also in Evelyn's driveway. I panicked, thinking of all the things that could have happened while I was taking my sweet time getting here. Images flashed in my eyes as I ran up to the house. Did she fall on the stairs? Have a heart attack? She was healthy as far as I knew, but she was in her seventies. My heart was pounding as I reached the two men standing on her front steps.

They had been watching me coming with sharp and suspicious eyes. I stopped in front of them and pushed my mess of wavy blonde hair back. I stood up straight, trying to look less like a crazy person.

"Is Evelyn okay?" I asked with a catch in my breath.

Both the men eyed me, then looked at each other, almost seeming to have a silent conversation as I waited anxiously. The dark-haired man on the left shrugged and pulled a notepad and pen out of his back pocket. The man on the right, with the salt and pepper hair and a bit of a paunch to his belly, squared his shoulders back as he spoke.

"Who are you, and what is your relationship to the d - to Miss Evelyn Heights?"

"I'm her friend! We were meeting here for lunch, she doesn't have any family, and she is an older woman who lives alone. I check on her sometimes and spend time with her because we were neighbors while I was growing up." All of that came out in a rush, and I realized I was babbling.

He quirked an eyebrow, and I took a deep breath. Right. I need to sound less defensive and more assertive if I was going to get anything out of them. I raised my chin a little. "And who are you?"

"I'm sorry, ma'am. We should have introduced ourselves. I'm Detective Finn, and this is Detective Myrtle," he gestured to his dark-haired companion with the notebook.

Detective Myrtle gave me a brief nod and went back to writing in the notebook.

"Detective Finn, I'm guessing that since two police detectives are standing in front of Evelyn's house..." My voice cracked, and I paused to take another deep, calming breath. Then I managed to continue to force the words out. "...that something...bad has happened." I tried to keep my composure, but my heart was pounding, and a deep sense of dread was slowly filling me.

Detective Finn gave me a brief evaluating look. "Miss Heights was found this morning by her neighbor, who was picking her up for church. The circumstances are under investigation at this time, but I can tell you that she has passed."

I stared at him in horror and disbelief.

I'm sure that Detective Finn caught on to the storm of emotions that were raging inside of me. He gave me what I guess was supposed to be a reassuring smile, but it came off as cold and impersonal. "I know that this is difficult, but I'm going to need to take down your info and have you come down to the station for a statement. I'm sure that as a friend of Miss Heights, you want to do everything you can to help with the investigation…"

His voice started to fade into just an indistinct blur, and a sense of numbness settled over me. His partner stepped in, and I robotically gave him my information as he wrote it down in the book.

"You live in Port Idris? Isn't that a bit of a drive?" His question drew me out of my daze as I tried to process his words.

"I'm staying in Seaside this weekend, and I'm housesitting to take care of my friend's dogs while she's out of town," I mumbled.

Detective Finn's eyes snapped to mine immediately. "What kind of dogs?"

I blinked, confused for a second as to why he would ask that. "Shih Tzus?" I replied, a question in my voice.

He seemed almost disappointed. "Those are small dogs, right?."

"Yes." I frowned. "They're about eight pounds now, but will probably be fourteen or so when they're full grown."

He lost interest again. Strange, why would…suddenly, it hit me. He was questioning me about dogs, but should he instead be asking about wolves? My heart started pounding again, panic chasing away the numbness.

His voice had faded out as my thoughts drowned him out, but I tuned back in when he reached towards me to hand me a business card. "…give you a call when we need you to come in." They both nodded at me and turned back to the front door to make it clear I'd been dismissed.

Another man in a full-on hazmat suit opened the front door. Both detectives stood up straight, giving him their full attention, and the three of them started to murmur quietly.

I started to back away, still in panic mode. Why would that police officer need to be wearing a hazmat suit? I was horrified, and a small part of me thought that if I could just get out of here, this would all just go away. I could drive back down the street and come back to Evelyn's house again. This time, she would be waiting for me at the front door with a smile, and we would have lunch, just like we had planned.

I turned to go back to my car and almost bumped into a uniformed officer coming up the driveway. "If the detectives have your info, then you're free to go," he told me sternly. The three men in the doorway stopped their murmured conversation and realized that I was still there. All four of them watched me with cold eyes as I headed back down the driveway to my car. Once I climbed into the driver's seat, they continued their conversation and then went back into the house.

I sat with my head pressed on the steering wheel. I tried to slow my breathing and get control of all the emotions running through my head. But maybe it wasn't her? They could have made a mistake. If there were wolves involved...I swallowed, not wanting to create any mental imagery, but hope slowly started to fill my heart. Maybe...

A sharp knock on my window brought my head up immediately. Mrs. Peterson waved at me. I got out of the car and leaned on the car door to support my shaking legs.

Mrs. Peterson reached out for my hand. "Isn't it so sad? I couldn't believe it! I'll *never* get the image of poor Mrs. Heights just lying there..."

"So, it was her?" I sharply interjected.

She looked at me with pity. "That's right, dear, I forgot you were so close to her. It was *definitely* her." She leaned in closer to me. "There are rumors, though."

I looked at her in disbelief for a moment. If she had come to pick Evelyn up for church, it would have been only hours ago that Mrs. Peterson had found Evelyn. Why is there gossip about this already?

Wait, I should know better. I grew up in a small town, so I know how petty and callous people could be when it came to gossip. I always thought of Mrs. Peterson as one of the good ones, though. I certainly hadn't thought she was a gossipmonger; she had three boys, was a working mom, and drove a minivan carpool to soccer practices for the team.

I guess I took too long to provide any new rumors or gossip for her to spread around because she straightened back up and sniffed. "I guess we should leave all that up to the police."

"Yeah..." I responded as my mind ground through the facts that I had so far. Mrs. Peterson turned away and started to head up the street, where a small group of Evelyn's neighbors were straining their necks to see what was going on at Evelyn's house.

"Mrs. Peterson!" I called out.

She turned halfway towards me reluctantly. Obviously, her heart was set on a more captive audience.

"When you found her, was she…I mean, do you think she suffered?" My voice cracked on the last word, and tears threatened to overwhelm the brief sense of calm that I managed to find.

Mrs. Peterson looked uncomfortable for a moment. "Well, I'm not sure I should say."

She looked at me sympathetically. "I know she's in a better place now, dear. Whatever she went through in the past, I know she's happy now and looking down on us from heaven." Mrs. Peterson turned back and hurried toward the group of neighbors who were now awaiting her arrival with rapt interest, no doubt to see if she had managed to get any more details out of me.

I got back in my car. I couldn't even catalog all the emotions I was feeling right now. Guilt for not being there when she needed me, for not being able to protect her. Grief from the thought that I would never see her smile again. I was angry that someone had taken her from me. I was embarrassed at how selfish I'd been for thinking of myself. What had she gone through? What had she been feeling in her last moments? And lastly, I was overwhelmed with sadness. I hoped she had reunited with her daughter in death.

My mind went back to "the talk" we had eight years ago. Had Evelyn moved on, or was she hanging around as a spirit, waiting to see if I would follow her directions? She had wanted me just to run and not look back if something like this happened.

But I didn't want to run. I wanted to find who her murderer was and rip them apart. If I was honest with myself, I wanted to find who was responsible for making her entire life miserable, for causing the death of her daughter, for making her run and live her life in fear.

I needed to do something other than sit here and wallow in my emotions. I couldn't help Evelyn while she was alive, but I had nothing left to lose now that she was gone. First things first, I needed to figure out who did this and if they were going to come after me next.

I needed to plan and be smart about this. If wolves were involved, I needed to get into the house to smell the crime scene. If I were in my wolf form, I would be able to detect if there had been wolves there. If I ever came across those scents again, I'd be able to identify them as the killers.

I started up my car with a purpose. I needed to get into Evelyn's house after the police were done, but before they finished cleaning up all traces of what had happened. My resolve started to slip when I thought of what they would be cleaning, and my horror at picturing the scene caused nausea to come back up. I took a deep breath and then stubbornly pushed away the images that were overwhelming me to focus on my plan.

I checked the clock with a quick glance to see that Kelsey would be back in a few hours. I still had time to get back to her house, pack up my weekend gear, and then take the pups out to the beach before she returned. The pups had just gotten a bath, but I needed to do something other than just sit and wait. Maybe the ocean would soothe some of the pain and allow me to stay focused on my new mission.

# Chapter 2

While waiting for Kelsey, I accomplished everything I put on my list of things to do, plus I also cooked her favorite dinner: chicken marsala. I'd thought that it would help if I kept moving and working on things to keep my mind busy, at least until I had time to be alone and process everything. Deep down, I wondered if this was me trying to stay in denial of what happened to Evelyn.

I was just putting the final touches on my culinary masterpiece when I heard the front door open and close. I knew it was Kelsey - her heels clicked down the hallway as she headed to the kitchen.

"Anna, OMG, that smells divine." Kelsey came into the kitchen, striding along in her super-high designer heels and cute little dress. Kelsey was a blonde like me, but that's where our similarities ended. Where I was tall, she was petite. She was a size zero to my size eight. She was heart-stoppingly gorgeous with perfect hair and makeup and dressed in stylish clothes; I was the girl in jeans and a messy ponytail.

Being around her always made me even more self-conscious about myself. I was usually uncomfortable with my height being 5'10," but towering over her made me feel even worse. I was tall even in grade school – taller than all the boys, so they had taken to calling me a "gorilla" or "big bird," and that's how I have thought of myself ever since. A big, hulking gorilla.

I confided in Kelsey one night after we had a few drinks, and she blinked at me in surprise before looking me up and down. "I guess I have always wanted to be taller." She paused and then looked again. "But I wouldn't want everything to be proportionally bigger, you know, like, I would still want to have slim thighs and everything." That had *not* made me feel better about myself.

I did yoga and ran daily, so I was fit and in shape, but I was more curvy than slender. On my good days, I tried to reassure myself by saying I was more Kate Upton than Kate Moss. When Kate Upton had first started modeling, everyone told her she was too fat to be in the business, but look at her now. On my bad days, I couldn't even convince myself of that.

Kelsey smiled and happily got a couple of plates out of her cupboard. "Kitchen or dining room?"

"Actually, Kels, I can't stay."

Kelsey pouted her perfect lips. "Annnaaaaa, I need you to catch me up on everything since I've been gone."

I rolled my eyes. "The puppies and I ate, went on walks, and slept. Consider yourself caught up."

"Oh, fine. What I wanted to say was that I want to tell you all about my weekend. I have pics!" She excitedly slid into one of the counter stools and scrolled through her phone. "Gregor is just so amazing," she gushed. "I can't believe I just spent the weekend on his yacht."

I was happy for Kelsey, but I couldn't keep the fake smile plastered on my face for much longer; I was barely holding myself together. I needed to get out of here and be alone.

"Kels, I really gotta go," I stated as I picked up my bag. "Enjoy the dinner, the puppies are sound asleep in their kennel." She looked surprised for a second, then frowned.

She cocked her head at me and tapped her fingers on the counter, setting down her phone.

Her eyes narrowed. "C'mon Anna. I know you don't have anywhere to be. It's not like you have a social life outside of hanging around my friends and me." She stood up and came towards me. "Why are you being so selfish when I told you that I need to talk to you?" she asked callously.

And here was mean Kelsey. Mean Kelsey made appearances regularly when she didn't get her way, but as her trusty sidekick, I wasn't usually on the receiving end of her bitchiness.

I felt a flash of irritation at her reaction to me wanting to leave. I was being selfish? How could she be so oblivious? I wasn't in the mood for a confrontation tonight, and I really didn't want to talk to her about what had happened to Evelyn. Kelsey was the person you called when you wanted to go out and have fun, not the shoulder you would lean on when something terrible happened in your life. I was at a loss for how to handle this situation, so I just sighed and stepped around her. "Bye, Kels."

"Fine, you can just forget about the party on Friday." The intensity of her viciousness stopped me mid-stride. I looked back at her for a second to see pure rage on her face. She picked up the pan of chicken marsala, stepped over to the trash can and dumped it while she looked me in the eyes the entire time. Hurt bubbled up inside me, and I felt betrayed. After all that happened earlier today, my only friend had turned against me.

I pushed those feelings aside. This was just how Kelsey reacted when she felt she'd been slighted. We were both fucked up in how we related to other people – just in different ways. About a year ago, I'd canceled my plans with her to go out on a date. I was excited but nervous because going out with a guy I was crushing on was a massive step for me. Partially because when I stand next to Kelsey, I'm utterly invisible to men, but also because of my trust issues.

It was difficult for me to open up and trust this guy enough to say yes to a date, but I'd been proud of myself for doing it. Kelsey wasn't at all impressed that I forced myself to step out of my comfort zone and try to live life like a normal twenty-something-year-old woman. Not only was Kelsey not happy for me, but she was also very vocal about me 'abandoning' her for some guy who didn't even like me. She then made a point to sleep with the guy a few days later after a disappointing date. I guess she proved her point that he didn't really like me after all. I'd been furious with her and had struggled to see it from her point of view.

I'd been devastated because I'd reached out to someone and attempted to leave my safe bubble of isolation, only to have it end in disaster. It could have been worse - I could have fallen for the guy and then had my heart broken. But even *I* couldn't believe that whole-heartedly. Sometimes Kelsey was just a bitch.

I hadn't told Evelyn the whole story, but I did tell her that I went on a date and wouldn't be seeing the guy again. She had looked sad but told me, "It's for the best. You shouldn't be going out and meeting strange men. What if you ran into another wolf?"

She was right, of course. I scolded myself for believing I could pretend to be a normal girl and resigned myself to being single for life.

I hunched my shoulders forward as I passed through Kelsey's front door and quietly closed it behind me. I tried my best to clear my mind on the drive home, but I was a mess of emotions. I was angry, but it wasn't completely Kelsey's fault. She might react harshly, but deep down it was just because she was hurt. She hadn't had the greatest childhood either, but her defense mechanism was going on the offensive before anyone had the chance to hurt her.

Kelsey and I became friends in our freshman year in college. We had been randomly placed together as roommates and had bonded quickly even though our personalities were opposites. I was quiet, shy, and awkward. Kelsey was outgoing, fun, and extroverted. I liked to stay in and study, she wanted to go out and party. I helped make her a little more responsible, and she helped make me a little more adventurous. We had struggled on occasion because we communicated differently, and sometimes things didn't quite translate. That was why I wasn't too worried about tonight; we would work things out like we always did. This wasn't the first time that I'd run from my emotions and avoided her.

As it wasn't yet dark by the time I got home, I figured I would go for a run and blow off some steam so I would be calmer for tonight's secret mission. I'd thought about staying in Seaside, as it was a forty-five-minute drive home and then another forty-five minutes back, but I realized that I probably needed dark clothes to sneak into the house unseen. The trip would help to keep me focused on something other than my volatile emotions that swirled just below the surface.

After my run, I showered and put my pale blond hair into a tight bun so none of the strands could escape. I headed to my closet to evaluate if any of the contents would be suitable for a nighttime reconnaissance mission. Black yoga pants were a yes; stretchy would help me move fast and comfortably.

I looked at the rest of my selection of black in disappointment. A black tank top would work, but it would leave too much of my pale skin exposed. A black dress was also a no, for obvious reasons. My only black blouse was too dressy and uncomfortable for sneaking around in. I did have a black hoodie - but it had bright graphics. With my luck, someone would see the Northern Peninsula logo glowing in the dark.

I pulled on the yoga pants and black tank and decided to stop at the store for a black hoodie and hat. A black ski mask would scream burglar, so if anyone did stop me, I would have absolutely no reasonable explanation for what I was doing. Maybe I would be able to find a black baseball cap. I pulled on some sneakers so I could use the 'out late for a run on the beach' excuse if I were stopped.

After a successful trip to the store for my black clothing items, I slowly drove past Evelyn's house to see if the coast was clear.

Unfortunately, I saw the Peterson's light still on; it looked like they were all in the living room with a direct line of sight to Evelyn's house. I sighed; I would have to have to wait for them to go to bed first before I could do any late-night snooping.

I drove around the block slowly while I considered my options. In all honesty, my plan was highly dependent on me being able to shift into a wolf, quickly get the scents I needed, investigate what I could, then shift back and leave. Now that I was here, I was doubtful about my ability to carry out this plan.

Could I sneak into the house unseen? Yes. Could I change into a wolf so I could investigate? Yes. Could I quickly get the scents and conduct a short investigation before changing back into a human and sneaking back out of the house unseen? Hmmm, probably not.

I liked to think that I had control over my wolf, and in a way, I do. I don't shift accidentally, but it's difficult for me to restrain my wolf once I let her out. Once I changed into my wolf tonight, she was going to want to run free and get out all her pent-up energy before she did anything that human-me wanted her to do.

And I wasn't sure that I could even convince her to change back into a human quickly - it was going to be a difficult challenge. I was kind of banking on the extreme importance of the mission to hold her to the task, but I wasn't quite sure I could do it.

There was a state park not too far from where I was now that I'd initially identified as a possible place to let my wolf out when I first moved here. But I'd crossed it off the list when I realized how close the nearby campground was. The chances of the campers going on late night explorations and running into my wolf were too high to risk. I wasn't worried about my wolf hurting anyone, but I did worry about being spotted and making it on the news.

The last thing I need is a bunch of humans spotting a "wolf" in Virginia and having that reach the ears of any wolf packs out there. I couldn't afford to have them sniffing around here and accidentally come across me. Evelyn had told me that this area was generally one of the places considered to be safe for lone wolves because there weren't any packs here. She had assumed it was because of the strong military and government presence. This area had the largest Navy base in the country, a large Navy airfield, shipyards, Army and Marine bases, and one of the most extensive military health care networks in the country.

I'd taken advantage of the lack of wolves here to attend college at the Northern Peninsula School of Pharmacy. I'd been lucky enough to be accepted into the pharmacy doctorate program after finishing all the requirements for a bachelor's degree in three years of undergrad studies.

After graduation, I accepted a job at the military hospital here. I thought that it would be doubly safe: pack wolves would keep away from this area because of its no-man's-land status, and wandering wolves wanted to avoid an area controlled by the government and the military.

I did regret not being able to join the military because of my fear as being caught as a supernatural masquerading as a human. But as a civilian pharmacist in a military hospital, I had the same daily pharmacist responsibilities as the military pharmacists but without the collaterals, politics, and deployments. Perhaps most importantly of all, I didn't have to submit to any medical tests. I didn't know if any of those tests would reveal my genetic abnormalities, but I didn't want to take the chance.

Evelyn had approved of my plan and followed me to the general area. She had moved to the beach, saying that she always wanted to live near the ocean. I lived near my school, and then near work after I graduated. I was close to Evelyn, but not so close that she would have to worry about wolves finding me if they found her.

I drove to the state park and headed through the entrance. It was off-season, so the gates were left open all day and night. There were no other cars in the parking lot, so it looked like I was going to be alone in the park tonight. I got out of the car and listened with every sense I possessed to make sure there were no humans around. Just to be safe, I decided to head into the woods and change there. I could hide my clothes somewhere and come back for them later.

As I got further into the woods, my excitement started to rise. That was my wolf; I could feel her anticipation and impatience to run free through the woods. I was glad I decided to do this beforehand; there is no way she would have agreed to a quick back and forth switch tonight.

I found a spot hidden from view so that I could change without the fear of being seen. The crisp autumn breeze caressed my bare skin as I looked around for a hiding spot for my shoes and clothes. I finally decided to reach up to a little nook between a couple of tree branches covered in their fall leaves. I wedged my things in there, making sure they wouldn't fall and get trampled by random woodland creatures. I kept a spare change of clothes in the car just in case, but I'd rather not walk naked back to the car. That would be difficult to explain if I crossed paths with a human on the trail.

Once I hid my clothes, I was finally free to shift. I let go and surrendered to the change as my wolf burst forth. I shook out my pure white coat and stretched out my legs. There were acres of land here that I was aching to explore, so I shot off in a run.

I felt the wind rush past me as I bounded through the woods. Graceful and sure, my wolf practically flew over the terrain. The exhilaration of pure freedom took hold of me, and I forgot about everything but the sheer joy of running. Miles passed, and I came to a river. I gently lapped at the water, eying my surroundings as I got my drink. During my run, I hadn't smelled evidence of anything bigger than a raccoon, but my wolf was always alert for danger.

I hesitated, indecisive about what I wanted to do next. I could head back to see if the coast was clear for me to break into Evelyn's house, but my wolf was in control now, and I could feel her desire to keep going and explore more of this new territory. *Another hour or so wouldn't hurt*, I thought to myself. I had all night to do this, and I needed my wolf calm and focused anyway.

Decision made, I eyed the river ahead of me. I was eager to see what was on the other side. The river didn't look deep, but the best option to cross was the path of rocks sticking partly out of the water. I could hop from rock to rock without ever touching the water.

I leaped onto the first rock and evaluated my chances of crossing the river successfully this way. The rest of the way seemed safe, so I bounced over to the next rock. I crossed the river this way, bouncing from rock to rock. A couple of the rocks were wobbly or slippery, and my paws got a little wet, but I was able to cross quickly.

The forest was denser on this side of the river, and the well-worn trails that led me through the park were absent here. There were fewer human scents on this side and even more evidence of wildlife. I caught onto the scent trail of a deer and followed it for a while out of curiosity. I eventually was bored with that and just played in the forest for a while. There were fireflies for me to chase after, and piles of fresh autumn leaves for me to roll through.

A few miles away from the river, my nose caught the scent of something new. I was curious because it wasn't often that I found something that I hadn't smelled before.

Interest piqued, I followed the scent. It was definitely mammal, and probably large, judging by the size of the markings left. My wolf hesitated for a second. It seemed like something had marked their territory, and perhaps recently, judging by the strength of the scent.

My interest and curiosity in something new warred against my keen sense of self-preservation and the need to avoid danger. I'd just decided to turn back out of caution when I heard the snap of a stick about forty feet to my left, behind some trees. I froze immediately and flicked my ears forward, straining to catch any other sounds that would give me a clue as to what was out there.

I couldn't tell what the sound was from, or if there was anything over there at all. Unfortunately, the breeze was heading the wrong way. It carried my scent over to where the mysterious sound had come from and didn't bring me any clues as to what was over there. My only option in the face of possible danger was to run. I'm a white wolf, so when I was under a full moon and a sky bright with stars, there was no chance of hiding for me. Especially if there was something out there that had my scent.

I quickly turned away from where I heard the sound and ran full speed back in a roundabout way to the river in the hopes of throwing whatever it was off my trail. I thought I heard some rustling of leaves at first, but the rest of the way back to the river was quiet. No sounds, no scents. Could I have imagined it?

I slowed as I got back to the river and looked for the stone path that I'd taken before. I just had to make it a little further down the bank, and then I would be back on my way back to the car. As I got closer to the start of the rock path, there was movement ahead of me. I froze and looked closer, listening attentively.

Suddenly, I saw the glint of eyes. To my horror, an enormous wolf rose from the ground where he had crouched in hiding. This wolf was definitely male, and at least twice my size.

He watched me, and I watched him as neither of us moved. He must have followed my scent back this way in the hopes of cutting me off, assuming I was headed back the same way I came. If I were in my human form, I would have panicked, but my wolf evaluated the situation clinically. Panicking wouldn't increase my chances of surviving this.

I decided my best option was to jump into the cold river. I could ride the current down a bit and emerge on the other side. The wolf could follow, but I figured my chances of getting away via water were better than here on the ground. I might get lucky and be facing off with a non-swimming wolf.

I crouched down in an attempt to gather momentum for a quick sprint and jump into the water when I heard rustling behind me. Backing up to the side and careful to keep the giant wolf in view, I quickly glanced over to evaluate a potential new threat.

My heart stopped and sunk down into my chest; another giant wolf was creeping up from behind me. That's why the first wolf was just patiently watching me; he was waiting for his friend to get into place behind me. The first wolf let out a loud howl, and I panicked; that was the sound of a wolf alerting his pack of prey. Desperation hit me, so I leaped up and sprinted for the water.

I heard panting behind me as I leaped into the water but was careful to avoid hitting any rocks. I went into the freezing cold water with a splash and struggled to get my nose to the surface so I could get a breath. After struggling for what seemed like an eternity, I finally broke the surface of the water and looked around as I frantically panted for air.

The current wasn't that strong, and I wasn't too far from where I'd jumped. One of the wolves was pacing back and forth where I'd jumped, and I felt a moment of triumph. It looked like I was partially right, because that wolf didn't look like he wanted to jump into the river after me.

I was paddling to the other bank of the river when I caught sight of the first wolf. He had headed right for my rock path and was hopping from rock to rock to cross the river, just like I had my first time. His heavier weight made the crossing much more difficult for him, and the next wobbly rock he landed on careened off of the pile it was precariously balanced on and slid into the river, taking the wolf with it. This destabilized the entire rock pile, and a couple larger stones fell into his direction.

I was thankful for the distraction, and hastily climbed up the embankment to get out of the water. I didn't even stop to shake the water out of my coat before I ran back through the woods. Initially, I was heading directly to my car, planning to just leave my clothes behind when I realized that's where my car keys were. I cursed and abruptly changed direction so I could get to my hiding place.

I've never run so fast in my life. I ran as if those wolves were panting at my hindquarters. I didn't hear or smell them behind me, but that didn't make me feel any safer. After all, I hadn't heard them tracking me through the forest until it had been too late.

I finally made it back to my clothes but stopped to look around before shifting. I didn't hear or smell any sign of my pursuers, and it seemed like I had a clear lead, so I changed back into my human form. I slipped my shoes on and gathered the rest of my clothes in a pile, hugging it close to my body. Then I ran naked through the woods.

I probably sacrificed some speed in my human form, but I didn't want to leave my clothes behind with my human scent on them. I was hoping that my scent would blend in with all the other human scents here on the trail, and they wouldn't be able to track me down. This was probably wishful thinking, but it got me back to my car.

I jumped in the car and backed up out of the space. I wanted to tear out of here like a bat out of hell but forced myself to stick to the speed limit. The last thing I wanted right now was to attract attention, especially considering that I was completely naked.

I stopped at the exit of the park and quickly slipped my shirt on. At least the people in passing cars wouldn't be able to see that l was naked at a glance. I was dripping water and mud all over my car, but that was the least of my worries right now - I was much more concerned with any wolves that might be on my trail.

I pulled out carefully onto the roadway and merged into the line of other cars. I breathed a sigh of relief because somehow, I'd made it out of the forest unscathed. I wasn't sure if luck was on my side or if Evelyn was now an angel watching over me, but I should be dead right now. There was no way I should have been able to escape those much larger wolves.

I pulled into the parking lot of a Burger King and parked in a shadowed parking spot where no one would be able to see that I was using it to get dressed. I hunched down in the seat and kept watch for anyone who might be heading my way. I wiped off the mud I could and pulled on my clothes.

Once I dressed, I banged my head against the steering wheel. How could I be so stupid?! In my arrogance, I just assumed I would recognize another wolf's smell instinctively. I'd just assumed it would smell like me. I banged my head again a few times. I've never actually smelled another wolf before! *Stupid. Stupid. Stupid.*

I groaned to myself. What are the chances that Evelyn just happened to die a mysterious death, and then I just happened to run into two wolves later that night? There was an excellent chance those wolves were the murderers.

I'd never felt so helpless before. My great plan had been to go sniff out the perpetrators, but I hadn't thought about what I was going to do after I identified them. I'm sure that I now know who they are, but what am I going to do about it? I know I couldn't win in a fight; one of those wolves could easily crush me, and it was likely that there was a whole pack of them. I couldn't let the police in on my suspicions. What would I tell them?

I pondered what I should do next in an attempt to push away my helpless and depressing thoughts. I could go to Evelyn's to carry out my original plan. But with those wolves so close and on the hunt, it would be dangerous to stay in the area for even a moment longer.

I kept thinking it through. If I didn't go now, I could lose my chance to inspect the crime scene forever. I didn't know when Evelyn's house was going to be cleaned, and I couldn't live the rest of my life knowing that I could have identified the killers but chose not to.

I groaned again. I already knew that going back to Evelyn's house was the wrong decision as far as my safety was concerned. But I also knew that I already made the decision to disregard my concerns and go back to Evelyn's house to investigate anyway. I couldn't just walk away from this.

I headed back in that direction to see if the coast was clear yet. To my relief, the lights in every house on the street were off as I drove towards Evelyn's house. It was completely dark and quiet in the neighborhood, so I decided to get this over with quickly.

I parked near the end of the street, where there was an empty lot and no streetlight to put me under a spotlight. I decided to go the sneaky way and crept along the back edge of the lots, where there was a border of trees to hide in until I could reach Evelyn's back yard. Once I was close, I quickly sprinted from the shadows and up to her back door to try and get in unseen.

I still had a key, and I held my breath that the police didn't change or add additional locks to the door to keep people like me out. There was a sign on the back door stating that this was a secured crime scene, but I ignored it. The lock clicked open, and I slowly twisted the door handle, not sure of what I was going to see when the door opened.

The back door opened into the kitchen, and I didn't see anything unusual. Some of Evelyn's stuff was out of place, but I was guessing that was from the police investigators who had been here earlier today.

Nostalgia rose in me when I caught sight of her cute little cookie jar sitting on the kitchen counter. She'd always kept it stocked for me when I came over and would try to make me guess what delicious goodies she had hidden inside. I felt the tears coming on, so I quickly pulled myself together, determined to stay on task.

Evelyn had always been careful not to leave anything with my name or information in her house. She'd wanted to keep me hidden, even if she were discovered. I'd never been in Evelyn's house while in wolf form before, and I wasn't sure if other wolves would be able to recognize that I was a wolf underneath my human scent that was all over the house from my many visits.

Just like I'd never met another wolf to be able to recognize the scent, I'd also never met another wolf in their human form to compare the two scents. I sighed; I was just now realizing all the hurdles I was going to face when I tried to track down the wolves who were responsible for this.

I finished creeping through the downstairs and still hadn't found anything unusual other than the signs of the police presence from earlier today. I slowly headed to the stairs with a sense of dread. I knew I should hurry, but I just couldn't make myself go up there.

I took a deep breath and slowly put my paws on the first step. I needed just to pull off the Band-Aid and stop being so scared of what I was going to find up there. Quickly and quietly, I ran up the stairs and stopped at the entrance to Evelyn's room. Since this was the only place I hadn't examined, I already knew that this is where the horrible events must have happened by the process of elimination.

I hesitated at the top of the stairs because someone had closed her door. It had probably been the police, acting out of respect for the dead. Another wave of sadness hit me as I realized that I'd just admitted to myself that Evelyn was one of the dead. I pushed away those thoughts so I could focus on the task at hand. I shifted back to human so that I could open the door to her room, I wouldn't be able to do that with my paws.

I turned the handle to her bedroom door and let the door swing open slowly. I knew the scene was going to be horrific, but I still wasn't prepared for what I found. Bloodstains were everywhere, and the room was a complete mess. As my eyes took in the scene, vomit rose in the back of my throat. I barely made it down the hall in time to reach the toilet of the guest bathroom.

I started to clean up when I was sure I was done and looked in the mirror as I wiped my face. My green eyes looked hollow and red from grief. As I stared at myself in the mirror, I knew that I was just putting off the inevitable. I needed to go back in there and complete what I'd come here to do.

I'd already opened her door and looked in the bedroom, so my human self was no longer needed. I stood there naked, hesitating on what I needed to do. I silently pleaded with my wolf: *Please just behave and do what we need to do.*

I let go of my human form and felt the change come over me with a rush of relief.

My emotions were always different when I was in my wolf form; some were muted while others were more vibrant. Changing into my wolf numbed the grief, the helplessness, and the guilt. But I also felt the need for vengeance more strongly.

I trotted back into the bedroom and gently placed a paw on the carpet. The blood was no longer wet, so I was able to make my way over to the ruined bed. The scene didn't affect my emotions as much now that I was in my wolf form, and I was able to examine things critically.

I sniffed around carefully, trying to identify and catalog all of the different scents. I could easily detect the distinct smell of wolves, now that I knew what I was looking for, and separate them from the scents of humans that had been in here.

I couldn't tell if all the human scents were from the police officers that had been here earlier today or if there may have been wolves here in human form at some point.

Done with my examination of the bedroom, I headed back downstairs to see if there was anything I may have missed while I was in human form. This time, I picked up on the addition of two more wolves. That makes a total of four wolves here that night, assuming none of the wolves were in human form. Why would two wolves stay downstairs during the carnage? As lookouts?

Done with my examination, I trotted back to the bathroom, quickly changed back into a human, and got dressed. I was more than ready to get out of here, so I ran down the stairs and to the back door.

I peered outside of the door to make sure it was safe for me to run for the wooded part of the backyard. It was, so I sprinted to the tree line and slowly crept back through the shadows to the empty lot. I made it to the back of the lot just in time for a black SUV to pull up to Evelyn's house.

I crouched down to watch as two men got out of the vehicle and looked around the neighborhood as they obviously looked for scents. Could they be wolves? How are they using their wolf senses while in human form?

I couldn't see them in any real detail, but it seemed like they had the same idea about dressing in black that I had, so that they appeared to be nothing more than two large shadows crossing the yard.

They strode confidently up to the front door, and one of the men crouched down as the second man kept an eye on the street. Were they picking the lock and keeping watch?

My eyes narrowed. If these are two of the wolf murderers, why were they here? Did they forget something while they were on their murder spree? They must realize that the police would have taken anything of interest.

Even after they disappeared within, I stayed crouched down and watched the front door for signs of them coming back out. I didn't see any movement in the house – I didn't have a clue as to what they were doing in there. I waited impatiently, but it was almost thirty minutes before they came back out and headed to their SUV. I was relieved to see that they were finally leaving, but one man hesitated before getting in the driver's side door and glanced back at my car parked in front of the empty lot.

My heart started to pound. My car had caught his interest. Belatedly, I realized it was weird to have a car parked here in front of an empty lot in the off-season. During peak season, all the streets are packed with vehicles from the tourists, but in the fall and winter months, it is just the residents that parked here.

They both got back into the car, and I let out a deep breath, thinking that I was safe. Then I froze as their SUV started to back up towards my car instead of driving off down the road. I ducked down and made sure that I was well hidden here in the woods, but my heart pounded as I watched their car stop right next to mine.

I started to count the seconds, but it felt like they were sitting there for an eternity. What are they doing? Finally, before I was about to explode from the tension, the car quickly drove away. I waited for another ten minutes before I decided to risk running over to my car.

I made it back without incident and started the drive home. Today had been insane so I should be exhausted - but I just couldn't shut my brain off. All the emotions and thoughts of the day were still churning around in my head, but nothing made sense.

When I finally got home and made it to my bed, I just laid there and stared at the ceiling in the darkness. A part of me didn't want to go to sleep, because I knew when I woke up it was going to be my first day without Evelyn here on this earth. The emptiness of the world hit me, and I realized that I now had no one. I was utterly alone.

I felt selfish for thinking like that. I shouldn't be thinking about how I was suffering. Evelyn was the one who was horribly murdered. Evelyn was the one who suffered.

Guilt hit me. Evelyn had asked me to do one thing: run. Instead of doing as she asked, I'd put myself in more danger by exposing myself to multiple wolves in the woods through carelessness. I'd also searched her house and left my wolf scent there along with my human scent. If the men who broke into Evelyn's house tonight were wolves, they definitely knew there was a female in the area, and they had both my scents now. Acid burned my throat when I realized that they saw my car. If they were the criminal masterminds that I suspected them of being, it wouldn't be difficult for them to track me down. I'd been so fucking stupid in my arrogance.

My heart pounded. What are the chances that they would put it all together? Were those men the wolves that had chased me from the forest? Or were they another two wolves that made up the four wolves in Evelyn's house that night? If they were connected, what were the chances they could tie my wolf to an oddly parked car in the neighborhood?

It might seem like I was just paranoid, but deep down, I had the feeling that they knew who I was and were coming for me. Evelyn had taught me to always to trust my instincts, and every fiber of my being was screaming that I was in danger. I took a deep breath and tried to settle my nerves - panicking wouldn't help. I needed a plan. *Because the last one went so well,* I thought sarcastically.

I turned to grab my phone off the nightstand and pressed my thumb down to unlock it. It was only an hour before my alarm was about to go off, and there was no way I was going to be able to sleep now, so I just shut off the alarm and got up.

I used the bathroom and went through the usual motions of getting ready for work and not really seeing anything around me. I made my way out to the living room and rubbed my face as I sat on my couch, staring into space. I had absolutely no idea what to do next.

I finally decided that leaving my house was probably my best option. If the mysterious burglars had run my plates, then they already had my address and could be on their way here. I ran upstairs to pack up a bag, thinking that I should stay somewhere else tonight after work. I felt reasonably confident that I would be safe at work, as I worked in a hospital on a military base with a ton of security.

According to Evelyn, wolves avoided any contact with the police or the government, and they definitely wouldn't be able to join the military. That means I should be safe on a military base.

I locked up my house and set the security alarm. Before I exited, I took one last look around at my home - there was nothing personal here that couldn't be easily replaced. I'd just purchased the house a few months ago and had decided to slowly add pieces of furniture as I could afford them instead of going further into debt. It's not like I ever had guests to impress.

I didn't have any memorabilia from my childhood, no family heirlooms, no scrapbooks or photo albums. As I gazed back into my dark and empty house, I thought about how it accurately reflected my life. After escaping hell to go to college, I threw everything I had into my studies, focused on proving everyone wrong. I wanted to make something of myself, and I wanted to become someone that mattered.

Looking back on it, I think sometimes I used my studies and work as an excuse to withdraw from my classmates and peers. While I did need to work hard to get good grades and put myself through school, I was also afraid of getting close to anyone. Now, I wondered if I'd made a mistake by keeping myself isolated. I had a good job, a house, and my own car - but I was utterly alone.

Why hadn't I made more time to spend with Evelyn while I still could? I always thought I would have more time later on, but it had run out far too soon. I drove to work slowly, even though I was practically alone on the empty roads. It was early enough that I didn't run any traffic until I took the exit to get on base.

Despite my slow pace, I still got to work too early and sat in my car for a moment before I could talk myself into going into the hospital. My coworkers were going to notice something was wrong with me. I'm usually the annoyingly peppy and positive person at work, but right now I doubted I could even pretend to be my usual self.

Confiding in my co-workers wasn't an option. I wasn't comfortable talking to other people about my emotions; I preferred to keep everything to myself and only present my happy face to the world. Before I got out of the car, I decided just to tell people that I was sick so I could try to do my work quietly and under the radar.

I walked into the hospital and got dressed in my scrubs like a zombie. Despite pasting a fake smile on my face, several of my coworkers asked if I was okay before I'd even made it to my spot at the pharmacists' table. I was trying my best to act like myself, but I knew that the smile on my face didn't look genuine, and I was probably missing my usual happy glow.

On a typical day, I would make the rounds through the pharmacy so that I could say good morning to everyone and get pass down from the evening shift. Today I just didn't have it in me, and I was barely holding in my grief. If people started to be too nice to me, I was afraid everything would come spilling out.

I sat down at one of the pharmacists' desks and organized all my references around me as my computer started up. I pulled up my pager list and Lexi comp before logging on to the hospital system to see what was in our work queue for today. I hoped that work would be a good distraction to get me through the day.

I tried to stay focused on things like renal dosing and whether the patient's antibiotic regimen was going to cover the offending bacteria that was growing in their cultures. I buried myself in my work and tried to ignore all the events in the past twenty-four hours completely.

Somehow, I made it through the first five hours and thirty-five minutes without bursting into tears or having a panic attack. Once I announced I was sick, everyone decided to stay far away in case I was contagious. I was given all the desk work so I wouldn't risk bringing any of my contagions out to the patients. This situation worked well for me, as it meant I didn't have to talk to anyone and could hide at my desk.

When it was finally my turn for lunch, I decided to go to the food court. It's usually the most crowded place on base for lunch, but I found it comforting to be lost in a crowd. I claimed one of the two-person tables for myself and pulled out a protein bar.

I still hadn't been able to make myself eat since breakfast yesterday, but I knew that I needed to. Shifting burned a lot of energy in the form of calories. I needed to eat more than the typical human female, and I'd shifted forms several times yesterday. Technically, I should be starving and packing in the calories. But right now, the thought of food just made me feel nauseous.

I took a sip of my water, sighed, and opened my protein bar. I was just about to take my first bite when a large man slid into the chair opposite mine.

"Hi." He smiled, and his beautiful blue eyes sparkled with humor when I just stared at him.

I looked around the food court to see that there were plenty of empty tables where he could have sat. Then I looked back at him. He was definitely speaking to me because there was no one else at my table.

"Hi?" I replied hesitantly, confused about what he was doing here right now.

"I thought this would be easier. In the reports, your co-workers said you're usually the friendliest person in the department." He gave me another dazzling smile, and I struggled to keep my wits about me.

"Oh, are you from security?" I asked, as I suddenly realized how weird I must seem to him with all the blank staring I'd been doing. It wasn't unusual for security to continually check up on people who looked suspicious. Everyone here had a security clearance, and with all the security breaches in the news lately, they had been under pressure to crack down on people with high-risk behaviors who had access to sensitive information.

"Not exactly," he replied.

"So, then what reports are you reading?" I asked suspiciously. *Please do not tell me I was part of some weird security drill where he was trying to see if I would give up "secured" information*, I thought to myself. I didn't have the time or patience for this today. As annoyed as I was, I didn't want to look unbalanced or temperamental, so I fought the urge to scowl at him until he went away.

Apparently, my attempt failed, because his grin faded a little. "Sorry, can we start over?"

"Um, sure?"

He stood up and walked a couple of steps away. I was surprised at how tall he was; he must have been around six and a half feet tall. He was also quite muscular, and I blushed a little as I admired the view of him walking away. He quickly came back and sat again. I was still just staring at him in disbelief, hoping he didn't just catch me checking him out.

He flashed another grin at me, seemingly oblivious to my staring. "Hi, I'm Cody. Can I have lunch with you?"

"Yes?" I felt incredibly awkward right now, but since I'd already embarrassed myself enough by staring at him, I figured a couple more seconds of it wouldn't hurt. He had light brown hair that was a little longer than was permitted by the military, so he must have been a civilian. He was dressed in civilian clothes and had a tattoo on his well-muscled arm peeking out of the bottom of the sleeve of his black T-shirt, but I couldn't see enough of it to recognize what it might be. Despite his hot body, it was his eyes that drew me in. He had unbelievably beautiful Caribbean blue eyes framed by thick eyelashes that I was jealous of.

"I'm Anna," I added shyly.

Cody was quite good-looking and had a great smile, which explained how easily he had invited himself to my table. He was probably used to girls fighting over who would eat lunch with him. I was the opposite - I didn't receive male attention here. Ever.

I wear hospital scrubs a couple sizes too big so that the pants would be long enough to cover my ankles. There are only six unisex sizes to choose from, and 'tall' wasn't one of them.

If wearing baggy scrubs that didn't fit correctly wasn't bad enough, I also don't wear makeup, and my hair is always pulled tightly into a bun at the nape of my neck. There are strict requirements for anyone who needs to go into the cleanroom to work on TPNs and IV medications, and they don't mesh well with 'looking pretty.'

It was also a requirement for me to wear a white coat over my scrubs whenever I left the pharmacy. I was forced to get a coat that was too big for me so that it could fit over my giant scrubs, and the entire ensemble made me look even larger than I was.

In comparison to me, the food court was full of nurses and female corpsman in tight scrubs who looked like they were on the prowl for a date with their hair and makeup on point. It made no sense that this guy would walk past all of those attractive women to sit with me - he must have an ulterior motive.

I glanced at the empty table in front of him suspiciously. "Where's your lunch?"

My suspicion didn't seem to deter him at all, as he just chuckled. "I didn't bring one today. I guess what I should have said was 'Can I sit with you while you eat your lunch?'"

I just looked at him thoughtfully. This guy seemed nice enough, so I didn't have a problem with him sitting here. I could wait until he was willing to reveal what it was that he wanted. Yeah, this was a weird situation, but as Kelsey was fond of telling me - I was a weird girl.

I sighed and reached into my bag to pull out a second protein bar and slid it slowly over the table to him. His smile brightened by a few watts, and he picked up the bar to tear open the wrapper. "Thanks!" he said enthusiastically, biting into it.

I mumbled something incoherent in reply and looked back down at my own bar. He finished his lunch in four bites and started to eye my water as he chewed. I reached back into my bag and sighed again as I passed him my afternoon water bottle. Yes, I also needed to drink a ton of water to go with all the food, and I liked to be prepared.

He smiled and thanked me before opening up the water and gulping down some water.

"So, what is it that you do here?" I asked, trying to keep a frown off my face.

"Oh, I'm just here for an appointment," Cody told me casually.

I leaned back in my chair a little. If he had an appointment here at the hospital, he must be active-duty, a dependent, or retired military. He was too old to be a child dependent, too young to be retired military, so that left spouse? I glanced down at his hands quickly, but I didn't see a ring.

"Are you active-duty?" I asked innocently.

He chuckled softly and slid a hand through his hair. "Nope, sorry to disappoint, but I can't offer you Tricare or BAH."

I laughed despite myself. A second later, the small smile that was starting to spread over my face immediately dropped when reality hit me. What was I doing here? I was sitting here flirting with a random stranger when I had all the other drama going on in my life? I needed to pull myself together and stay on task.

He seemed to sense my shift in mood as he put a more serious look on his face. "Looks like I owe you lunch one day. What are you doing tomorrow?"

And I was back to staring in disbelief. I wasn't sure if my lack of reaction was due to my sleep deprivation or the total lack of understanding of why this good-looking stranger was asking me to eat lunch with him for the second day in a row. All I'd done so far was stare at him and awkwardly mumble useless sentences because my brain was on the fritz and not functioning at all.

"I'm working tomorrow," I admitted hesitantly.

"So, you're going to have lunch here?" he asked persistently.

"Yes, but I -"

"Excellent. I'll see you tomorrow." He stood up, gave me another grin and a wave and then sauntered off before I could gather my thoughts enough to be able to state my objections. I didn't even get a chance to ask him why he would be reading reports on me if he was just here for an appointment. What reports?

I think that this had been the strangest interaction of my life. I didn't expect to see him again. Maybe he was the loser of a bet or the recipient of a dare. I quickly dismissed all thoughts of the awkward encounter with Cody when I started thinking about my wolf problem again. All too soon, lunch was over, and it was time to go back to work.

# Chapter 3

As I got closer to the end of my workday, my numbness started to wear off, and my work was no longer a distraction as anxiety took hold of me again. The more I thought about it, the more convinced I was that wolves were waiting at my house to murder me.

I chewed on my lip as I stared at my last kinetics calculations for the day. But then I suddenly realized something: I didn't have to go home. The hospital frequently ordered staff to stay on the premises under a variety of circumstances. I perked up a little at that thought because the base would be the safest place for me to stay tonight.

Last winter, I'd been stuck here for forty-eight hours because the command didn't want to risk on-duty staff not being able to make it back to work the next day through a blizzard. They'd given me an uncomfortable cot in a room that I shared with someone else for the duration of the storm, but it was something.

I somehow made it through the rest of my workday, despite my anxiety and sleep deprivation. After my shift was over, I went back to where I'd stayed overnight last year. I was hopeful that I would be able to work something out with the corpsman who was on duty.

Last time, I just had to show my hospital badge and CAC card, and they gave me an assignment for the night. Of course, the last time I was here, every department in the hospital had people assigned to stay the night because of the blizzard. I figured it wouldn't hurt to try again; the worst they could say was no.

*Just act like you're upset that you have to stay here overnight, and they won't question it,* I told myself in a pep talk.

I walked up to the desk where the corpsman on duty was sitting. He was a young HM3 who clearly didn't want to be here. Shockingly, I was able to bond a little with him because we both shared the same 'dead man walking' look of fatigue and hopelessness. He informed me that he had been sitting at this very same desk for twenty-six hours now.

I commiserated with him as he explained that he couldn't leave until someone showed up to relieve him, but there had been some kind of mistake on the schedule. The corpsman scheduled to relieve him after his twelve-hour shift had gotten out of the military a week ago. This being the military, he was told to cover the next shift, resulting in over twenty-four hours of duty straight. That sucked.

"My relief is due to be here any minute. She's only two hours late," the corpsman told me sarcastically, not looking hopeful at all. He was more than willing to assign me one of the open rooms for the night and couldn't care less about whether I was authorized to do so. As he put it, "Who in their right mind would stay here willingly?"

I was consumed again by dark thoughts when I entered the room, and the door clicked shut behind me. There was an uncomfortable cot, a ratty old chair that had seen better days, and a wobbly looking desk, but at least I had a single room this time. The light was giving off a yellowish glow on the dingy white brick walls, but I felt like this room matched the state of my soul at this moment.

I shrugged out of my white coat and draped it carefully on the back of the chair so it wouldn't wrinkle. I slipped my shoes off, but my kept my socks on after taking a look at the cold tiled floor.

Knowing that I would never be able to sleep without some help, I pulled a bottle of Unisom out of my bag. I swallowed double the standard human dose with the help of a sip of warm water from the bottle that had been in my bag all day. I grimaced as it went down and then laid on the cot, not even bothering to change out of my scrubs.

I was physically and emotionally exhausted. I'd gone too long without sleep, and my body ached. I could feel a deep pit down in my stomach which was probably due to the starvation that I put myself through the last couple of days. I hadn't really eaten all day Sunday or today.

The little I'd eaten on Sunday had come back up while I was in Evelyn's house, and the small protein bar I managed to choke down at lunch today was hardly a sufficient meal for a human or a wolf. Despite the emptiness inside me, I couldn't make myself care enough to leave the room in search of food.

I just wanted to sink down into the oblivion that sleep could offer and forget everything for now. I could figure everything out tomorrow, I told myself. For now, I was safe - even though I felt anything but. That was my last thought for the night as the sleep meds kicked in, and darkness rose to swallow me whole.

# Chapter 4

Almost twelve hours later, I woke up. My initial confusion at waking up in a strange place faded as the events of the last couple of days came back to me slowly. I sat up in the bed and leaned forward with my elbows leaning on my thighs.

I still felt a little drowsy, but that was most likely due to the after-effects of the sleep medication I'd taken. The nausea in my stomach had faded and had been replaced by a gnawing hunger. I reached over to the desk by the bed to grab my phone and check the time. I saw that I had two hours until I needed to be back in the pharmacy for my next shift, which was more than enough time to find something to eat before I had to report for duty. I didn't have any missed calls or messages, but that wasn't surprising; Evelyn was gone, and Kelsey wasn't speaking to me.

I swung my legs over the side of the cot and stood up slowly. My body still ached, and I took five minutes to stretch out a little. I needed a good thirty minutes to go through my yoga routine, but I decided that a shower and food were higher up on my list of priorities at the moment.

A hot shower helped to soothe the aches from sleeping on the lumpy cot. I decided to dress in my gym clothes for now and stop at the scrub machine for some fresh scrubs before reporting back to work. I picked up some snacks at the NEX and headed over to the food court to take advantage of the Wi-Fi there.

I spread my selection of snacks out in front of me and opened my bottle of diet Mountain Dew. My appetite had come back with a vengeance, and after inhaling some food, I was feeling a little more like myself. A full night of sleep, food, and an influx of caffeine had helped to clear my head, and I was ready to make a game plan. I needed to stay focused and not let myself get lost in my emotions. I could give myself time to grieve after I figured all of this out.

I pulled out my phone, ready to make a list of everything I needed to do. I decided to start by listing what I already knew. I think now it was safe to assume that wolves had murdered Evelyn. I was guessing that the pack Evelyn had grown up with was responsible.

I chewed on my lip as I thought about my next step: identifying her old pack. Evelyn had never told me where she came from, but she had occasionally dropped hints without realizing it. Over the years, she had mentioned taking day trips to the mountains, snowstorms in the winter, and a waterfall that was in biking distance of her house. But that list wasn't exactly something I could Google and have a location pop up.

The one helpful hint that I'd obtained was the photos that she had shown me all those years ago. If Evelyn had found them on the Internet, then so could I.

If only I knew her real name, I sighed in frustration. I knew she kept her past secret from me to keep me safe, but right now, I regretted that I'd never pushed her to reveal more of her previous life. I thought that we'd have years before I ever needed to worry about anything happening to her. I felt tears start to form in my eyes, and I struggled to push them back so I could stay focused on my current mission.

I tried my best to try to picture the yearbook pictures that I'd seen so briefly, but it was a struggle to bring those images back in my mind. I vaguely remembered that there had been a photo of Evelyn's daughter at a football game. I racked my brain to try to remember what the high school team was called - it might have been something like Wildmere High or Windfall High. I glanced down at my phone and held back a curse. I could try searching for those names after work, but for now, my time was up. I was going to have to rush to get my new scrubs and report to work on time. I sighed in frustration but stood up to start my day.

# Chapter 5

Within the first couple of hours at work, I realized that I wasn't going to be able to focus on anything pharmacy-related today. I was squirming in my seat and antsy to get out of here and back to solving a murder. It was taking me ten times longer than usual for me to do the simplest tasks, and I couldn't say that I'd accomplished anything productive yet today.

I caught a flash of my supervisor's curly red hair out of the corner of my eye as she walked through the pharmacy, and after only a second of hesitation, I followed her.

I caught up with her just as she made it to her office. "Good morning, Carol! Is there any way that I could talk to you for a minute?"

She turned and frowned at me, but I gave her a small smile with a hopeful look in my eyes.

"All right, come to my office." She sat down in the chair behind her desk with a sigh of unhappy anticipation. I doubted anyone chased her down the hall this early in the morning to give her good news.

"You remember Evelyn?" I'd brought Evelyn to a couple of civilian work functions where attending with your family was expected. Just as I'd hoped, Carol's eyes lit with recognition. I didn't have anyone else to bring to events like that, so I introduced Evelyn as my grandmother. No one had questioned it, maybe because Evelyn was the type of grandmother that everyone wanted as their own. Evelyn had felt safe attending the events on base because she was sure that wolves wouldn't be able to infiltrate my workplace.

"They're too rough to be able to blend with civilized folks," she had sniffed.

"Of course," Carol said with a smile. "How's Evelyn doing?"

Carol and Evelyn had bonded over their love of baking when they had both brought a pecan pie to the same potluck. The memory of that event brought my pain of losing her sharply back into focus. I had to swallow the lump that had formed in my throat. I looked down at the floor to take a moment to let the emotion pass before I could speak.

"She passed the other day," I managed to whisper. My attempts at pushing my grief and despair down weren't going well, and I could feel tears forming in my eyes yet again. I blinked them away and squared my shoulders back, determined not to be so unprofessional as to cry at work.

I met Carol's sympathetic eyes when I was able to look back up at her. "I could tell that you weren't feeling yourself yesterday." She leaned back in her chair and folded her hands. "If you need time, we just received word that the Solace isn't going out on their planned training exercises this week, so I have two extra pharmacists to add to the schedule."

I was genuinely grateful for her offer. I was the type of person who never called out and hated to ask for time off. Our hospital was responsible for staffing the USS Solace, which was a medical ship that was mainly deployed for humanitarian efforts after disasters occurred. The Solace had just recently gone out to Puerto Rico after hurricane Irma had left a trail of destruction through the country. Almost a quarter of the hospital staff had gone on the ship then, but for training exercises, a much smaller crew went.

"Yes, thank you." I blinked away the tears that had formed and were threatening to drop at any moment.

She stood and motioned to the door. "Take the rest of the week, go home and get some rest. I'll have LT Giles and LT Michaels cover your shifts."

I tried to smile and murmur my thanks, but I needed to hurry out the door before I managed to embarrass myself by letting any tears drop. I wiped at my eyes as soon as I left the office and tried to summon back my determination. I was getting frustrated with all the sudden mood changes and overwhelming emotions that kept hitting me. I tried not to make eye contact with any of my co-workers as I headed back to my desk. My emotions were still dangerously close to the surface, and I didn't want to have to explain my emotional state to anyone.

I grabbed my bag on the way out and was soon changed into civilian clothes and sitting in my car, unsure of where to go. The business card that the police had given me on Sunday was still on the passenger seat of my car where I dropped it. Since I was indecisive about where to go, I decided to stay right here and make some phone calls.

I dialed the number the detective had given me, but I was forwarded through a few other people before I reached Detective Finn on the phone.

"Hi, this is Anna. We met the other day concerning the Evelyn Heights case." I hesitated. I wanted to get info from him, but he might be more likely to share if I offered to help first. "I was calling because you had mentioned that you needed me to make a statement?"

There was quiet on the other side of the phone, but right before I was going to check and see if he had hung up on me, I heard his voice. "We've closed that case already, but thank you for checking in," he told me gruffly.

"Closed it?" I said in disbelief. "I heard that she was murdered? Did you catch the guy who –"

"Ma'am," he interrupted me, "it was ruled as a natural death. There's nothing to be investigated."

My jaw dropped. "Natural?" I asked in disbelief.

What could possibly be natural about a werewolf attack?

"Yes, ma'am. It's my understanding that the family has already claimed the body. You may want to contact them for details on the service they have planned."

"I wasn't aware that Evelyn had family," I told him with a frown. Who would have claimed the body? Could it be the same pack that murdered her? Now were they trying to hide the evidence?

"I can give you the number for the liaison to the morgue. They might be able to help you," he told me. I could tell by the impatient tone in his voice that he had already told me everything he was going to, so I accepted the phone number he gave me and thanked him for his help.

After I hung up the phone, I sat in the car for a few moments in disbelief. This wasn't what I'd been expecting at all. Could someone be covering up the fact that Evelyn was killed by wolves? How could they convince anyone that had actually seen her body that she died of 'natural causes?'

I shook my head but still called the number that Detective Finn had given me. A polite young woman named Violet answered the phone and informed me that the body had been sent for cremation by her son. I knew for a fact that Evelyn didn't have a son, so this made me even more suspicious.

I asked her for contact details for the mysterious son, and I told Violet I needed it so that I could help with planning the services and offer my condolences to the family. She was more than happy to provide a name and a phone number and told me that Evelyn's son's name was Robert Heights. Evelyn's real name wasn't Evelyn Heights, so I highly doubted that this man's real name was Robert Heights. As soon as I was able to get off the phone with Violet, I called the number she had given me for 'Robert Heights' with my heart pounding.

Who would be on the other end of the phone? I was disappointed when the phone line rang once and then gave the 'you have reached a disconnected number' message. I sat in my car and stared down at my phone blankly. I'd gotten nowhere fast with my investigation, and I now had even more questions than I did an hour ago.

I was having a difficult time processing that Evelyn was truly gone. It seemed unbelievable that she was suddenly torn from my life, not leaving much evidence behind. I was sad that I wouldn't get to hold her hand one last time and say goodbye. It seemed unfair that someone had just gone into the morgue, taken her body, and disposed of it. She deserved to have her remains treated with love and respect, not disposed of by a stranger.

Rationally, I knew she was gone and that she wouldn't care what had happened to her body, but I did care. I wanted to be able to say goodbye to her and make closure with her death. I wanted to plan a service for her, and I wanted to celebrate her life with all the people who loved her.

I decided I wasn't giving up just yet. How many places could there be in this area that provided cremation services? I could call them directly and see if I could stop things in time. I Googled cremation services, and there were a lot more than I thought there would be. Nineteen different places came up in my search, and I sighed - this was going to take a while.

I called each one of those places and pretended to be Evelyn's daughter, 'Emily.' I figured if the mysterious 'Robert Heights' could get away with it, then so could I. Each one of those places had never heard the name Evelyn Heights before, and I'd listened to quite a few sales pitches on why I should use their services for the death of my beloved mother. After I'd called each and every place within a thirty-mile radius, I felt the weight of failure pressing down on me.

It was possible that 'Robert' had taken Evelyn further away to avoid people like me, but I couldn't call every single place in the country. The more I thought about this, the more upset I started to get.

Why had I waited this long? I should have done this immediately, but instead, I'd waited around and let someone steal Evelyn from me. I'd buried my head in the sand and avoided dealing with the problem because I was too weak to handle it. It was difficult for me to process the emotions that came with loss, and so I tried to distract myself with other things.

Why did I have to be like this?

I'd also made a mistake in assuming that I had more time. I'd watched plenty of episodes of Law and Order, and investigations always seemed to take forever. I guess that's what I got for trusting TV representations of real life. I should know better - I've seen quite a few episodes of *Teen Wolf.*

I took a deep breath as I realized that I needed to regroup and come up with a new plan now. I needed to figure out a different way to approach this problem because nothing I was doing was working. I was going to have to take a step back and look at this from the outside. I needed to get a different perspective.

My stomach chose that moment to growl, and I looked down in irritation. I hadn't eaten yesterday, other than the protein bar I ate for lunch. I'd eaten a bunch of snacks and Mountain Dew this morning for breakfast, but it clearly wasn't enough to make up for the past two days of starvation. Lunch would probably give me an opportunity to clear my head and then start over.

I decided to err on the side of caution and avoid my home for the time being. There was a bar and grill called Greenies not far from the base that had great burgers, and I was craving real food. The snacks that I'd hurriedly consumed earlier today weren't ideal fuel for a wolf. The restaurant staff there didn't care if you sat outside on their patio for an extended amount of time during their off-season slow hours, so I would have a place to gather my thoughts for a while.

I headed in and waited in line to speak with the hostess. "Anna!" I heard a slightly familiar voice call. I looked around through the crowd of people that had formed behind me. My eyes were caught by a familiar pair of blue ones. It was the random guy I met yesterday, Cody. Was it only yesterday? It felt like that had happened years ago.

His eyes glanced quickly up and down my body as he headed in my direction. "I almost didn't recognize you without your white coat, but not many people have your hair color."

I ran my hand over my ponytail self-consciously, trying to smooth it down a bit. Cody was right - not many people had white-blond hair without the help of peroxide. I was dressed casually right now in jeans and a long-sleeve tee. The jeans were snug, but the T-shirt was comfortably loose. Although, in comparison to my clothing from yesterday, it probably looked like I had instantly shed thirty pounds.

Cody looked good in dark wash jeans and a snug T-shirt that showed off his fantastic physique. All rational thoughts went out the window when he was close enough for me to pick up the faint scent of his aftershave; my body was responding to him despite my best efforts.

"I was just coming here to pick up lunch. There aren't exactly any decent options on base," Cody told me with a warm smile. He stepped a little too close to me, and I instinctively flinched away. I hated it when I reacted like that, so I tried to pretend that I hadn't.

I grinned a little to try and hide my discomfort. "You don't want to try your luck at the galley?" I teased him. The galley was the cafeteria in the hospital that sometimes had decent options, like Taco Tuesday, but most of the time it was a roll of the dice.

He smirked. "Last time I braved the galley, I asked them if my chicken was supposed to be pink on the inside. They told me yes, it was just cooked medium rare."

I snorted and then quickly covered my mouth in embarrassment. But Cody didn't seem to notice the awkward moment and continued.

"I was going to just pick up a few options for you since I don't know what you like, but I'm glad you're here, so I don't have to agonize over the decision."

I gave him a confused look.

He pouted jokingly, "Oh, don't tell me you forgot about our lunch date. You would have broken my heart if you stood me up."

My eyebrows raised in surprise, but the hostess saved me from answering. "Table for two?"

Cody looked at me. "Patio okay?" he asked.

I blinked in surprise, and the hostess took that as consent. No doubt she wanted to get everyone moving; the waiting area was filling up fast with the early lunch crowd. She grabbed some menus and led the way to the patio as Cody gestured for me to go ahead of him. I really didn't want to waste time on social interactions right now, but I felt like a jerk for completely forgetting about him. To be fair, though, I never actually agreed to a date.

Cody and I were the only ones on the patio since it was a cool day for Virginians. Not a lot of people wanted to hang out here after the temp went below 70, and today it was a crisp 63 with a breeze. But I enjoyed the cooler weather and looked forward to fall here every year.

I slid into a chair at the table that the hostess had indicated was ours. She waited for Cody to take a seat before leaning forward to put a menu in front of him, giving him a great view of her cleavage.

To my surprise, he didn't seem to notice her attempt at seduction and had kept his eyes on me. She tossed a menu across the table in my direction before huffing and turning on her heel. I fought the urge to roll my eyes as she shot me a dirty look over her shoulder before she opened the door to go back inside.

If I'd been asked on a date by a handsome guy like this a week ago, I would have been ecstatic but nervous. But right now, I just wanted to get this over with, so I could get on with my planning.

Neither of us had opened the menu yet, so I decided to break the ice and move things along. "So, do you know what you want?"

"This place has amazing burgers!" he told me enthusiastically. I chuckled at how excited he was about food, but he probably had to eat a lot to maintain his muscle mass.

I smiled at his gusto, but he looked a little embarrassed at my amusement and rubbed his chin. "Or you know, they have girl stuff like salad or chicken, too."

I rolled my eyes at the assumption. "Nah, I want the barbecue bacon cheeseburger. Have you tried that one? It's a true culinary masterpiece."

He looked surprised but pleased. "Oh, yeah. That's what I'm getting."

We grinned at each other, and I relaxed a little as the waitress came over to introduce herself. She positioned herself so that her body was angled towards him and away from me. As she spoke, I could see that she had flirt mode turned on high. When she got to the part of her spiel where she asked if we wanted to start with drinks, Cody smiled at me.

"I think we're ready to order. What would you like?"

As I placed my order, she scribbled impatiently on her notepad. No doubt, she was eager to get back to flashing her bedroom eyes at Cody. He placed his order as well, then thanked her and leaned forward toward me and put his elbows on the table. She looked irritated, as it was clear he was politely dismissing her, but she flashed one more smile at him before heading inside to put our orders in.

"We're finally alone," he said in a joking manner.

I glanced down at the table as my brain scrambled for something to say. "Yeah," is all I managed to come up with. I was entirely out of my depth here, because flirting and dating weren't things that I regularly did.

A rational thought from deep down in my brain tried to surface through the web of confusion that clouded my mind. I had wanted to ask Cody something yesterday. Ah, yes. The 'reading reports about me' comment he had made. I looked at him as I tried to think of a way to bring it up. Why did he have to be so good looking? It was challenging to focus when he was looking at me with those gorgeous eyes.

He drummed his fingers on the table and tilted his head to one side. "You know, I haven't ever seen a female wolf out in public before without at least one of her pack-mates with her. Where's your pack?"

I froze, ice running through my veins. All thoughts instantly left my brain. How could he know what I was? Was he one of the wolves who had chased after me? Was he one of the men who broke into Evelyn's house? Could he be one of the murderers?

He saw the wide-eyed panic on my face and raised his hands defensively.

"I didn't mean that in a threatening way. I was just curious," he said gently.

I could try to run from him and hope he wouldn't chase me in public, but I thought about my determination to find Evelyn's killers and raised my chin. I could run, or I could hold my ground and try to get some justice for Evelyn. I hid my shaking hands under the table and replied with a bit of challenge in my voice, "Where's your pack?"

"Touché," he grinned, then hesitated for a moment before continuing. "I'm part of the Seaside Pack."

I frowned. "I thought there weren't any packs in the area?"

"There weren't, at least not until about six years ago." He crossed his arms over his chest, leaning back in his chair. "Which means you had to have been out of the loop for at least that time. We were huge news when Austin claimed some territory out here and started gathering wolves to him."

I groaned to myself. I'd been 'out of the loop' for a lot longer than six years – I'd never been in the loop to begin with. But this gave me a chance to get some information out of him.

Cody seemed relatively unthreatening, and even though Evelyn was continually telling me how dangerous other wolves were, I did have a craving deep down to be near my own kind. There was so much I didn't know about myself and the world I was excluded from. Evelyn had been adamant that all male wolves were evil, but could that have just been her pack? There were good and bad humans out there, is it really that unreasonable to think the same about wolves?

It wouldn't be a bad idea to talk to him for a bit and see if I could learn anything useful from him. It was unlikely that he would harm me in such a public place, and he had done nothing so far to indicate he intended to try.

I focused on what my gut instinct was telling me about Cody. People could put on fake smiles and lie, but deep down, I'd always had the ability to know when someone meant me harm. Maybe it was because I'd lived so long with an abusive uncle. I'd spent years watching his every move, trying to anticipate when the fake smile would slide away, and the evil monster inside would be released. Even though my Aunt and cousins knew what he had been doing, they had always been willing to sacrifice me to save themselves.

I didn't get any bad vibes from Cody, and I sensed that the friendliness he was exhibiting was genuine. There was no doubt in my mind that he had sensed what I was yesterday, and that was why he had sat down at my table, but I didn't believe he meant to harm me. I got the impression that he was curious.

The waitress picked that moment to come out with our drinks and try to flirt with Cody some more. He once again politely assured her that we had everything we needed. Still, I was grateful for the interruption because it gave me time to compose my thoughts and figure out the best way to question him without giving up too much info about myself.

He finally succeeded in getting her to return inside. "She's certainly persistent."

I rolled my eyes. "That's one word for it."

He chuckled, and I switched our water glasses.

"Just in case," I assured him as he laughed.

I plunged right in. "So how much of this area is your pack's territory?"

"Most of us live in Seaside, but our pack goes all the way out to Emporia, up to Richmond, and down to the North Carolina border."

I paled. Emporia was more than an hour west of where I lived in Port Idris, so my home and my job were both within their pack lands.

I couldn't just come right out and ask if his pack had murdered any older ladies recently, so I decided to start with a more natural question. "So, uh, how friendly is your pack to random wolves that you might find on your land?" I ran my hands up and down my thighs nervously as I waited for his answer.

He considered his answer for a moment. "Depends on the wolf."

"Could you perhaps give some example scenarios?" I asked hopefully.

He laughed. "I guess. So, in our hypothetical scenario, is our mystery wolf hiding from another pack?"

"No."

He gazed into my eyes steadily. "Has she ever harmed another person, human or not?"

I held his gaze without flinching. "No."

"Would she be willing to meet with the pack master?"

I dropped my eyes down to the table at that question. Evelyn had taught me that there is nothing I should fear more than meeting a pack master. I took a deep breath to stay calm.

"Why would he want to meet me?"

He raised an eyebrow. "You're on our land. Of course, he would want to meet with you to see if you're a danger to his pack."

I looked at him incredulously. He wanted to know if I would be a danger to his pack? I couldn't help it and started to laugh. Cody also saw the humor in that statement but quickly regained his serious look.

"Looks can sometimes be deceiving. You could be a spy for another pack looking to move into our territory. There's been some evidence lately of other wolves near here..."

I sat up abruptly in my chair. Could Cody be talking about Evelyn's murder? Was it possible that his pack had nothing to do with her death? Cody had already caught me on their territory, and he knew where I worked, could I somehow turn this situation to my advantage?

If I were completely honest with myself, I'd have to admit that I had no idea what I was doing trying to investigate a murder by myself. I knew very little about other wolves and was clueless about where to even begin in my hunt for Evelyn's murderers.

I eyed Cody carefully. Appearances could be deceiving, but I had a good feeling about him. He was warm and friendly, but I could also hear the honesty that echoed in his words. If he had been lying to me, I would know it.

Cody and the Seaside Wolves might be motivated to help me if they were angry enough about another pack killing on their lands. Maybe I could bargain with them so that they would give me time to find a job outside of their territory. I was going to have to meet with their pack master regardless of whether I wanted to or not, and I preferred to go on my own power rather than be dragged there.

I returned Cody's serious look. "Can you honestly promise me that no harm will come to me if I agree to meet with your pack master?"

"I promise," Cody said with a smile. "Austin is a good man, and we don't mean you any harm unless you intend us harm."

I stared into his eyes, wondering if I could trust his word. My gut was telling me yes, this wolf was okay. But how could I be sure?

What were my options? He knew where I worked, how long could I hide from him if I ran? If this were a movie, I could just move to a new town and start over. But this wasn't a movie, this was real life with a mortgage and student loans to pay. It would take months for me even to get a license to practice pharmacy in another state, and the board of pharmacy would publish my place of practice on their public website, anyway.

My only option was to trust my gut and go along with Cody for now. If these wolves turned out to be bad news, then I'd come up with a new plan. But for now, I'd see if they could help me find Evelyn's killer.

"All right," I agreed hesitantly. I wondered what I'd just gotten myself into, but I was determined to turn what could be a hopeless situation to my advantage.

A man came out on the patio carrying a tray with our food. Our waitress must have given up on Cody, because she was nowhere in sight. My mouth watered, and I was eager to sink my teeth into the first real meal that I had in days. I might as well enjoy it, as this could end up being my last meal if things didn't go well with meeting the pack master.

Cody and I devoured our meals in contemplative silence. My mind was on how I was going to manage this situation so that instead of being murdered by a pack of wolves, I convinced them to help me hunt down some murderers. I don't know what was on Cody's mind, but he seemed deep in thought.

I cleared my throat. "Um, I haven't heard anything about your pack specifically, but I was always warned to stay away from male wolves."

Cody looked up in surprise. "Yeah, there are some packs out there that can be real assholes to the females, but we're not like that."

"How do I know that?" I asked softly.

Cody reached for my hands. "You're going to have to give me a chance to show you. Austin has made it his mission to change the way things are done in our world. Everyone in our pack is treated fairly and with respect." Cody flashed another devastating smile my way. "Plus, I'll be by your side the entire time."

Our waitress sauntered outside towards our table, so I guess we hadn't seen the last of her yet. She asked Cody if he liked his meal and if he needed anything else. He declined, and she turned back in disappointment. She flicked a glance in my direction, and I took the opening to ask for separate checks out of habit. After a couple meals with Kelsey and her friends, I'd quickly realized that if I didn't ask for a separate check, I got stuck with the entire bill.

The waitress shrugged and headed back inside.

"You're not really like other girls, are you?" Cody asked softly, almost to himself.

It was my turn to shrug, and I played with the last lonely fry on my plate, trying to scrape up enough ketchup onto it to be able to eat it without pouring more from the bottle.

Cody's phone vibrated, and he pulled it out. "Austin wants to know if you can come to the house tonight after work?"

So, their pack master already knew that I was here with Cody. Good thing I agreed to the meeting; I wonder what he would have done if I said no. I wasn't sure if I should lie and pretend I needed to go back to work to buy myself some more time, or just try to get this over with as soon as possible.

I opted for as soon as possible, because having to sit and wait in a state of pure anxiety seemed like torture to me.

"I'm done work for the day," I admitted.

"Huh, I guess I should have guessed that because you don't look dressed for work."

I just sighed. "Do I need to wear fancy clothes or anything to meet your pack master?"

He grinned. "Fancy clothes?"

"You know, something other than jeans and a T-shirt? I kinda want to make a good first impression." I wanted to make sure that I could convince this guy to use his resources to help me.

Cody just smiled. "Believe me, what you're wearing now will impress him just fine."

I frowned at him, not sure what he meant by that.

Our waitress came out with both of our checks. Her phone number was written on his, of course. I didn't bother to hide my eye roll this time, but she didn't even notice. I pulled some cash out of my bag because I didn't want to wait for her to run my card and come back again. I had enough interaction with her already.

Cody must have followed my train of thought because he also drew some cash out of his wallet and placed it on his check. We stood up at the same time as the waitress continued to chatter at him. Now that he was standing, she had to tilt her head up at him, as he was at least a foot taller than her.

Cody looked at me in exasperation, but I just grinned and headed for the door.

"Excuse me, I think my date just left," I heard him say to her as I opened the door and started to walk through. He had called this a date earlier as well, but I was sure that he was just using that as a pretense now.

Cody must have recognized me as a wolf during our first meeting and had intended to bring me to his pack master. I felt a twinge of sadness when I realized that I'd been deluded to think that a guy like him would ever be interested in asking me on a real date.

Cody caught up to me, and we walked through the restaurant towards the front door.

"Do you collect stalkers everywhere you go?" I teased him, once again resorting to bad humor in my anxious state.

He opened the door to the outside and gestured for me to go first. "The stalkers are never the girls that I want to have following me," he answered, and I laughed.

"She seemed pretty, though," I told him shyly. I wasn't sure about how he felt about having to ignore the advances of a pretty girl to take me to meet his pack.

"Yeah, pretty annoying," he reassured me.

We shared another grin, and he gestured to a black truck. "This is me."

"Okay, I can follow you there." I started to turn to where I was parked.

He looked embarrassed. "I need to bring you there," he said with a sheepish shrug. "Orders."

I looked at him suspiciously, thinking of all the nefarious reasons behind that decision.

"I promise, I will take you home right after," he assured me. "No funny business." He had turned on his most charming smile, and I tried my best to remain immune to it.

"What about my car?"

Cody looked over to where I gestured to my car.

"I can follow you home, then we can go to the house," he offered.

I thought about pointing out that the logistics didn't make sense. My house was in the opposite direction from Seaside. But I decided to let it go because it had been a while since I went home, and I should attempt to fix my hair and put on a little bit of makeup before meeting the pack master. Plus, I needed a bit more time to get to know Cody and get a feel for the situation that I was about to walk into. I wanted to be fully prepared for whatever awaited me at the pack house.

"All right, so you can follow me," I told him with a small smile.

He smiled back at me. "Don't worry about losing me, I have your address."

I gulped. I was right about the wolves being able to track me down. I murmured something to Cody before I walked over to my car and got in. The wolves at Evelyn's house must have been sent by Cody's pack to investigate her death. That actually made me feel a lot better, because the evidence was pointing toward Cody's pack *not* being the killers. And if they were already after Evelyn's murderers, then it shouldn't be difficult to convince them to help me.

# Chapter 6

I drove home slowly, making sure I didn't lose Cody on the way. I felt apprehension that something unpleasant might be waiting at my house, but I was confident that just about anything would be scared away by Cody's 6'5" heavily muscled frame.

I eyed my neighborhood carefully as we drove through, looking for any unusual people or cars. Nothing seemed out of place as I pulled into my driveway, but I waited at the front door for him before going in.

My security alarm started going off as I pushed the front door open, and I quickly entered my code. Cody hovered behind me as I checked the alarm activity on the security panels. There had been no activity while I was gone, and everything looked normal.

I led Cody into the house and gestured to the couch. "I'm going to shower and change if you want to watch some TV," I offered.

Cody plopped down on the couch, and I tossed him the remote. "Do you want a drink? I have water or diet soda?"

"Water is good."

I tossed him a bottle, then headed upstairs. I was eager to get a hot shower with decent water pressure; the locker room showers on the base weren't exactly five-star quality. After a fantastic shower, I was feeling more like myself. I wrapped a towel around my hair and pulled on my fluffy robe. I went into my closet and eyed my selection of clothing.

I had no idea what to wear to a meeting like this. Cody was wearing jeans, so I figured that would be fine. I owned some black skinny jeans that Kelsey had picked out for me. I decided to dress up a little with a sweater instead of a long-sleeved T-shirt.

Shoes? I had a choice of cute but uncomfortable ankle boots, flats, or Uggs. Since I was already nervous about the meeting, I went with Uggs. I know so many people out there think they're the ugliest shoes in the world, but I'm convinced that's because they've never slipped on a pair and walked on the clouds. They're the most comfortable shoes on the planet, and I desperately needed some comforting.

I towel-dried my hair the best I could, then stared at the wavy blonde mess in the mirror. I sighed and pulled out my hairdryer, I might as well go all-out today. After my pale blonde hair was looking shiny and bright, I swiped some mascara over my eyes to darken my eyelashes. I eyed myself critically in the mirror, then added some bronzer to my pale skin and a little bit of lip gloss. That was more than enough primping for me.

I headed back down to the living room, where Cody's large frame sprawled over my couch. He was intent on playing a game on his phone but glanced up when I jumped down the last couple of stairs.

Cody took a second glance, then stood up. "You look nice...not that you didn't look nice before..." He rubbed a hand through his hair. I was starting to realize he did that when he was nervous. I felt surprised, then flattered. Did I make him nervous?

"Uh, thanks," I said awkwardly. I was eager to change the subject. "Are you ready to go?"

During the ride to the pack master's house, I peppered Cody with questions. Where exactly were we going? How long would it take? What was Austin like? Would more of the pack be there? How many wolves were in the pack?

He answered almost all the questions with a grunt or "You'll see."

I sat in silence to rethink my strategy for getting some answers from him. By that time, the shipyard traffic was out, and the tunnel was backed up for miles. We were going to be sitting in the car for a while if we were heading to Seaside. I chewed my bottom lip and looked across the car at him from under my lashes. Maybe I should try to get him talking about casual stuff and then ease in some questions about the pack.

"What kind of music do you like?" I asked him.

He looked at me with a glint of humor in his eyes. "Giving up already? I thought you had another twenty minutes of questions in you, at the very least."

I narrowed my eyes at him. "This might seem funny to you, but this is my life that's on the line," I told him angrily.

He looked repentant and ran his hand through his hair. "I already promised we aren't going to hurt you. If it makes you more comfortable, I guess it won't hurt to tell you some things, because you're going to see them yourself when we get there." He took a breath, and I leaned forward eagerly.

"The pack house is in Seaside. Austin has a kick-ass mansion where most of the high-ranking pack members live."

"With all their families? That must be a huge house." I tried picturing it.

He looked at me out of the corner of his eye. "The whole pack is a family."

"That sounds nice," I murmured wistfully. What would it have been like to grow up like that? Surrounded by a huge family, full of love.

Cody cleared his throat. "Yeah, you might meet some of them. I don't know who's there right now or if Austin has anything planned..."

That caught my attention. "So how long have you guys known about me?"

He looked embarrassed. "Well, our grounds border the state park that's out that way. There's a river that separates the park from our territory."

I felt incredibly stupid, because Sunday night I'd not only met two of their pack members, I'd also been directly on their hunting grounds.

It was unbelievable that had Evelyn lived so close to them. Would they be angry when they realized how much time I'd spent just under their noses? I was surprised I'd never run into any of them before since I'd spent plenty of time in Seaside or with Evelyn. Or maybe I'd crossed paths with wolves before and just hadn't realized it. Once again, I lamented the knowledge I lacked about my own kind.

Both of us got quiet, and traffic started to go faster once we got through the tunnel. I tormented myself with visions of what was going to happen to me once we got to the house and tried to come up with different ways I could turn this situation to my advantage. I came up with nothing.

Cody turned off the main road and onto a dirt road that was mostly hidden. I looked at him dubiously. "Are you sure you aren't taking me into the middle of the woods to murder me?" I asked him.

He laughed. "You'll see the house in a second. We don't like anyone being able to see the house from the road. We like our privacy."

I nodded, and true to his word, we drove up to the long driveway towards the house. "Are you close to the beach?" I asked him, curious as to why they would put a mansion in the middle of the woods instead of at the beachfront.

Cody nodded. "There's a path that goes from the house, through a small section of a wooded area, and then onto the beach. We also don't like beachgoers or passing boats to know that there's a mansion back there."

That made sense to me. I could see why a house full of werewolves would want to stay hidden from casual human viewers.

I started to squirm as we pulled up to what Cody had described as a "kick-ass mansion." He wasn't exaggerating; if anything, he had undersold it. I looked down at my jeans and Uggs...why hadn't I decided to put on some fancy clothes?

I imagined standing in a room with beautiful men and women dressed to the nines and sneering at me as if I'd tracked mud into their gorgeous house. I hunched down in my seat even more as we pulled up the driveway.

There was what looked to be an eight-car garage – eight! Additionally, there was a small parking lot off to the side. Who needs a parking lot at their house? The lot was half-filled with mostly trucks and a Jeep. So, it looked like there were some members of the pack here after all.

My stomach churned, and I was glad that I'd eaten that burger a few hours ago. Any sooner, and it would be coming up right now.

Cody parked in front of the house and hopped out of his truck. I hesitated to get out, so he came around to the passenger door and opened it. He gave me an encouraging look. "I promise, it isn't going to be that bad."

I just gave him a dirty look. Easy for him to say; he wasn't the one who was about to be on trial here. He tapped his thumb on the door where he was holding it and looked at the ground, considering his next words carefully. "Not all of us here were exactly ideal candidates for a pack. Austin gave us all a chance. I'm sure that he will do the same for you."

"So, he's not…evil or anything?" I asked quietly, searching his eyes.

He burst out in a laugh, and I realized how childish that must have sounded. I was essentially asking him to tell me that the monster under my bed wouldn't hurt me.

"No, he's not evil," he told me with a massive grin on his face. He shook his head and chuckled again before holding out a hand to help me out of the truck. I jumped down, and he shut the door behind me. He tossed his keys up and down in the air as he strode confidently toward the front door.

He opened the door and waved me in. I stepped inside and tried not to stare. I'd never been anywhere this nice before. The entryway looked empty as if someone hadn't gotten around to decorate just yet, but it was undeniably expensive. Cody tilted his head to one side, almost as if listening, then stated, "Office."

He strode off, and I slunk along slowly behind him. He reached a door around the corner and down the hall and stopped. He looked back at me as if he just realized that I hadn't been right behind him the entire time.

I hurried a little, as I realized he was waiting at the door for me. The closer I got to the door, the harder my heart was pounding. I fought the urge to turn and run the other way. Almost in slow motion, Cody turned the door handle and opened the door.

My eyes were drawn to the two men across the room. One was sitting behind a giant desk, and the other was half-sitting, half-leaning on the front right side of the desk. Both had their eyes on me with weighted stares. Cody had to nudge me forward a little until I was entirely in the room.

"Thanks, Cody," the man behind the desk stated. I couldn't tell how tall he was while he was sitting, but he was certainly good-looking, with dark golden hair and light eyes. He wore slacks and a button-down shirt with a few of the top buttons opened. His sleeves were rolled up, and I could see tattoos on his arms, which was an interesting look for someone dressed as a businessman.

I heard the click of the door behind me, and I turned to look for Cody. He was gone, and he had left me here with there with two strangers. I took a few steps backward until my back was pressed up against the door.

The man with the dark hair stood up from the desk he had been leaning on and started towards me. I just stared at him with huge eyes. He was almost as tall as Cody, but he was more lean than bulky. He had dark hair and olive skin that told me that he might be Italian or maybe from somewhere along the Mediterranean. He stopped three feet in front of me, and we just stared at each other.

I stood up straighter, unwilling to cower in front of either of these guys. I came here to get some answers, and I wanted help to find Evelyn's killers. I wouldn't let them scare me out of doing either of those things.

"James," the man at the desk murmured softly. My eyes snapped over to him where he was now leaning forward on the desk with his hands folded in front of him.

James relaxed a little. "Anna, you're not an easy person to track down."

"Well, why were you tracking me, James?" I answered snarkily.

He snorted. "I received word from two of our wolves on patrol that they had found a fluffy little white wolf prancing around on our territory."

I huffed. "I'm not fluffy, and I don't prance."

"In my report, there was mention of firefly chasing." He smirked. "Do you also chase butterflies in the daytime?" I turned bright red, mostly because he was right. My wolf loved to play and chase things. Fireflies and butterflies were included on that list of items.

I squared my shoulders back and stepped forward. I wasn't going to cower in front of this...ass.

I decided to ignore him for the moment and focused on the man with the golden hair at the desk. "I guess I can assume you're Austin?"

He smiled and leaned back in the chair. "I am."

"That's the way you're going to petition to join our pack?" James asked incredulously.

I just looked at him. I had no idea how I was supposed to petition for a pack. I was a little surprised that joining their pack was an option. Cody had promised to keep me safe, so I hadn't expected the torture and murder that Evelyn had frightened me with all of the years, but I'd expected them to ask me to leave their territory. Although, by the way that James was looking at me now, torture and murder might still be on the table.

"James is our security expert. He does the initial screening to see if a person is a potential candidate for membership in our pack, " Austin explained.

James scowled. I had the feeling that if it were up to him, I wouldn't be a potential candidate.

"From a security perspective, we do have some questions for you before we can move forward. I see you have a security clearance with the military already. That's good." Austin turned the page in an open folder, and I slid a little closer to his desk. Was that a folder on me?

James swung his arm wide. "Please, come in, have a seat." Sarcasm dripped from his words.

I didn't even give him the satisfaction of glaring at him. I just stalked across the room with my head held high and settled into one of the two plush chairs sitting in front of the desk. I folded my hands in my lap and got comfortable. James followed me and took up his spot at the front of the desk. He crossed his arms over his chest and glared down at me. I ignored him.

Austin just smiled at me again. "You currently work for the Navy. That's also good. Almost all of us here are prior or active-duty military."

My jaw dropped. "How could any of you have been in the military? I thought wolves couldn't join?"

James chuckled. "Who told you that, little wolf?"

"I…" I didn't want to mention Evelyn to him. If he did anything to disrespect her memory, I would probably launch myself at him in an attempt to wipe that smirk right off his face.

I just shrugged. "I guess I just thought it would be too difficult to hide what we are."

Thankfully, he left the topic alone, and Austin continued. "One thing that James couldn't figure out is where you came from initially."

Out of the corner of my eye, I saw James' face tighten. I imagine that he wouldn't like to be reminded of his failings. I made a note to myself to mention them often. And repeatedly.

"I don't know either," I answered honestly. "All I know is that I was adopted. I tried to go online to see if I could use one of those services that links up adopted kids with their birth parents, but I didn't have any luck."

I'd desperately searched for years, praying that someone would come to save me from my uncle and the hell I lived in. No one ever did, and I learned an important lesson. Hoping and praying wouldn't get you anywhere, you had to save yourself. I stopped looking and used college to get out of that life. I figured that if my birth parents wanted to find me, they would have done so already. Evelyn was more than enough family for me.

However, I wasn't about to let James know about any of that. I'm sure his research would have shown that I had a relatively normal childhood; Uncle was cautious about what was said about him in the community.

Austin just gave a quiet hum at my answer and continued to look through the folder. I leaned forward as far as I could without being obvious about it, but I wanted to know what was in that folder.

James tapped his fingers on the desk impatiently. "Do you mind if I get straight to the heart of the matter?"

Austin waved a few fingers in the air without looking up, giving James permission to ask his questions.

"Why was your scent all over the scene of my murder investigation?"

My heart stopped. James must have been talking about Evelyn. "What murder are you investigating?" I asked cautiously.

"Have you pranced through multiple crime scenes lately? You're having a difficult time telling which one I'm talking about?"

I ground my teeth. I really didn't like this guy.

"Well, if there were butterflies involved, I might not have noticed a crime scene," I replied sweetly.

A laugh burst out of Austin, and James' face got redder than I thought possible.

"I'm talking about Evelyn Heights," he ground out.

"That was *my* crime scene investigation," I told him. "And if you were a good security expert, you would know exactly why I was there."

I crossed my arms across my chest as I sat back in the chair and gazed at him defiantly.

At this point, I was sure that he was one of the two men I saw breaking into Evelyn's house, so I decided to instigate him further. "And you should have also realized I was watching you go through her house later that night. I still haven't crossed you off *my* list of suspects."

James spluttered, so I'd assumed correctly, and he had been one of the burglars.

Austin chuckled. "I can assure you that James isn't the murderer," he told me. "I kept a close eye on him all Saturday night."

"While you were sleeping?" I looked at him doubtfully. "And what about early that morning?"

"We were on a pack run that night out in the country. I assure you that his alibi is airtight." Austin still seemed amused, which I took to be a good sign.

"It sounds like James could probably use your help with the investigation," Austin told me with a twinkle in his eye. It turned out I was wrong; James' face could get redder. I think Austin might be trying to see just how red he got before he exploded.

"I guess I could help him out," I groused, playing along with Austin.

"Excellent," Austin stated. "We don't offer anyone pack membership right away. We have a thirty-day trial, then a year-long probation before you can officially join the pack."

"That seems fair," I answered. Maybe these wolves weren't as bad as the ones Evelyn grew up with. There are bad humans and good humans out there. It makes sense that wolves would also be a mix since we're human part of the time.

"I need to go over the pack rules with you, to see if you would be able to live with them," Austin told me seriously.

My anxiety crept back up, this where he was going to tell me about horrible things that I was going to have to do.

"The first rule is that we always support each other."

I nodded in confusion.

Austin smiled reassuringly. "What I mean by that is, we treat each other as family. We're organized with a rank structure, but at the end of the day we're all brothers, and we always have our brothers' backs."

That didn't sound too bad. That actually sounded nice.

"The second rule is that you respect the rank system that we have in place. You don't issue challenges, and you don't disrespect anyone higher ranking or disobey orders. If you have a problem with how you're treated by a superior or bothered by something that they ask you to do, you can come to Cody, James, or myself. We'll sit down with you and work out the problem without having violence involved. Violence within the pack is forbidden."

I nodded again. None of that would be a problem for me; a non-violent pack sounded exactly like something I would want.

"The next rule is that everyone works for the good of the pack, and everyone contributes. We make sure everyone has a home, a good job, and everything that they need. In return, we ask you to work for the pack or work for one of the businesses that the pack operates."

I looked at him nervously. "Does your pack currently have an opening for a pharmacist?" I asked dubiously.

James snorted, and Austin shot him a look.

"I understand that you currently work for a military hospital?"

"Yes," I answered, probably unnecessarily. I'm sure my entire life was written in the folder that he had in front of him.

"We have some pack members who are currently serving active-duty or who are enrolled full-time in college, so we're flexible with how we can work with you. I will most likely assign you duties that serve the interests of the pack directly, instead of assigning you to a work detail at one of our companies."

"So, you don't have a problem with me keeping my job?" I asked hopefully.

Austin gave me a warm smile. "No, I can see that you like your job. I don't want to take that away from you. We'll work around your schedule."

My heart started to get lighter. Maybe this could work! Never had I ever thought that I might be able to join a pack one day. I certainly never thought that I would get to be part of a pack that was so opposite to everything Evelyn had told me about. I was starting to get excited at the thought.

Austin nodded. "Let's talk about rank," he continued. "We don't fight for dominance like a lot of other packs do. You probably think that's odd."

I shook my head no. I had no idea how other packs worked, not that I wanted to admit that to James.

Austin looked more animated as he spoke. "We use more of a military structure here. We determine your rank by your desire and ability to lead, job skills, and merit. Physical strength might factor into some of the work assignments we take on, but strength and the ability to fight well don't always make a good leader."

I nodded along as he spoke. Austin was very charismatic, and I could tell this was an important issue for him. What he was saying so far made sense, and I could this pack was much different from what Evelyn had told me about wolves.

"We do a lot of things differently in this pack, as you will start to notice as you spend more time with us. Not everyone in the wolf community likes that we're doing something unconventional here, and not everyone is a good fit for our pack. If we decide this isn't a good fit for you, I'll do everything I can to find you a pack that would be a good fit."

I was surprised at his earnestness and a little touched by his concern for my well-being.

"I take it you're most familiar with the Navy rank structure?" Austin asked.

I nodded in agreement.

"We have two prior Navy in the pack, but the majority of us are former Army or prior active-duty Marines," Austin told me. I smiled a little that he had called the Marines "prior active-duty." Most Marines strongly objected to being called former Marines or ex-Marines; they believed 'once a Marine, always a Marine.'

My attention went back to Austin as he continued. "You're a civilian at the hospital. Where do you fit in the military ranking system there? Are civilians kept separate or incorporated into the military structure?"

Finally, here was a question I could answer. "Our mission at the hospital is patient care. The CO runs the command similar to the way a ship would be run, with some obvious differences."

James and Austin seemed to be listening carefully, so I continued. "In my department, all the pharmacists are expected to do the same job, whether they're active-duty, reservists, GS, or contract. The military officers do have some additional requirements and command duties that they're expected to complete. Still, for the most part, we're all interchangeable and work on a rotating schedule."

He nodded. "That's unusual to see in the field, but I can understand how health care would be different."

I nodded. "While at work, a nurse is a nurse, a doctor is a doctor, and a pharmacist is a pharmacist."

"So, if you were in the Navy, what would your equivalent rank be?"

"Pharmacists are lieutenants when they first come in. In the first few years, they do mostly staffing, and then transition into more leadership positions. As a staff pharmacist, I would be doing the job of a lieutenant for life. In contrast, most of the lieutenants I work with now will move into Division Officer or Department Head positions once they reach Lieutenant Commander or Commander."

"So, an O3?" Austin mused.

James laughed. "There's no way. We would only consider a status like that for someone who we were recruiting with significant leadership experience in both the military and their prior pack. You have neither of those. I don't see that you have anything at all that you can bring to our pack."

The tiny tendrils of hope that had been growing in my heart shriveled at his words. He was right. What did I have to offer any of them?

"James," Austin said softly.

"It's better to be harsh now than to give her false hope."

"Anna, can you step outside for a moment while James and I consult?" Austin said gently.

I nodded and walked to the door quickly. The solid wood door was more substantial than I'd expected, so I needed to use my full strength to open it. I stepped out and allowed the door to sink closed behind me with a thunk.

I didn't see anyone else in the hallway. Cody had disappeared completely, and I listened for signs of anyone nearby. Seeing no one, I couldn't help my curiosity and placed my ear against the door to see if I could hear anything.

Nothing.

I slid down the wall and sat down to wait. I had a feeling this was going to be a long conversation between them. I fantasized for a moment about what it would be like to be accepted into a pack as a family member. I'd spent most of my life being on the outside looking in. What would it be like to be one of those happy, smiling people at barbecues and Thanksgiving dinners? I imagined feeling safe, protected, and loved. But what could I offer them in return?

I looked around the hall of the giant mansion I was in. They had money, they probably had professional chefs, maids, and other workers to fill the typical "female" duties of a household. I wasn't looking to be a housewife, kept at home to take care of the house anyway, but I couldn't think of what other duties they might assign me.

Austin had never explicitly said what jobs their pack was involved in, but I was guessing that those jobs relied heavily on military skills. Skills that I didn't have. I hoped that whatever military-like jobs this pack was taking on were on behalf of bettering the world. Austin seemed like a good guy, but I could see James being the head of an international league of assassins.

I heard voices coming towards me, and I scrambled up off the floor. It sounded like several people were coming in the same way that I had earlier; they were headed this way. Just as they were about to turn the corner so I could get a look at who it was, the door to Austin's office opened back up.

James scowled at me and gestured for me to come back in. Austin smiled at me from his chair behind the desk, and I took a seat back in the same chair I'd occupied earlier.

"We have decided that it wouldn't be fair for us to place you in a position of authority over anyone in our pack."

My heart sunk. This was it, they were going to toss me out of the house, out of their territory. I would be homeless, jobless, friendless, and family-less - if that last one was even a word. I tried to push those thoughts away so I could think of what I was going to do.

Austin continued. "But we still want to offer you a position here in the pack."

I looked up hopefully. "So, I'll just be ranked at the bottom?" That couldn't be that bad, could it?

They both looked uncomfortable.

"That wouldn't be a good idea either," Austin told me hesitantly.

I was confused.

"So…where does that leave me?"

James and Austin looked at each other, then at me.

"We're not sure just yet," Austin murmured.

Suddenly, a crazy idea came to me. "Did you know that the Vatican is actually its own country inside of Rome?"

James looked confused at the abrupt change in subject, but Austin cocked his head at me, and a grin suddenly spread over his face. I could see that he knew where I was going with this right away.

"So, what you're saying is that you have essentially been maintaining your own pack lands inside of my territory."

"Not exactly. It's more like your territory just happens to surround mine," I told him confidently.

Austin laughed.

James looked at Austin incredulously. "You're not seriously thinking about this. She can't have a piece of our territory to have a pretend-pack."

"I think that what Anna is suggesting is that we merge our packs," Austin said with amusement in his voice.

I nodded in agreement. "So, I wouldn't need to be incorporated into the pack hierarchy right away."

"That's not how this works," James ground out, his teeth clenched.

Austin nodded to agree with him. "That wouldn't work. But your idea of a separate pack gives me another idea. Females could be ranked separately from males in the pack. Everyone would still fall under my authority, but females would have a different chain of command that reported directly to me."

I nodded. The only problem would be the other females in the pack. How would they feel about being considered 'separate' from the men in the pack? I could see this not going over well.

"How many females are in your pack?"

Austin paused. "Including you? That would be one."

My jaw dropped. "You don't have any females in your pack? Isn't that unusual?"

"We didn't see a need for any," James arrogantly told me.

Have I mentioned how much I really didn't like this guy?

"What James means to say is that we haven't found any females who would mesh well with our mission and our pack. Most female wolves tend to be...difficult."

"Not all females are the same." I was steaming. "I understand that females aren't welcome in all parts of the military, and I even understand some of the reasoning behind it. But females aren't worthless and can contribute a lot to your mission and your pack."

"And that's one of the reasons why I want you here," Austin interrupted. "A lot of the guys in the pack have had negative interactions with females, and it has affected the way they view females in general. We need a good female to show them how awesome the female half of our species is."

I did feel a little better at that. I could understand how they felt because I had a somewhat negative view of men, both from my experience with my uncle and the fear of male wolves that Evelyn had instilled inside me. I knew that I had some issues to work through, so I would be a hypocrite for judging anyone for having similar issues.

"So, we agree to merge our packs," Austin announced with a grin. James rolled his eyes.

"It's not going to be easy to introduce the pack to this," Austin warned me. "You're going to have to work hard to prove yourself. Plus, James and I are going to have to figure out a plan to introduce you to the pack. It's going to take some time for you to be fully incorporated, but I'll let you know what your next step is. For now, I need you to keep your head down and not attract any attention from outside wolves."

I nodded again. I had a lot of competing emotions swirling around in my head. I was excited that I was going to get a chance to be a part of the pack, but I was worried they would never really accept me.

Would this be like going back to high school? Surrounded by mean girls and tormented daily? Only in this scenario, the mean girls from high school would instead be vicious wolves.

*I can't see this going badly at all*, I thought sarcastically to myself.

Austin considered me. "It has also been obvious during our conversation that you don't follow the usual customs."

I just looked at him with a confused look on my face.

James snorted. "She's never been part of a pack before. How would she know?"

"Yes, that makes sense," Austin said with a nod. "So much of what we are is ingrained in us since birth. You'd have missed out on a lot being raised as a human."

My face turned bright red with embarrassment. "Uh, I hope I didn't do anything to offend you?"

"Well, you certainly didn't act appropriately for a lone wolf coming to speak with a pack master and ask for admittance into his pack," James told me sternly.

I just glared at James. I wasn't asking him if *he* was offended.

Austin didn't seem to be insulted and still had a grin on his face. He stood up, and I sensed that our meeting had reached its conclusion.

But there were still so many questions that I needed to be answered before I could walk away. I decided to stick with the most important of all of them. "What about the investigation? Whoever murdered Evelyn is still out there, and they think they got away with it," I growled.

"This seems more personal than just investigating a wolf kill near your territory." James eyed me suspiciously.

Had I given him too much credit? He must not know as much as he thought he did. However, there probably wasn't any documentation to link me with Evelyn. She had always been careful not to have my name associated with hers. I guess the only way we could be associated together was from one of my co-workers mentioning I brought her to events, or by realizing that we were neighbors when I was growing up.

I decided that since Austin was taking a chance on me and trusting me by letting me into his pack, I should also make an effort to trust him.

I cleared my throat. "Evelyn was like a grandmother to me. She was a neighbor when I was growing up, and she was the one who told me what I was. She guided me through my change, and I may not have survived without her."

James and Austin both looked shocked. Austin sat back in his chair, and James pulled out the chair next to mine and sat. Of course, he was careful to pull it a safe distance away from mine.

They both looked at each other, having a silent conversation.

James put his head in his hands. "I can't believe I missed that."

Austin looked at me sharply. "She wasn't a wolf?"

I shook my head no. "Not exactly. Her father was a wolf, but her mother was human. Her father kept her in the pack for...breeding purposes. He gave her to another male wolf, and she had a daughter. The pack kept both of them as prisoners to keep the generations going, but her daughter didn't survive the...breeding efforts." Even James looked horrified at that.

"Evelyn ran from the pack, and she's been in hiding ever since. She figured out what I was and took care of me despite everything that had been done to her. She loved me as if I were her own granddaughter and taught me everything I know about wolves."

"That definitely explains why you were so terrified to be brought in here." Austin gazed at me sympathetically. "If I'd known a little more about your past, I would have handled this situation much differently.

James looked guilty. "I..."

"Not your fault," Austin assured him. "It seems like our new wolf is good at hiding and keeping secrets. I think she is going to fit in here just fine."

James glanced at me, and I think he was feeling a little repentant for being such an ass to me, but he didn't speak.

"So, did you guys steal Evelyn's body, or was that the murderers?" I blurted out.

Austin's eyebrows rose, and he looked at James. James scowled. "No one stole the body. I notified the appropriate chain of command that there was a possible wolf kill on our territory. They have a protocol for how they dispose of the evidence."

Rage rose inside me, and I growled. "Evelyn wasn't evidence to be disposed of," I told him angrily. "She was everything to me!" Furious tears leaked out of the corners of my eyes, and I brushed them away impatiently.

"I didn't mean it that way," James said softly with an apology in his eyes. I tried to push my rage down; being angry would only hurt me, not them.

Austin cut in. "What James meant to say is that we're both sorry for your loss, and we're here for you. We're your pack now, and we're going to help you through this."

I took a deep breath to calm down. I was reassured by Austin's words and by the sincerity in his eyes. I'd been at a complete standstill in my investigation, with no idea of where to turn next when Cody had tracked me down. Maybe being found by these wolves would turn out to be a good thing if they could help me track down Evelyn's killers and get justice for her.

"Thank you," I told him quietly. "Could you help me locate her remains? I want to plan a service for her, to say goodbye." I tried to finish my sentence without breaking down in tears in front of these guys, but I couldn't get the words out without my voice breaking at the end.

I cleared my throat in embarrassment, and both of them pretended that I wasn't about to have an emotional breakdown. I appreciated that and tried to pull myself together.

Austin turned to James. "I'm sure we could coordinate that. James, could you make the necessary arrangements?"

"I'll see what I can do," James answered without any expression on his face.

I looked at him doubtfully, but his answer seemed to satisfy Austin because he nodded at James.

"And her house?" I added. I didn't want some stranger going through all of her things.

"She didn't name you the executor of the estate?" Austin asked, looking confused.

"She didn't want my name associated with hers in any way, in case her old pack came looking. She didn't want anything of hers to lead them to me."

James nodded. "That was smart. If she had named you, you would have been the first stop on my investigation."

Austin gave him an unreadable look. "If she didn't name anyone specifically as an heir, we can make sure the house goes to the pack. We'll help you to go through her things and decide what to do when you're ready, but there's no rush."

I was relieved. "Thank you."

Austin drummed his fingers on the tabletop and changed the topic of conversation. "So, the reason you were hiding on base was from Evelyn's old pack, and not from us?"

I was surprised - they knew that I'd been hiding on base?

"I didn't even realize there was a pack here," I answered honestly.

"Hmmm...I think we're going to change our plans. I'm going to have you stay here for a while until we can determine if Evelyn's old pack knows about you," Austin told me as he tapped his fingers on the desk thoughtfully.

As much as I wanted to protest, I was also afraid to go home alone. I was uncomfortable with the idea of staying here - I wasn't the type of person who belonged in a fancy mansion. I also felt awkward knowing that the mansion was full of wolves that I had yet to meet. I wanted to go home and snuggle up in my own bed, but that wasn't an option.

"I could stay at a hotel or something. I don't want to impose," I suggested cautiously.

"I know this place must look kind of small, but I promise we can find some space for you," Austin said with a sparkle in his eye. He turned to James. "Can we have Cody take her back home to get her things?"

"Cody's busy."

"Who else do we have?"

James winced. "The twins should be done with classes for the day."

Austin groaned.

"It's them or one of us," James pointed out.

"You're going to have to talk with them first," Austin told him. James nodded and rose. He headed towards the door without another glance at me.

It was just Austin and I alone in the office now as James closed the door behind him.

Austin cleared his throat and looked awkward. "I know you may have heard the worst about our kind, but I want you to realize that not all packs are like that. There are still a lot of packs out there who are old-fashioned and believe that we're ruled by violence and instinct, but my pack is unique. I'm trying to prove that we can evolve, we can be better."

That explained why he was so passionate about how he ran his pack. He was essentially running a social experiment in an attempt to convince wolf society that they needed to change.

"I understand. I want you to know that I'm on board with the mission, and I will do whatever I can to help," I told him readily. It was true. From everything that he'd said to me about his pack and his mission, this was something that I wanted to be a part of, and I was hopeful that I could find a place to belong here in the pack.

He smiled at me. "I appreciate that. James should be back with the twins in a moment. I have to warn you that they can be a little rambunctious at times, but their hearts are in the right place."

"They *are* adults, right?" I asked hesitantly.

He barked out a laugh. "Yes, it'll be quite obvious they're adults when you meet them."

I blushed. I had one more question that I needed to ask, but I had no idea how to approach Austin with the issue. I was embarrassed to be asking at all, but I wanted to be prepared.

"Um, so you know, Evelyn had told me some stories from her old pack and how they treated the females. I have to ask... am I safe here, in the mansion with other wolves around?" My voice ended in a whisper, and I could feel my face burning in embarrassment.

Austin started to reach out for me, then stopped when he saw me flinch. He dropped his arms to his sides. "I'm sorry about anything that happened to Evelyn, or to you in the past, but I promise you that no one in my pack will harm you or lay a hand on you." He spoke softly with a worried look in his eyes. "This pack is unique for a lot of reasons, but one thing I will tell you is that no one was born into this pack. Everyone here was hand-selected to join by me."

I was surprised. "I thought your pack was hereditary unless you were traded to a different pack."

"Normally, it is. But I claimed a small amount of land and built my pack from nothing. I trust every single person in this pack. They're all good men. And now I have a good woman here as well." Austin smiled at me encouragingly.

I hoped I would be able to meet his expectations. I wasn't exactly sure what I would be doing for the pack, but I had the impression he didn't have a clear plan either.

"James should have briefed the twins by now. Let's go introduce you to them," Austin suggested.

I stood up and headed to the door with him close behind me. I started to open the door, and he pulled it open the rest of the way and held it so that I could step through.

James was in the hall with two men. His back was to me, but the other two men were facing me. One was scowling at James. "So, you want us to teach her how to be a wolf?"

The second man nudged him and tilted his head towards Austin and me coming out of the office.

James turned toward us with a look of exasperation on his face, and the two twins eyed me curiously.

"Anna, this is Mason and Jason." Seriously? Their parents gave them rhyming names? Poor guys, they probably had to wear matching clothes, too, while they were kids. I kept my thoughts to myself and tried to smile through my nervousness.

It didn't help that these guys were insanely hot. James was good looking in a scary way, and Austin was handsome but a little intimidating as the pack master. These guys were just gorgeous. They were tall like James and Austin but not quite as tall as Cody. They both had light brown hair with some gold highlights from the sun. Their matching hazel eyes were both trained on me.

What was it with this pack and tall, good looking men? I felt a little self-conscious because I didn't look like I belonged in this group of beautiful people; I was more of a plain Jane.

I gave an awkward wave at the twins. One smiled in a friendly way, the other still had the hints of a scowl on his face but nodded at me in greeting.

"Your orders are to stay with her. Keep her safe, teach her what she needs to know to fit in the pack, and keep your hands off her. Any questions?" Austin barked out at them.

"No, sir," they both replied in unison, standing up straight.

"Very good. James, I believe we had a few more things to discuss?"

I could tell already that Austin was gentler with me than he was with the other pack members. He had a little bit of softness in his eyes when he looked at me that was missing when he interacted with the guys.

I wasn't sure if that was going to bode well for me, or end up causing trouble with the rest of the pack. If they thought I was being treated favorably because I was a girl, that would undermine my goal of teaching the pack that women could be their equal.

I sighed to myself, but brushed those thoughts aside for now. Right now, I had twins to deal with. There was a moment of silence after the door clicked shut behind Austin and James.

All three of us stood there awkwardly. I decided to break the ice. "So, um, Austin didn't say which one of you was which?"

They both laughed. The scowly one answered me. "Most people tend to treat both of us as one unit, 'the twins' or 'Mason and Jason' together as one phrase." He made air quotes with his hands.

"I'm Jason," the friendlier of the two answered. So, that means Mr. Grumpy was Mason.

I looked at them both carefully, cataloging any distinguishing marks that would keep me from embarrassing myself by calling them by the wrong names.

"I heard Mary-Kate and Ashley had the same problem growing up," I blurted out, falling victim to my nervousness, which caused my awful humor to emerge. The scowl lifted from Mason, and he looked amused. At least that got him moving in the right direction.

"James said we need to take you home to pack up your stuff?" Mason asked with only a slight frown.

"Which room did he say you could have here? Is he going to let you have the big room next to his?" Jason added.

The twins asked me questions right after the other, without giving me time to answer.

I took a deep breath. "I do need to get some stuff. Austin didn't mention how long I was staying, but he said he could find space for me here," I said, meeting each of their eyes as I answered their questions.

They both shrugged. "Let's go."

Mason tossed his keys up in the air absentmindedly as he walked, and Jason snatched them out of his reach before they came back down.

"I'm driving this time."

"Fine, but I call shotgun."

They both glanced at me as if expecting an argument. I just shrugged. "Fine with me."

We walked out the front door, and Mason headed toward a silver Jeep parked in the parking lot next to the house. Jason hesitated and looked at the garage with a mischievous look in his eye. Mason looked back at him curiously. "What?"

"We should take the Range Rover. Austin and James are going to be in that meeting for a while."

Mason's eyes twinkled back at him. "James is going to be pissed."

That was all I needed to hear. "Then I vote yes." They both looked at me in surprise, and huge grins broke out on their faces. Good lord. I thought they were good-looking before.

Jason bounded back into the house, shouting over his shoulder, "I'll bring it out front."

"James keeps his spare keys in the garage in case of an emergency," Mason told me as Jason disappeared into the house. "He changed his hiding place from last time, but you would think he would learn his lesson." Mason shook his head with a shit-eating grin on his face.

I chuckled. "So, I'm not the only person that James is a complete asshat to?"

Mason laughed and reached out to put his arm around my shoulders. "I like you."

I tried not to flinch, but my body was tense. I hated the fact that I reacted like this to any type of physical affection, but I took a deep breath and concentrated on making sure it wasn't noticeable.

The sound of one of the garage doors opening caught our attention, and Mason dropped his arm as we walked over to the slowly opening garage bay. Jason was sitting in the driver's seat of a brand new, very shiny black Range Rover.

Mason opened the front passenger side door and gestured for me to get in.

I put my hand over my heart. "Are you offering me shotgun?"

He smirked. "Don't get used to it. I'm just being nice since it's your first day with us."

I hopped in, and he shut the door behind me. This was a nice car; the inside of it was just as impeccably kept as the outside. I looked up at Jason. "So, we're definitely going to get this car muddy before we bring it back, right?"

"I like you," he answered. He met Mason's eyes through the rear-view mirror. "I vote we make her part of the team."

"Agreed. You're in trouble now," Mason warned from the back. "It's not often we agreed to let just anyone in on our shenanigans."

I laughed and leaned back in the seat. Maybe being in a pack wasn't going to be as terrifying as I thought. It might turn out to be even better than I hoped for.

# Chapter 7

The playful and mischievous attitude of the twins was exactly what I needed right now. The intense amount of pressure that I felt squeezing down on me the last couple of days was slowly lifting, and I felt almost giddy with relief.

After my meeting with Austin, I had high hopes. I knew James would be forced to work with me to find Evelyn's killers, and once we found the pack responsible, we could figure out what was going on. Had one of her old pack mates wanted revenge on her? Had the pack master wanted to make an example out of her to prevent others from trying to escape?

I wish Evelyn were here with me now. For as long as I'd known her, she had always lived in fear and had never felt safe. She'd never let herself get attached to a home because she always said that she may have to leave at a moment's notice. I wish she could have met Austin and had the feeling of being welcomed into a pack and kept safe.

I comforted myself by daydreaming of what would happen once we found Evelyn's old pack. I was fairly confident that I could convince Austin to save any females who were still left there. I'm sure he would agree that they shouldn't have to live under the oppression and slavery that Evelyn had described to me. It comforted me to picture her smiling down on me in satisfaction from heaven once I'd accomplished all of that.

I wasn't a religious person, but I was sure Evelyn was in a good place now. She had such a kind soul, and she had sacrificed so much that she deserved an eternity of happiness, comfort, and security. I only wished I could have provided her that while she was on Earth.

I snapped out of my daydreaming to referee the twins. Jason was tormenting Mason with his music choices, and Mason had finally lunged up front to try and reach the console. I smacked his hands away from the controls.

"Don't you guys know that the navigator is always in charge of the music selection?"

Mason settled back down in the back. "We'll see." He crossed his arms over his chest as I flicked through the radio.

"C'mon, where's some Britney Spears?" I teased them.

Both guys groaned. I stopped going once I recognized the first chords of Wonderwall by Oasis. "Everyone knows the words to this song." I grinned and theatrically started to sing along. They both got in on the fun, and we all tried to outdo each other with our terrible renditions.

As we got closer to my house, I needed to do more navigating and less karaoke.

We pulled into my neighborhood, and I admired the fall colors of the trees that lined the perfectly manicured lawns and walking paths.

"This is nice," Mason said. "It's not what I expected when you said you lived all the way out here." I lived pretty far from Seaside in an area that, up until recently, had been mostly undeveloped forest or farms. Most people didn't realize how much construction had gone up this way in such a short time.

I purchased a house in one of the new neighborhoods a few months ago. The advantage of living this far from the beach was that houses were a third of the price, so I could afford one. I'd worked two jobs for a while after I graduated, and I'd lived in a tiny studio apartment when most of my classmates were spending their first 'real' paychecks on new cars and parties.

My sacrifice had paid off because I saved up enough for a down payment and achieved something I'd thought would never happen - I owned my own home. I spent so many years being unwanted in my uncle's house; sleeping on a fold-out bed in the den, and having to erase all signs of my presence when I got up in the morning.

I'd never had a place to call my own before now. When I finally left my uncle's home, it had been to a college dorm where I shared a room with two other girls. I never had any type of privacy in that situation, and my roommates were always borrowing my stuff without asking.

Once I was in pharmacy school and working on my doctorate, I'd been able to move into an apartment that I shared with only three other girls. It was less crowded than in the dorm, where I shared communal showers with twelve other people, but it was nothing compared to owning my own home.

I didn't have the words to adequately describe the flash of joy I felt every day knowing that when I came home from work, my stuff would still be there, exactly how I left it. I could wake up in the morning and take a shower in my own bathroom. I didn't have to clean or cook for other people, and if I cleaned up a mess, it was because I made it. Having my own house gave me a sense of freedom that I'd never felt before.

We pulled into the driveway of my house. It was a cute two-story with a one-car garage, not nearly as impressive as the colossal mansion we just came from, but it was mine, and that made it the best house in the world. I hopped out of the car and skipped to the front door, entering my code into the electronic lock. Mason followed me in as I put my code into the security system to stop its insistent beeping.

"Jason is going to take a look around outside the house and check for anything unusual." I nodded in acknowledgment and kicked off my boots in the entryway so that I wouldn't track anything on the new carpets. I went to the fridge and peered in; it was pretty empty because I stayed the weekend at Kelsey's house and then avoided coming home yesterday. It had been hours since the burger, and I was starving.

Mason stood behind me as I gazed forlornly into the fridge. "I think you need to go shopping," he told me earnestly.

I just grunted in answer.

"We can probably stop and get something on the way back. Jason and I haven't gotten dinner yet."

My stomach picked that moment to growl loudly. We both laughed, and I grabbed some chips from the pantry. I plopped down on the couch with them and picked up my iPad. "Do you care if I order some stuff to make dinner?"

"Where are you going to order from?" he asked, sounding confused and reaching a hand out to grab some chips. He was probably confused by the "make dinner" part of my question.

"The grocery store down the street will deliver," I told him.

He looked a little impressed. "I didn't know they did that."

"Oh, yeah. The best part is that they'll also deliver alcohol."

"Really?" he asked doubtfully.

I quickly logged onto the app. "Do you guys like Mexican?"

"Yeah." He sprawled down on the couch next to me and nudged my leg with his foot. "Order beer."

I rolled my eyes. "What kind?"

I selected my quick list named "Mexican" that already had all the items I needed for tacos and fajitas and then added his request for beer.

The front door slammed, and Jason came into the living room. He eyed us both just sitting on the couch and claimed the loveseat for himself. "What are we doing?"

"Anna is going to cook us dinner."

"Really?" He looked surprised.

"No," I corrected him. "I'm going to make you guys help while I supervise, especially with the chopping."

"That's cool, we like knives," Jason grinned. He mimed throwing one, and I rolled my eyes.

Jason jumped to his feet. "Where's the food? Let's get started. I'm starving!"

I explained that we were waiting on the groceries to be delivered, and he looked just as impressed as Mason had. Judging by the house they lived in, I would have guessed they had a team of servants to take care of them.

They both laughed when I asked, and they explained that the two of them did the grocery shopping and procuring of food since they were the lowest ranking wolves living in the house.

"So, they just bring you all your stuff without going to the store? How long does that take?" Jason asked.

"It will probably be an hour or so."

"Huh, that's probably how long that would have taken if we ordered pizza."

I turned sideways on the couch, positioning a pillow against the armrest behind my back and swinging my legs up and over to my side of the sofa. My knees were up so I could keep my legs on my side of the couch, and I leaned my iPad up against my thighs. "Teach me some wolf stuff."

Mason scooped his arm around my feet and gently laid them over his thighs so my legs could stretch out.

He leaned back into the couch with his hands behind his head and gave a deep sigh as he relaxed. I tensed up when he first touched me, unsure of what he was doing. But I relaxed as I looked over at him.

My calves were across his thighs, but other than that, he wasn't touching me. I wasn't familiar with this kind of casual touching but decided I kind of liked it. It was comforting in a friendly way. With him reclined and exposed like that, he was the opposite of threatening right now.

Jason had taken advantage of the distraction and snatched the bag of chips off the coffee table, happily crunching away.

Mason opened one eye and looked over in my direction. "James didn't tell us anything other than you were a new addition to the pack. It's a little strange that you already have a house here and everything. When did you move here?"

Austin hadn't mentioned whether I should share my past with the pack, but I had a gut feeling that I could trust these guys.

"I have been in the area for almost eight years now. For seven years, I went to school at North Peninsula University, and I've been working on the base for about a year now."

They both looked surprised. "So you were here before Austin started the pack?"

I nodded. "So technically, you guys moved in on *my* pack lands."

They both laughed. "Please tell me that you told James that," Mason begged.

"Well, he was there when I told Austin that his land surrounded mine, like the Vatican in Italy."

The guys were both rolling in laughter now, so I continued. "And Austin did agree to merge packs, so I guess technically you guys are also in 'The Anna Pack' now, too."

Jason had to wipe tears from his eyes, he was laughing so hard, and it took a few minutes for the guys to settle down. "I wish I'd been a part of that meeting," Mason told me.

"What pack did you come from originally, though?" Jason asked. "I'm surprised they would let you move out here on your own. This was the Wild West of wolf country before Austin moved in and cleaned things up."

"I've never been in a pack before," I admitted softly with my eyes down.

Mason moved his arms down, placing one on his armrest and the other resting on my shins. I squirmed uncomfortably, and he absentmindedly wrapped a hand around my ankle, gently stroking the delicate skin right underneath my ankle bone. I guess this was okay.

Jason had finished the bag of chips, and after gazing longingly into the bag to see if he missed any, he tossed it onto the table. "Where are your parents?" he asked with a frown.

"I was adopted as a baby. By humans." I didn't want to get into the whole story about being adopted a second time by my uncle.

"I wonder how that happened." Mason murmured with concern in his eyes. "Wolves rarely let offspring out of the pack - especially females. Someone else in your pack should have stepped forward to take care of you if your parents couldn't."

I just shrugged, trying to think of something to say that would change the subject.

Jason did it for me as he sprawled out over the loveseat, making himself more comfortable. "So, James wasn't exaggerating when he said you needed 'how to be a wolf 101'."

"Nope, I really need to know how to avoid embarrassing myself in front of other wolves."

They both laughed. "You definitely don't act like any other females I've ever met, but I don't think we should teach you how to be like that."

"Yeah, most of them are super-spoiled and use the fact that they're so rare to manipulate and take advantage of the single males in the pack."

"A lot of them think it's a game to make the men compete and fight over them."

I turned my head from one to the other as they took turns speaking. I must have had a disbelieving look on my face, because Jason added, "It happens."

Mason nodded. "That's why we don't have any females in the pack now. Austin is building a good thing here, and he doesn't want it torn apart by fighting or jealousy."

That made sense to me. "Well, I'm independent and can provide for myself just fine."

Mason grinned. "Don't worry, we'll make sure no one spoils you."

"I call first dibs on any presents that pack members try to give Anna!" Jason called out.

I threw my pillow at him and sat back up. I put my legs back down on the floor to sit up straight. I was surprised to realize that now that I'd been getting used to feeling Mason's touch, I felt the absence of his warmth.

The doorbell rang. "Food's here!"

# Chapter 8

The guys explained what they knew of wolf etiquette to me as we prepared dinner together. I assigned each of them slicing and dicing duties as we prepared lime chicken fajitas and ground beef tacos with homemade guacamole and salsa. They both thought it was a little excessive for me to use steak to make my own ground beef, but I promised they would taste the difference.

I was confused as to why Austin and James thought the twins would be a useful resource for wolf etiquette. Most of what they told me was about dominance struggles, which Austin didn't allow in his pack. They were clueless about having females in the pack, and they both admitted they preferred to avoid female wolves altogether. Mason was quick to add "except you."

A short time later, we sat down to eat, and they admitted I was right about making everything from scratch.

They ate enthusiastically, and while I thought we would have plenty of leftovers, the food was gone quickly. I'd underestimated the amount of food that two grown male wolves would eat. I could only imagine how much it would take to feed a pack.

After cleaning up dinner, we went back to the living room and relaxed with full bellies. Jason checked his phone. "You get anything from James yet?"

"No, but he might be hunting down his car by now, though," Mason grinned.

"We haven't even given it a mud bath yet," I said with a frown. "We can't let him find us yet!" I jumped up, and they both laughed.

"Hurry up and pack up your stuff. We'll get the car dirty on the way back and have it back in the garage while he's out looking for us," Mason told me.

"I'm pretty sure we'll get at least one threatening phone call before he comes after us," Jason added. "So, we'll get some warning."

I laughed and ran upstairs. Kelsey had given me one of her old luggage sets when she upgraded to a Luis Vuitton set. It was black with hot pink hearts and the Guess logos. Not exactly my style, but it was free and worked for my purpose.

I tossed all my toiletry items in one of the bags, and after a moment of hesitation, I added my hairdryer. Hey, I might want to look nice again one day.

I dragged the larger bag into my closet and just starting piling things in it. Gym clothes, sweaters, jeans, bras and panties, all of it went in there. My strategy was to pack as much as the bag would fit, so I would probably have what I needed when I got wherever I was going.

I sat on top of the suitcase, so I could zip it and look around my closet. Crap, I forgot shoes.

I wasn't about to repack my bag, so I just grabbed my backpack and threw some sneakers and flats in it.

I decided the most efficient way to get all three of my bags down the stairs was to stand at the top of the stairs and throw the backpack down. I watched it bounce down a couple of stairs and then slide to the bottom of the staircase. It seemed to work well, so I just gave the other two pieces of luggage a push over the edge of the stairway. They thunked down the stairs quite satisfactorily, so I went back to my bedroom to grab my charger.

I bounded down the stairs and jumped over the pile of stuff that had landed at the bottom of the stairway. Mason watched with an amused look on his face from where he sat on the couch. Jason was nowhere in sight.

"Are you guys ready?" I asked.

Jason walked into sight from where he had been standing in the kitchen. He glanced at his phone. "That was, like, five minutes of packing."

"Dude, when a girl gets ready for something in a reasonable amount of time, you don't question it." Mason joked.

I rolled my eyes at Mason. It wasn't that difficult to pack when you just threw most of what you owned into a suitcase. I didn't need a lot of clothes since the hospital provided me with a fresh pair of scrubs to wear to work every day, so it's not like I had a lot to choose from.

I picked up my purse and shoved my phone and iPad into it, along with my charger. I hesitated for a moment, thinking about if I forgot anything important. *Nope.*

To my surprise, the guys had already picked up my bags, and we were ready to head out. I said a sad goodbye to my house; I might not be back until the end of the week.

I set the security alarm and locked the door on my way out. It looked like Mason was driving this time, and Jason had already called shotgun. The back seat was fine with me.

"Let's go to the park around the block, it's always muddy because it's part marshland," I suggested.

The close proximity to the park is one of the reasons I decided to live out here. The best part of the park is that there were no streetlights, so everyone stayed away once it got dark. I lived in the type of neighborhood where everyone had their kids to bed by nine and houses dark by ten. It was perfect for my wolf to be able to roam the park without fear of interruption.

Both of the guys agreed with the plan, so we headed up the long driveway of the park that led to the docks and fishing pier. I directed them to go past the paved parking lot and down the dirt road to the gravel parking lot. While driving there, mud sprayed up the sides of the car all the way up to the windows. Mission accomplished.

"I think we might have time for a run since Anna is so delightfully efficient," Mason teased.

My ears perked up. My wolf could use a run after being cooped up for so long.

"Is it safe?" Jason asked me.

"I come here all the time to let my wolf run free," I answered enthusiastically.

Mason parked, and I got out of the car eagerly. "There's a picnic shelter over in the woods that's hidden from view and is the perfect place to change," I told them.

They both shrugged and followed me as I practically skipped ahead of them. The cool night air was invigorating, and the sky was bright with the moon and stars.

I entered the picnic shelter and stopped. I looked at them both nervously as they followed me in. I hadn't thought the logistics of this out. All three of us were going to have to get naked. There was no way was I okay with undressing in front of one guy, and definitely not two guys.

"Do you guys mind if I change first, and then you can come in and do your thing?"

Jason looked surprised, then grinned. "Anna, are you shy? You know, nudity is perfectly natural -"

Mason punched him in the arm. "Shut up." He looked at me. "We'll wait out here."

He gave Jason a stern look. "And turn our backs so that we don't see anything."

Jason jokingly scowled but stepped out and turned his back. Mason followed and stayed a step behind Jason, probably to punch him again if he tried to peek. I appreciated that.

I quickly undressed and gave the guys a nervous look. My wolf had never met other wolves before the other night; I wasn't sure how this was going to go.

I relaxed and let my wolf come to the surface. I was relieved that she seemed curious and playful as she went to the surface, and I shed my human form.

I bounded out of the shelter and ran top speed into the field in front of me. I made a wide circle and then slowed as I came back to where the guys were standing there, watching me. They were both grinning as they crouched down to greet me, and I sniffed at the hands they offered me, taking in their scents.

Mason reached his hand towards my head and hesitated as if asking for permission. I rubbed my head against his hand, and he gently stroked my fur. "You're a pretty wolf, Anna. I've never seen anyone with a pure white coat before."

Jason stood. "I've never seen a wolf that fluffy before," he teased me.

I playfully growled at him in return.

Mason stood as well. "I think that means she's ready for us to change so we can run."

I trotted back out in the field to sniff around while I waited, eager to stretch my legs out and race the twins.

Two wolves ran out to join me quickly. They were both twice my size, and their coats were a mix of browns. They crowded me a little and boxed me in between them as all three of us took in each other's scents. Once I was sure I would be able to track them by scent, I was bored with the meet and greet. I shoved my way through them and ran. I loved the feeling of freedom as I flew through the night.

The guys quickly caught up to me, and we had a great time running and chasing each other through the woods. They may have been larger than me, but I had the advantage of agility and maneuverability that their size didn't allow them.

I led them on a merry chase through the woods, and eventually, I came to the end of the trail. The wooded area ended abruptly, and there was an eight-foot drop down to where the marsh was. The tide was out, which meant it was a muddy mess. I stopped abruptly, but Jason came barreling though after me and tried to skid to a stop. His larger size kept his momentum going forward, and I took advantage of the moment to pounce on him as he teetered near the edge. He lost his balance and fell into the muddy mess below us with a plop and a muddy splash.

If I were in my human form, I would have been laughing hysterically. Jason struggled to stand as the muck clung to his body. He pulled one of his paws free, and the mud released it with a sucking sound.

I heard Mason coming up behind me; he was more cautious than his brother and approached slowly. I could see the look of amusement in his wolf eyes as he gazed down at his brother. I crept a little closer to the edge to watch Jason's progress in freeing himself.

Mason backed up a little, and I glanced back at him in just in time for him to shove me over the edge and into the mud with Jason.

I landed in the muck almost on top of Jason, who couldn't move quickly enough to get out of the way. I was soon quite familiar with his struggle. The muck was so soft that I just sank right down in it. It was too thick to swim through but too mushy to get any type of purchase to stand.

I decided to try to get out by climbing up Jason's much larger body. He realized what I was doing when the extra weight caused him to sink deeper. He attempted to throw me off, and we engaged in a wrestling match.

We both froze when we heard low growling from Mason. He was looking down the trail we had come from. Suddenly, he headed toward the edge of the cliff-like border and leaped in after us. Both Jason and I frantically scrambled to avoid being crushed by him, but we couldn't make it far.

All three of us were now tangled in the mud, and Mason snapped at us to stop struggling. All three of us were quiet as we heard rustling and branches snapping as someone walked our way.

The footsteps were definitely human. There was a chance that whoever it was would just keep walking by without looking down the drop to see what was below. The marsh didn't smell good when the tide was out, so most people avoided it.

No such luck. The footsteps came closer, and we all watched with apprehension to see who it would be. There was no way we could get away unnoticed.

A shadow separated from the trees, and a man's silhouette appeared. As he came forward, the moon shone on his face.

James.

"Are you fucking kidding me right now?" he raged, trying to keep his voice low.

"What are you idiots doing with her?" He took a deep breath. "Never mind, I don't want to know."

He gestured towards us. "Get up here. I have a plane to catch, And you're making me late."

We all just looked at him; that was easier said than done. I started squirming around, but didn't have any more success getting out than the twins did. When James realized the dilemma, he began to laugh.

He pulled out his phone. "I hope the camera's good enough to capture this moment in the dark." He continued to laugh as he took multiple pictures. Jason and Mason started to growl, and I could feel their bodies vibrating against mine.

James sobered up and eyed the situation critically. "You could either try to make your way through the mud and into the deeper water to swim to where you can climb out, or you can change back to human and try to climb up."

I weighed both of those options. The muddy route would be time-consuming and difficult. Alternatively, we could scale back up the face of the cliff-like drop by using the tree roots sticking out - but only in human form.

Mason had the same idea because he worked his way free of us and changed to human. In his human form, he was able to stand, and the mud went up to his knees. He laboriously walked up to the wall of dirt, rocks, and roots. With each step, he had to pull his leg out of the mud forcefully before it would let him go with a loud squelching noise.

Jason watched his brother's progress for a moment, and then he, too, maneuvered away from me and changed back to human. Mason had started to climb up, and James was reaching down to pull him the rest of the way up.

My only choice looked like I was going to have to follow them. However, I was terrified to change in front of them. I would be naked. In front of three men. I couldn't just stay down here for the rest of my life, though.

I did my best to relax my body so I could change back to human. After I changed, I made sure I was fully covered in stinky mud before standing up. I decided to pretend that the mud I was wearing was actually a bodysuit, so I wouldn't feel so exposed.

I tried my best to follow in their footsteps as I laboriously made my way through the mud. Jason had stayed near the bottom of the cliff to help me up. As he lifted me up, Mason reached down to grab ahold of me and pull me up.

I didn't even want to consider what the view must have looked like to either of them as I climbed back onto solid land. Mason and James were both staring at me when I reached the top, and I was scrambling onto the grass so Jason could climb up after me. I was so embarrassed that the only thing I could think to do was rapidly change back into my wolf.

I instinctively shook out my coat. Mason laughed, and James looked at me incredulously as he wiped splatters of mud off his face. Mason reached down to help Jason up as James glared at me. I flicked my tail at him and sat to stare back at him defiantly.

Once the guys were both back on solid land, James started in on them.

"What were you thinking? Were you thinking at all?" When he took a breath, Mason interrupted.

"We were teaching her how to be a wolf and got caught off guard by the terrain."

James just looked at him and then turned to head back up the trail. "I track my car down here, find it covered in mud, and then what do I hear? Wolves growling and barking, chasing each other through the woods and doing everything they can to attract attention."

I trotted after the twins as they followed James back up the trail. The two guys had stayed in human form and weren't at all embarrassed by their nudity. Mason continued to offer reasonable explanations for what had happened, but Jason just smirked as James continued to chastise us.

I was quickly bored with trailing after them and pushed my way to the front so that I could run free again. I made it out of the woods and rolled around in the grassy field to wipe some of the mud off me.

I paused and eyed the boat ramp that led down into the river. I glanced back at the trail; it looked like I had some time until the guys would catch up. I ran over to the water and splashed around. The water was freezing, but it felt good to get the muck out of my coat. I used the textured concrete boat ramp to scrape the mud off my back by rolling around on it in the shallow part of the water.

I heard the guys coming out of the path, so I shook out my coat and ran back in their direction. I rolled around in the grass some more while they headed over to the cars. James had driven the silver Jeep here.

I trotted up to them. James was no longer finding creative ways to express his displeasure, but steam was still coming out of his ears. I briefly considered shaking out my coat again while he was in range but stopped when he shot me a look.

"Where are my keys?" he barked.

"I'll get them," Jason volunteered. I'm pretty sure that Jason just wanted to get away from James. He ran off quickly towards the picnic shelter, where we had left all of our belongings, still naked.

James included me in his glaring as he continued to berate us. Jason came back toward us after a few minutes. He had wiped what mud he could off him and pulled his pants on. Mason still stood there unabashedly naked. Jason unlocked the doors to the Range Rover before handing the keys to James.

"We need to get Anna's stuff out of the trunk." He tossed a shirt and pants to Mason and then headed towards the back of the Range Rover to get my things.

Jason unloaded my things out of the back while James examined the interior of the car. I had to fight the urge to jump in and shake off my still wet and muddy coat. I could just imagine the look on his face when he saw me splattering mud all over the interior of his fancy car.

"I think six months of detailing everyone's vehicles is an appropriate punishment for stealing my car and taking it on a muddy joyride."

The guys groaned. James glared at me. "That's for all three of you."

I just curled my tail around me and looked at him impassively.

"Don't think you're going to be treated differently from any other pack member," he warned me.

Even though he was handing out punishments - which apparently he could do - I felt oddly reassured. He clearly didn't like me, but he'd just admitted I was an equal member of the pack.

The warm feeling of pleasure that started to fill me took me by surprise. Honestly, being forced to spend more time with the twins didn't seem like a bad thing. I was pretty sure they could manage to make whatever we did fun.

# Chapter 9

After James peeled out angrily in his filthy Range Rover, both Mason and Jason burst out laughing.

"That was pretty awesome!"

"Did you see his face? Totally worth it."

I bounced up because the cold air in my wet coat was starting to bother me while I was sitting still. The temperature tonight was only in the lower fifties, but the water had soaked through my thick coat down to my skin, and I was ready to be dry.

Jason tossed the rest of our clothes into a pile in the back seat, so I jumped in through the open door and made a nest in the collection of clothing.

Mason grinned. "I guess Anna's ready to head out."

I just yawned in response.

During the trip back, I took advantage of having access to the guys' scents on their clothing. I inhaled deeply and picked out Mason and Jason's individual scents. Under the human scent, I could pick out a muskiness that I now recognized as a wolf.

Their wolf scents were faint and hidden under the stronger human scent, but I could now understand how their human and wolf scents were related. I think now I'd recognize wolves in their human forms.

My investigation done for the night, I settled into a nap. I was lulled to sleep by the warmth of the Jeep and the scents of my new pack members surrounding me.

I was awakened by the sounds of the car doors opening. I stretched my back out before I leaped out of the door Mason held open for me. I started to head for the front door, but Mason stopped me. "Sorry, pretty girl, no wolves allowed in the house. Austin's rules."

I gave a wolf pout. I'd made a mess by lying on the clothing with my muddy and damp fur, and I didn't want to have to put those clothes back on.

The front door opened, and Cody stepped out. My ears and tail perked up in interest.

"Sorry, dudes, James told me not to let you back into the house until you were relatively clean. I saw the pics." Cody smirked and then caught sight of me with a smile. "Hey, is that Anna?"

I ran up the front stairs to greet him with a wolf grin.

Cody crouched down to let me smell his hand. This time, I could easily recognize the musky scent that identified him as a fellow wolf under his human scent. He ran his hand down my back and grimaced a little, as my coat was still damp and slightly muddy.

He straightened back up. "I'll take Anna inside—"

"No way!" Jason interrupted.

"Yeah, we aren't going to let you turn her into a spoiled brat," Mason added. "She gets the hose just like the rest of us."

Cody gazed down at me. "Well, I'm not really spoiling her. It's only her first day -"

"Nope," Mason interrupted again.

"Get down here and stop trying to disrupt our pack with your cuteness!" Jason teased me.

I flicked my tail at him but bounded back down the stairs toward them.

"You should grab her stuff out of the Jeep, Cody," Mason added as an afterthought in Cody's direction.

Cody sighed and grabbed the keys that were tossed at him.

I nervously ran circles around the twins as they headed down the stone path that lead around to the back of the ridiculous mansion. We weren't really going to be hosed down with freezing cold water, right?

They led the way up to a fenced-in area that included an Olympic-sized pool and looked like it belonged at a five-star resort. The pool was surrounded by cushioned chairs, cabanas, and there was even an outdoor bar attached to the pool house in the back. Behind the bar and under the alcove there was a giant outdoor TV - I didn't know that was even a thing.

Mason walked over to an outdoor shower. "This is pretty cold water. It's not bad in the summer, but -"

"Fuck that," Jason said and launched himself into the pool.

"Austin and Cody are going to be pissed if they find swamp muck at the bottom of that pool!" Mason shouted at him.

"Now that I'm already in, we're going to be in trouble anyway!" Jason yelled back. "The water in here is nice and warm, it's heated to a delightful seventy degrees." He floated in the pool on his back, the caked mud slowly streaming off him and drifting in a dark cloud around him.

Mason shrugged and looked at me. "They installed the outdoor shower so we wouldn't get the pool dirty, but he's right, we're going to be in trouble now anyway. Might as well make it worth it." He grinned and launched himself into the pool, trying to splash Jason with his cannonball.

I trotted over to the edge. I couldn't tell how deep it was, but it was definitely too deep for my shorter wolf legs to reach the bottom. I decided to jump in and change back to human once my body was mostly submerged.

Jason saw that I was back to human once I came up for air. "Well, since Anna is naked..." He pulled off his pants and chucked them back onto land.

Mason punched him. "You're embarrassing her. Don't talk about being naked."

Jason punched him back. "She needs to learn how to be a wolf. Wolves are naked a lot."

I ignored them. I'd spent enough time with the twins now to realize that play fighting was just something they did.

They got into a splashing match, and I dunked my head under the water, scrubbing out what was left of the mud. I felt terrible getting the pool muddy, but the amount of dirt on me was minuscule compared to what was coming off the twins.

Their splashing fight had escalated to a wrestling match. I decided to take advantage of their distraction and see if I could make it out of the pool without them seeing me naked. The splashing noises had stopped when I made it over to one of the cabanas, and hurriedly wrapped a towel around myself.

I shot a glance back over my shoulder to see both of them carefully not looking at me.

"Are you getting out already?" Jason asked disappointedly.

"I think I need a shower more than a dip in the pool," I replied. "I did get almost all of the mud off, but I'm a little sticky now from the saltwater."

Mason nodded and dipped his head under the water, scrubbing his hands through his hair. Jason was splashing around and wiping mud off himself, too.

They both headed for the side of the pool to climb out after a few minutes, and I averted my gaze. Mason's pants were lying on the side of the pool near Jason's, so he had stripped down at some point as well.

They got out and wiped themselves down with towels. I avoided looked at them as I took a second towel and wrapped my dripping hair.

Once we were all dry enough that we wouldn't drip water through the house, we headed toward the back patio area. This also looked like a resort area with a few tables placed on top of the stone patio. The giant area had a sunroom off to the left, but we headed through the glass doors that led into a sitting area inside.

The boys headed through the house and to a stairway that looked like it belonged on the Titanic. The floor was cold under my bare feet, and I looked down. Was this marble?

"Cody!" Jason shouted as we went up the stairs.

There was no answer. "We need to know where he put your stuff," Mason added.

Jason was impatient. "Just look in the guest rooms as we pass by. We'll see her luggage." They opened a couple of doors as they headed down the hall.

"That's weird. I know Cody would have brought it upstairs," Mason said.

Jason shrugged. "Guess that means she's going to have to shower with us." They both grinned, and I turned bright red.

"We each have our own room here, but the two of us have to share a bathroom," Mason explained.

I nodded in understanding. That didn't sound too bad.

"We can let you use one of the guest showers, but we don't have any extra girl clothes," Mason said apologetically.

"I guess you'll just have to wear mine," Jason added.

"She's not wearing your clothes. When is the last time you did laundry?"

"My stuff is cleaner than yours."

I just rolled my eyes as I listened to them argue.

"Where's the shower I can use?" I interrupted, knowing this could go on for a while.

Mason headed back down the hallway and opened the door to one of the rooms we had looked in for my luggage. "This room has its own bathroom, and it's empty right now."

I nodded. "Just how many rooms does this house have?"

Jason shouted down the hallway, "A lot!" and went into one of the rooms, closing the door behind him.

Mason shrugged. "I think, like, twelve. Only six of us live here full-time, but we always have pack members staying here for pack events or guard duty."

I thought back to the two wolves who had chased me through the woods. They would have been pack members on duty. I was sure that I hadn't officially met them yet, now that I knew the scents of James, Cody, and the twins. It would be a challenge to see if I'd be able to recognize them if I saw them in their human forms.

Mason gestured into the room he had offered to me, and I walked in.

"I'll leave some clothes on the bed for you," Mason offered with a smile. He closed the door behind him, and I heard his footsteps head down the hallway.

I walked toward the bathroom attached to the bedroom. I was surprised to see that the large room only had a bed in the corner – no other furniture.

I entered the bathroom, and it seemed normal but nice. There was a shower with a glass enclosure and a garden tub. I needed a nice hot shower with good water pressure, so I fiddled with the knobs until I got the temperature just right. I slid under the cascade of water and enjoyed the moment.

There were a couple of bottles of shampoo and conditioner for me to choose from. To my surprise, there was a flowery-smelling body wash for me to use. I thought this pack didn't have females? Maybe they had human girlfriends?

I took my time showering and washed my hair several times until I was completely free of the marsh smell. When I stepped out of the shower, the bathroom was full of steam, so I flicked on the fan. I wrapped a towel around myself and stepped out into the bedroom. There was a pile of clothes on the bed.

There were hoodies, sweatpants, T-shirts, socks. Some smelled like Mason, and some like Jason. So, they were going to let me choose whose clothes to wear?

I picked out a T-shirt and sweatpants to wear from Mason and socks and a hoodie from Jason. Now that I was warm and comfy, I headed back into the bathroom to see what I could do about my hair. I looked in the still foggy mirror. My hair was a tangled mess.

I looked through all the drawers in the vanity until I found a small plastic comb and a little trial sized bottle of leave-in conditioner. This would have to do.

I heard pounding on the door. "Anna! Are you still naked?" That would be Jason. I finished doing what I could with my hair, so I just left it down to dry in waves and headed to the door to meet Jason.

When I opened the door, he was leaning there, waiting. "We're going to have movie night! Mason's getting the screening room ready. It's our job to get the snacks."

Of course, this gigantic house has a screening room. I wouldn't be surprised if they invited me to the bowling alley in the basement next.

I followed him as he led me to the kitchen, looking around the house as we walked. Jason started to raid the pantry. "We're going to have popcorn - do you want cheesy or butter?" he asked me.

"Both, obviously," I answered with a shy grin.

"I knew there was a reason I liked you." He winked at me.

"What's taking so long?" Mason interrupted as he walked in the kitchen.

"I had to wait for Anna to make herself pretty," Jason answered with a teasing look at me.

I shot him a dirty look and crossed my arms.

"I know you were the one who wanted to look pretty for Anna," Mason told him. "Don't even try to put it on her."

I relaxed and laughed as I walked over to the microwave to start making the popcorn that Jason passed over to me from the pantry.

Jason grabbed drinks out of the fridge and grabbed three pints of ice cream out of the freezer. "I knew there was a reason *I* liked *you*," I told him with a smile.

Mason grinned at me. "I'm pretty sure you like me just as much as my brother, because I can smell my scent on you."

I blushed. I was wearing some of each of their clothes; was that more significant to wolves than to humans? I decided it would be better not to ask right now.

Mason started scribbling on a whiteboard that was attached to the front of the fridge. I looked closer to see what he was writing.

Sorry about the mess in the pool. We'll clean it ASAP in the am.

-J&M

Jason read over his shoulder and then took the marker from him and added "&A" to their initials.

"You're going to get her in trouble," Mason scolded him.

Jason just grinned. "She's one of us now." Warmth flooded through me. I'd never been accepted into a group like this before.

# Chapter 10

Our arms full of snacks, we headed downstairs to the screening room. It was a huge room with two rows of movie theater seats in the back, there were couches a couple steps down, and then the "pit" of the room was lined with cushions and full of different shapes and sizes of pillows. This was where we plopped down with our treasure trove of snacks.

It was times like this when I was thankful I had the metabolism of a wolf. Under normal circumstances, I would have already eaten more than I should for today, but the stress had me burning calories at a higher rate.

"We're on the Avengers theme this week. That okay with you?" Mason asked.

"Yup." I loved Thor and Ironman, so no complaints here.

"We just saw Captain America and Agent Carter, so today is Ironman," Jason informed me.

"Cool." I settled back and made myself a comfortable nest among the pillows as the beginning credits started to roll. It was quite late at night, so I wasn't sure how long I would be able to stay awake; I was nice and warm after my hot shower and quite comfortable in my nest of pillows.

We were towards the end of the movie, and the latest popcorn fight between Jason and Mason was on the way to progressing to another wrestling match when Cody came in.

"Dude, what did you do with her stuff?" Jason asked as both guys disengaged from each other.

"It's in my room," Cody answered. "I didn't know where she was staying."

"Not in your room," Mason stated adamantly. I looked over at him in surprise.

Cody rolled his eyes. "I know that." He turned to me. "What room are you staying in?"

I shrugged. "Austin didn't really say…" I trailed off in embarrassment.

"I'll put her into the room between Austin and me," Cody decided. He stood up. "C'mon, Anna, I'll get you settled."

The twins protested him interrupting movie night, but I said I was tired anyway, so I headed up with Cody.

We walked upstairs, and I played awkwardly with the sleeves of my borrowed hoodie, trying to think of a way to start a conversation. "So, where is James going on a trip to?"

Cody glanced at me in surprise. "He had a lead to check out."

"On an investigation?"

He frowned and ran his hand through his hair. "Something like that."

I wondered if he was working on the case with Evelyn. I missed her. There was so much that I wanted to tell her, and I wished she was here now.

Cody must have sensed the sadness that settled over me because he smiled reassuringly at me. "I'm glad you're here," he murmured and reached out to squeeze my hand.

I gave him a smile in return. These guys were pretty awesome, I was glad I'd taken a chance on them.

Cody led me to one of the bedrooms and gave a dramatic bow as he opened the door for me. I laughed and walked in ahead of him.

This bedroom was even larger than the first one, but there was still only a bed in the corner of the room, no other furnishings. I thought it was odd for such a fancy house to be so sparsely furnished, but I didn't mind because all I really needed was a bed. I just moved into my house a few months ago, and had yet to fully furnish it, so I couldn't judge.

Cody took a step into the room behind me, then stopped. "I'll go get your stuff."

I followed him back out. "I'll help." I was a little nervous about being left alone in a new place, and I left the door open on my way out of the room.

Cody led the way back to his room and handed me my backpack and purse, then picked up my other two pieces of luggage to carry for himself.

I led the way back to my room, and Cody followed close behind me. He set down my luggage, and there was an awkward silence where neither of us knew what to say. He ran his hand through his hair. "My room is right next door if you need anything."

I tried to think of something to keep him here for a little longer but fell short. "Thanks," was the only thing I came up with.

He nodded and closed the door behind him as he left. I stood in place for a moment and gazed at my pile of luggage. Loneliness overcame me, and I tried my best to push it away. It was already late at night, and I was tired. I thought about unpacking and finding some PJs, but I liked wearing my borrowed clothes.

I jumped on the bed and snuggled down under the covers. The scents lingering on Mason and Jason's clothing were comforting and helped lull me to sleep.

# Chapter 11

Blinding white light woke me up as the sun shone through the window and right into my eyes. I reluctantly rolled out of bed and walked over to the window, squinting as I gazed out at the view that was much different than the one that I was used to. A bright green lawn stretched to the edge of the forest, but my window wasn't high enough to see the ocean that lay beyond the treeline that protected the house from curious eyes. I could see the patio and the sparkling water of the pool right beneath me, but there were some dark shadows on the bottom, and I winced - that would be from the mud the twins and I left there last night.

I decided to get ready for the day with pool-cleaning on my mind. I brought my bag filled with toiletries into the bathroom and dug through it to find the items I needed. I didn't want to fully unpack and leave my stuff everywhere because I wasn't sure if I was supposed to be staying in this room, so I just used what I needed and then replaced it in my bag.

After a shower and an attempt to make myself look presentable, I started digging through my luggage to find appropriate clothing. I decided yoga pants, sneakers, and a T-shirt with a zip-up hoodie to layer over it would work for any cleaning I needed to do today. I left my borrowed clothes folded on the bed to return them to their owners later. Before I left the room, I repacked my bags just in case I was going to be kicked out of the room.

I was ready to go downstairs in search of breakfast, but I was nervous at the thought of who I might run into. Four out of the five of the guys I'd met so far had been welcoming, but how would the other fifty or so pack members feel about my presence here?

I squared my shoulders back and marched to the door in determination. I certainly wasn't going to hide in this room because I was afraid of people not liking me. I didn't see or hear anyone as I left my room, walked down the hallway, and drifted downstairs. I headed toward the kitchen to hunt for any breakfast food they might have available.

I made it to the kitchen without seeing anyone, and while a part of me was relieved that no one jumped out and said, "Hey, what are you doing in my house, stranger?" The other part of me was disappointed that I hadn't run into any of the guys I'd already met and liked.

I was rummaging through the fridge when heard footsteps come into the kitchen. I closed the fridge door and turned so I could introduce myself to the newcomer. He was about my height with chestnut brown hair and warm brown eyes and was dressed casually in jeans and a long-sleeved tee. He looked lean and not as heavily muscled as the other guys in the pack.

I smiled at him in greeting. "Hi, I'm Anna."

He flicked his eyes down to my feet and then back up to my eyes. "Caleb. Austin mentioned there was going to be a girl here, but I expected you to be more…" He waved a hand in my direction.

I narrowed my eyes at him. More what? I thought to myself. More pretty? More petite? More well-dressed?

He realized that wasn't the best way to start out and backpedaled. "That's to say, I'm happy to meet you."

Mmmmhmmmmmm…I decided not to let it bother me; he could think whatever he wanted.

"What do you guys usually eat for breakfast?"

He smiled. "Breakfast is usually every man for himself. The twins have the tendency only to visit the meat and deli departments when they go to the grocery store. The rest of us pick up food occasionally to go along with all the meat, but no one ever wants to cook."

"Ahhh," I said. "Would anyone object if I start cooking with the food you guys do have here?"

"You're going to cook?" He looked at me incredulously.

"Why does everyone look so shocked when offer to cook?" I was curious but also a little irritated.

"Because you're hot. Everyone knows beautiful girls don't cook; they just lounge around and wait for people to bring them things," he stated bluntly.

My jaw dropped. Hot? Beautiful? Did this guy need to put on his glasses? Also, I was a little offended that he thought so poorly of women, but I thought about the Kelseys of the world. If the only girls he had ever met were like her, then he might not know any better.

This made me determined to show these guys that not all women were awful. I walked back over to the fridge and started to pull things out. They had bacon, eggs, and cheese in the fridge that I could use for what I had in mind. I was pleasantly surprised to find that the pantry had flour and other baking necessities in addition to the extensive array of snacks I expected.

"Where are all the other guys?" I asked curiously as I gathered the items I would need from around the kitchen.

"James is out of town, Austin should be down for work in a half-hour or so and will probably drag the twins down with him. Cody's probably still out on his morning run," Caleb answered as he watched what I was doing.

I started pulling out pans, bowls, and measuring utensils as I searched the kitchen for what I needed. I decided I had everything I needed for bacon, egg, and cheese sandwiches on biscuits. With an extra side of bacon, of course.

Caleb dubiously watched me measuring out ingredients but took a seat at the counter. "You're not going to use a recipe?"

"Trust me, once you've made something ten thousand times, you don't need a recipe," I told him confidently. "Do you have to go to work this morning, too?" I asked him, trying to make some light conversation.

"I do, but I work from home."

I smiled at him. "That sounds cool. What do you do?"

"Oh, I'm the tech guy for the pack." He grinned ruefully at me. "In case you haven't noticed, I'm not great with people."

I laughed a little and shrugged. "I get nervous around new people." I gestured toward the mess I was making as I formed and then placed biscuits onto a baking tray. "It helps me to keep moving and focus on physical tasks, so I don't worry so much about what other people think about me."

He nodded thoughtfully. "I can see that. So that's why you like to cook?"

I shrugged. "Part of it was a necessity; I have to cook if I want to eat. But the other part of it means I have something to keep me occupied when I go to gatherings. If I'm busy with food, I'm not standing awkwardly in the corner, trying to think of things to say to people or being too nervous to walk up to them and start a conversation."

He looked stunned. "You don't look like the type of girl who would have a difficult time socially."

"What type of girl do I look like?"

He tilted his head. "You look like the girl who everyone else would be too intimidated to talk to."

I gave him a weird look. "You mean because I'm freakishly tall or something?"

"Nah, you look like a model."

Was he just messing with me? I looked in his eyes, but it didn't look like he was mocking me. With the biscuits baking in the oven, I started putting the bacon on another baking sheet that I found.

"You're going to put that in the oven? I thought you were supposed to cook it on the stove?"

I rolled my eyes at him. "Trust me, this is going to be good."

I could tell he wasn't a believer. The bacon was going in the oven once I popped out the biscuits in another couple minutes, but I needed something else to keep me busy, so I started cracking eggs.

I started opening and closing all the cupboards, looking for something round I could use to make the eggs into the right shape for a sandwich. I eventually found several of those metal rings used to make hamburger patties and figured I could make it work.

Caleb watched me curiously as I put a pan on the stove to heat up but didn't say anything. I tried to ignore his eyes on me so that I could finish making my egg mixture. I looked around for their spice rack, and I found what I needed just as the timer went off for the biscuits. I switched the biscuits out for the bacon and reset the timer before I went back to the eggs.

"Jason and Mason have both eaten my food and lived to tell the tale," I assured him. "I'm pretty sure I hear them coming now."

I started cooking the eggs and slicing biscuits as I went along. Austin was the first one in the kitchen, and he raised an eyebrow at me standing at the stove. The twins were right behind him.

"Good morning!" I chirped out.

"Anna!" Jason exclaimed. "I checked your room this morning, and you were gone. Why are your things packed?" he asked worriedly.

I glanced at Austin. "Well, I wasn't sure if I was going to be staying there or..." My voice trailed off, and I was interrupted by the timer.

"I think that room is the best choice," Austin answered. "Cody and I can keep an eye on you."

I nodded and pulled the bacon out of the oven.

"All right, bacon!" Mason exclaimed. He was picking up a cup of coffee he had just made from the Keurig.

Austin took it out of his hands. "Pack master gets the first cup."

I laughed as Jason snatched a piece of bacon off the tray and tossed it from hand to hand, trying to blow on it and cool it off.

I finished assembling the first two sandwiches and handed them to Austin on a plate. "I'm guessing that goes for sandwiches, too?"

He grinned. "You learn fast."

I started on the next batch of eggs I needed for more sandwiches. Mason and Jason took turns making coffee and stealing pieces of bacon.

Eventually, all of us had sandwiches and coffee. Austin clapped his hands together to get everyone's attention. "Caleb, you already have your assignments for today?" Caleb nodded in confirmation.

"Anna, I need you to work with Caleb at some point today. He needs some info from you for the investigation that you're helping with." It was my turn to nod.

"Mason and Jason, you're going to class as per usual, but I want you back before dinner and to stick with Anna while you're home."

"We can't skip class today to take care of Anna?" Mason asked.

"No," Austin answered sternly.

Caleb cleared his throat. "Don't you guys only have class from one to four today anyway?"

They both mumbled an assent.

"That gives all three of you plenty of time to clean the pool and take Anna shopping for anything she needs. I'm guessing she can't live on meat alone," Austin told them.

I smiled; it sounded like Caleb wasn't the only one with complaints about the guys' shopping habits.

Mason got a glint in his eye. "So, we can shop the way Anna usually does?"

Austin glanced at me. "Within reason, and stick to the budget."

All of us nodded. Everyone turned to look as the glass door out to the back patio opened, and Cody stepped through - shirtless and sweaty.

Oh my god, that man was built. I tried not to stare or drool in his direction, but it was a pretty hopeless situation, my eyes were drawn to him like magnets.

"Cody, excellent. I need you in my office by ten this morning so we can review some things before contract negotiations."

Cody nodded and looked sadly at the remnants of breakfast. "It looks like I came in a little late."

"We still have eggs. I can make you an omelet," I offered shyly.

"You cook?" he asked in surprise.

I groaned. "Why does everyone keep asking that?"

"She's an awesome cook," Jason told him enthusiastically.

Mason chimed in and told him about the feast they had helped me prepare the previous day. All the guys looked impressed, and the twins only exaggerated a little.

"I vote we put Anna in charge of food procurement," Caleb suggested.

Austin looked at me thoughtfully. "We haven't decided what Anna's responsibilities are going to be for the pack yet. I need some more time to get to know her."

The twins groaned in disappointment.

"You two didn't think it was going to be that easy to pawn your duties off, did you?" Cody teased them.

"All right, everyone, time to get started on the day. I need to go debrief the night guards unless anyone else has something they needed to bring up?"

Everyone shook their heads no. Austin put his dishes in the sink and headed upstairs. Caleb hesitated after he stood, looking in my direction.

"We'll bring you Anna when we need to leave for class," Mason assured him. Caleb nodded and headed after Austin.

Cody wiped his sweaty face with the shirt he had thrown over his shoulder before heading to the fridge. "I already made myself a protein shake for this morning, Anna, but thank you for the offer."

I smiled at him. "Sure."

He took his protein shake and a bottle of water back upstairs with him. I was guessing he needed to rush to get ready for the day of meetings with Austin.

It was just me and the twins left standing in the kitchen.

"Help me tidy up here before we go out to clean the pool?" I asked them. They grumbled a little bit but agreed once I asked them where they planned to get dinner tonight.

We spent the morning cleaning the giant pool. To my surprise, the twins remained on task, and all three of us stayed relatively clean and dry. Once we finished, we all plopped down in the cushioned chairs.

"We only have one of our tasks done so far, Anna," Jason told me.

Mason added, "We need you to do your magic grocery trick so we can be free to do fun stuff for the rest of the day."

"Yeah, we need something good for lunch."

"My iPad is upstairs." I laughed.

They both groaned.

I decided to take advantage of the fact that neither of them wanted to move right now. "So, what is it that your pack does for money? It seems like whatever it is, you do it well."

Mason opened one eye to look at me from where he was lying. "Mainly, we get contracts from the military for 'security.' You know, like Blackwater."

I nodded in understanding, and he took it as a sign to continue. "We do well with that because almost everyone in our pack is prior military. We also have a lot of ex-special forces like rangers and SEALs to take on projects that no one talks about."

I looked at him doubtfully. The bars around Seaside were packed with 'special forces' on Friday nights. Everyone and his brother claimed to be a Navy SEAL when it came time to impress girls like Kelsey.

"If you're not deployed overseas or busy with training, you can work for one of the companies Austin has here. He has a construction company and is a part-owner of an engineering firm and some kind of financial company that makes investments," Jason added.

Mason looked at him. "Don't forget about the bar."

Jason nodded. "Yeah, so everyone in our pack can always get a good job through Austin's connections."

"You guys go to school?"

They both nodded. "We're using our GI bill to get a degree in business."

I thought it was a little odd that Mason made it sound like the two of them together were earning the same degree and using the same GI bill. I'd noticed both of them speaking like that before but had just brushed it off. I decided to bring it up this time delicately.

"So, you guys do everything together?" I asked softly, avoiding their eyes.

They both nodded. "I can tell by the look on your face that you think it's a little weird," Jason said with a soft smile.

Mason changed the subject. "You know, you're a little weird, too."

"Believe me, I know."

They both laughed at my response, but Mason continued. "I didn't notice it at first, but I can tell that you think of your wolf form as a separate person."

I gave him a confused look. "Isn't it, though? I'm a person, and she's a wolf. I have different thoughts and ways of thinking than she does."

Jason shook his head. "You're Anna. Sometimes you look human, and sometimes you look like a wolf, but you're still always Anna."

Mason frowned. "What do you mean, you 'have different thoughts' from her?"

I struggled a little to explain. "You know, when I'm human-Anna, I might feel insecure or nervous, and I'm always thinking about how other people will interpret my actions, or what they might think about me. My wolf - I mean, I guess when I'm in my wolf form, she - I mean, I act more on instinct. I feel free, and I just want to run and play and explore."

They both exchanged glances as I struggled to speak.

"Do you think it might be because you were raised by humans?" Mason asked.

Jason chimed in, "You probably felt like you had to separate your wolf form and hide it from everyone. That made all those aspects of yourself more repressed and must have seemed almost like another person was emerging once you finally let it all out."

I was a little shocked at how smart they were. The twins were a lot more than just fun pranksters.

"So how do I...recombine myself?" I felt like an idiot for not being able to find the right words, but they both understood why I was trying to say.

"You need to stop suppressing everything that makes you a wolf while you're in human form. You can relax around us and be yourself - we're your pack now."

I nodded. I wasn't sure that I could do that because I hadn't even realized that I'd been hiding parts of myself. Mason scooted over and patted the seat next to him. "I'll help you practice."

Jason looked over at us curiously while I moved over to Mason's cushion.

"I noticed you don't even try to pick up on scents while you're in human form," Mason told me.

I blushed. "I didn't realize I could."

I think Jason realized what Mason was planning because he nodded approvingly.

"Close your eyes," Mason told me. I hesitated.

"You can trust us," Jason murmured softly as he came over to sit on my other side and nudged me closer to Mason so he could have enough room on the cushion. I was now wedged between the two twins. I'd never felt small before, but being squeezed between these two big guys made me feel petite. I imagined this was what Kelsey felt like all the time.

I tried to relax and closed my eyes. I knew the twins didn't intend me any harm; they were trying to help. But despite my best efforts, my body was still tense, as if waiting for a blow to fall.

I felt Mason pick up my right hand and hold it in his. He gently caressed my wrist with his thumb. Jason did the same with my left hand.

"Concentrate on what you're feeling right now," Mason coaxed me quietly.

I first focused on the feel of their hands on mine. Their hands felt calloused, as though they spent a lot of time working with them. I idly wondered if they spent time at the construction company they mentioned; they definitely had the physiques for it.

I expanded my senses from my hands. I could feel the warmth of their bodies pressed against each of my sides. Their thighs against mine…I started to flush with the heat of embarrassment in addition to the heat their bodies were giving me. I decided to abruptly move on because my thoughts were going in the wrong direction.

I decided to focus on the cool breeze I could feel across my face and ruffling my hair.

"You're doing great," Mason encouraged me. "Now, reach deep inside yourself where 'your wolf' resides. Instead of just letting go and giving that part of yourself complete control, try to use that part of yourself to extend your sense of smell. Try to identify us by scent alone, as if you had no idea who we were."

I struggled with this part. I reached down and connected with that part of myself that yearned for freedom. I felt 'her' trying to emerge, and I clamped down to prevent myself from changing.

I opened my eyes, filled with disappointment and a little bit of shame. "I tried, but…" The words came out in a whisper, and I tried to hold back tears that were threatening to fall.

"It's okay." Mason patted my thigh encouragingly.

"That was just your first try," Jason added and released my hand.

"You should keep working on exercises like that, though. Keep trying to expand your senses and draw in that other part of yourself," Mason told me.

They exchanged glances. "We can try letting her human side out to have more fun," Jason suggested.

Mason nodded, his eyes lighting up.

"We're banned from using paintball guns on the property, for reasons I'm sure you don't need an explanation for."

I rolled my eyes. "I can imagine."

"We aren't even allowed to use them outside," Jason told me mournfully.

I tried not to laugh. Where were they going with this?

Mason grinned and rubbed the top of my head, messing up my hair. "Paintball actually isn't just a fun game -"

"Although it is fun," Jason interrupted.

Mason ignored him and continued. "It lets you use all of your wolf senses and indulges your urge to hunt." I started to see where he was going with this.

"The adrenaline from the hunt should bring some of those instincts to the surface for you," Jason explained helpfully.

"But you'll be having fun, so you shouldn't feel the urge to suppress those senses automatically. You might even use them without realizing it," Mason added.

I nodded. Their explanation made sense.

"We just need to clear it with Austin. The best place to go for this is about a thirty-minute drive from here. But he told us not to take you out of a five-mile radius from our property."

I frowned in disappointment. "Does that mean we can't go on another run?" The run we had yesterday was a lot of fun. "I think it was beneficial for my wolf – I mean..." I decided just to start over. "I think it was beneficial for me to interact in my wolf form with other wolves and people."

Both guys grinned at me with approval. "We're definitely making progress here," Mason told me. "It would be a shame to slow that down. Austin did tell us to teach you about wolves..."

"Technically, he told us a five-mile radius from the property, not the house," Jason said impishly.

"And our property extends for miles...we're on the very edge of Seaside. Not many people head this way and out into the wilderness." Mason grinned roguishly.

They were both laughing, and I think we had just talked ourselves into getting in more trouble. That didn't stop me from grinning right along with them.

Jason jumped up. "We have to finish our tasks for today before we can have fun."

Mason stood and pulled me to my feet. "Let's go get your iPad so you can make food magically appear again."

Jason stretched out. "The last one to Anna's room has to clean up after lunch!"

Mason and I looked at each other, and all three of us exploded into motion. They might have been larger than me, but I was quick. I used it to my advantage; every time they were shoving at each other, I used the distraction to slip under their arms or around them. I also wasn't above tripping anyone.

We were all laughing as we pushed and shoved our way up the stairs at top speed. Jason was the first to make it to my door. When he paused to turn the handle, I used my momentum to push him to the side and fall into my room first.

The twins pushed through the door at the same time. I was laughing too hard even to stand, so I just rolled around on the floor, watching them argue.

"I said the first one *to* the room, not in it. I was the first one here," Jason insisted.

"Nope. Anna made it in first; you lost."

They were pushing each other back and forth until Jason tripped over the luggage that I'd packed up and left near the doorway this morning. Mason and I laughed at the surprised look on his face as he fell.

"You think that's funny?" he asked as he rolled over to where I was standing. "I'll show you funny." He started to tickle my ribs, and I tried to wiggle away while laughing hysterically. I'd never been tickled like this before, and I couldn't decide if I loved or hated it. But my anxiety over having a man close and touching me had dissipated. The twins had somehow made it onto my trusted list without me realizing it.

I screamed with laughter and begged Jason to stop while he ignored my pleas. Mason decided to get in on it and pulled off my sneakers before tickling my feet. We were all laughing hysterically and rolling around on the floor when Caleb walked in.

"What the fuck? I could hear her screaming from down the hall. I thought you were murdering her!" He tried to keep a serious look on his face, but I could see a grin forming and a sparkle in his eye.

Austin and Cody pushed past Caleb and into the room next. The twins and I froze. Now we were in trouble.

Austin and Cody were both impeccably dressed in tailored suits and looked amazing. I tried not to stare and sat up on the floor. Damn, they cleaned up nice.

"Let her up," Austin ordered.

Both twins just held their hands up to show they weren't touching me. It seemed like Austin was more amused than angry while Cody just looked exasperated. "We could hear you from all the way downstairs as we were about to head out the front door."

"Did you get your assignments done already?" Austin asked. "If you need something else to do –"

"Nope," Jason quickly interjected.

"We just came upstairs to help Anna find something in her room before we did the shopping," Mason added.

Austin eyed my luggage, still packed and sitting near the door. "After you go to the store and get her what she needs, make sure you help her unpack and settle in." He smiled at me. "I want to make sure you feel comfortable here."

Both the twins nodded enthusiastically. "We'll make sure it's done right after we feed her lunch."

I tried my best not to roll my eyes. I think it was much more likely that they would try to con me into making them lunch. But I could always hold them to their promise. Cody thought the same because he snorted and rolled his eyes. "God forbid you miss lunch."

Austin glanced at his expensive-looking watch. "Just don't be late to class."

Both the twins murmured an affirmative and nodded.

"Cody and I have meetings out in town. We won't be back until late tonight, so don't wait for dinner."

All of us nodded, and they headed to the door. "Have a good day!" I told them out of habit.

Cody and Austin both looked surprised and turned back to me. "You, too," Cody told me. Austin nodded and smiled at me. That was odd; was I not supposed to say things like that?

The twins and I stayed on the floor until we heard Austin and Cody go down the stairs and out the front door. Caleb was still watching us and laughing a little.

"Make sure you bring her to my room before you leave," he told the twins. They nodded, and he gave me a smile and a wave. "See you a little later."

I smiled back at him and gave him an awkward wave. "Yup."

Then the twins and I were alone again. "Well, that went better than I thought it was going to," Mason said with a chuckle.

"Yeah, thanks for being cool and not tattling on us," Jason said.

Mason gave him a faux stern look. "Anna wasn't 'being cool'; she is cool."

"That's true," Jason said. "I think the other guys stormed in here thinking they were going to find you crying or whining, but you looked just as guilty as we did when they burst in. I think it threw them off, and they weren't sure how to react."

Mason threw his head back and laughed. "Yeah, I think they kinda realize you aren't like the other females, but they don't get just how different you are. The pack isn't going to know how to interact with you."

I wasn't sure if I should take it as a compliment or be worried that I was so far from the norm.

"Do you think your pack would prefer a more...traditional female?" I asked hesitantly, wondering if I should try to start acting more lady-like.

"No way!" Jason said adamantly.

"Yeah," Mason added. "Don't start wearing dresses and heels all the time and get mad if your hair gets messed up."

"And don't start wearing tons of make-up and acting fake."

"Uh, okay." I looked at both of them, not sure of what else to say.

Mason stood up and held out his hands for me. I put my hands in his, and he pulled me up. I went over to my pile of stuff, grabbed my iPad, and jumped on the bed. I piled a couple of pillows up against the headboard so I could sit comfortably. Mason sprawled out on his stomach next to me, and Jason lay across the foot of the bed.

I searched for another location of the grocery store close by to see if they would deliver to this address. It turns out that there was a location five miles away, but they didn't deliver. I could still order online, but we would have to pick up the groceries.

The twins were okay with that. They shouted out things they wanted, and I added them to the list. Eventually, we were satisfied that we had enough food to prepare breakfast, lunch, and dinner for the rest of the week.

I clicked through the prompts to check out and finalize the order, but my heart dropped when I saw the total. "Uh, guys? Is Austin going to be okay with this?" I flipped the screen around so they could see the outrageous sum.

Mason chuckled. "That's over the budget, but I don't think we should mention it to him until after he eats a few meals you cook. He won't care about the cost then."

I blushed at the compliment. "I think you meant to say 'we,' not me."

"Huh?" They both looked at me.

I patted Mason on the arm. "There's no way I could prepare enough food for six wolves without my two helpful sous chefs."

Jason shrugged. "Technically, it is our job."

Mason groaned but nodded. "We'll make the food if you do the planning."

"Our order will be ready to pick up in ninety minutes," I announced once I got the confirmation notice.

Mason rolled off the bed. "Next task, get Anna unpacked."

I sighed. "It's okay, guys. I can unpack my own stuff."

"Nope," Mason said.

"Yeah, we all know you'll just leave your stuff in your luggage if we leave you alone with it," Jason added.

I shrugged; they weren't wrong.

Mason went over to the largest bag. "What's in here?"

"Just clothes," I answered. "Dump it out on the bed so I can figure out what to do with it."

Mason dumped it, and Jason started going through it. "Damn, Anna, where's all your girl stuff? I don't see any dresses or anything."

I just laughed. "Hey, sometimes I wear jeans instead of yoga pants. I even wore a purple sweater the other day."

Mason grinned. "Don't you remember? We just told her not to wear dresses."

"Yeah, but I don't see any lacy thongs or anything in here either."

Mason punched him in the arm before I did. "Don't go through her underwear; it's creepy."

"I'm not going through it, it's all mixed in," he complained, rubbing his arm. I wasn't embarrassed about any underwear he might find. I wore mainly sports bras to hide my 34Cs and either cotton boy short or bikini panties to be comfortable. My underwear usually covered more than what most girls wore to the beach.

I just rolled my eyes at them and went to work. We had everything put away in a short time. The closet was one of those insane rich people closets, with built-in drawers and shelves to keep your stuff organized.

There were enough shelves to fit at least a hundred pairs of shoes; I thought it looked funny with just my two pairs sitting there. The hanging space for the closet was also mostly empty, with only two hoodies hanging there. I couldn't imagine owning enough clothes to fill this space.

"I'm glad your stuff is put away in here; it makes it feel like you're really here," Mason said quietly, standing next to me and gazing into the closet.

"Yeah, like you're not going to suddenly disappear the same way you appeared one day," Jason added as he walked up to us.

I was surprised at the emotion from these two pranksters. I'd felt myself grow attached to them fairly quickly, and I was surprised at how comfortable I was becoming with them, but I hadn't considered that the affectionate feeling could be mutual. Evelyn was the only person who truly loved me; Kelsey was my friend mostly when it suited her needs.

I'd slipped into an easy camaraderie with the twins, and a part of me wondered if they were like this with everyone. I found it difficult to believe it was just me. I was nothing special. They probably had leagues of human females that wanted to hang out with them just as much as I did.

I felt a flash of jealousy and chastised myself for it. Why was I jealous? Of course, they would date other girls; it's not like they could both date me anyway.

"When are we getting the rest of your stuff?" Mason asked.

I didn't know how to break it to the twins that I was only here for the week. It seemed like they wanted me here longer. I guess it would be worse if they found out later from someone else and I hadn't said anything to them about it.

"Well, Austin only invited me to stay here for the week. Plus, I'm on a trial membership in the pack. And isn't the house only for the high-ranking pack members anyway?" I spewed all of that out in a rush and then took a deep breath.

The twins exchanged glances and replied together, "We'll talk to Austin."

Jason glanced down at his phone as the alarm went off. "Time to get the food!"

The mood was broken, and I followed them downstairs and to the Jeep. We had just enough time to get to the store and unload the groceries into the kitchen before the twins needed to leave for class.

"Hurry up and get your stuff. I'll make you some sandwiches to take with you for lunch," I told them. "I don't want you to get in trouble with Austin for missing class."

They both broke out in huge grins and ran out of the kitchen and up the stairs to get whatever they needed for their classes.

I looked around at the mess of groceries piled all over the kitchen; it looked like I was on my own to figure out where all this went.

I'd just put together some sandwiches when they came back in the kitchen with a backpack slung over each one of their shoulders.

I handed Mason his sandwich. "Roast beef and Swiss." Jason held out a hand expectantly. "And for you, turkey and American." I wrapped their sandwiches in foil to keep them warm since I toasted the bread.

They both looked happy and gave me an enthusiastic 'Thanks,' so I remembered their preferences correctly from our earlier shopping session. Mason reached out a hand and mussed up my hair on their way out, and then I was alone.

I looked around at the mess and sighed. I decided to start with the fridge and freezer items first. I hoped they didn't mind if I reorganized so I could fit everything.

I was rummaging around when I heard, "Hey." I turned around to see Caleb heading into the kitchen.

"Hey, Caleb," I called to him. "I didn't forget about you. I just wanted to get some of this stuff put away before I headed up to see you."

He laughed. "I was heading down here for lunch anyway. Got anything good?"

"I have sandwich-making items," I offered, gesturing to where I still had everything out from making the twins lunches.

"Cool," he answered. "You want help getting all this put away?" He gestured to the food items covering every available surface of the kitchen.

"Nah, go ahead and make lunch. I enjoy a good organizational challenge." I grinned. "I didn't spend all those years of my childhood playing Tetris for nothing."

He laughed. "We wouldn't want those skills going to waste."

"Hey, do you think the guys would mind if I got rid of some of the expired stuff and...mystery items?" I asked as I held up a GladWare container that may have contained food at some point. "I'm guessing this isn't a science project for one of the twins' classes?"

He chuckled. "I'm pretty sure no one will mind, especially if you're replacing it with edible food."

"Excellent," I replied.

Caleb made his sandwich while I sorted through the contents of the fridge. "I brought my iPad down. Do you mind if I get some info from you while we're down here?"

"No, that's cool." Truthfully, I was glad to have something to do while we talked. I would be a lot more anxious if I needed to sit still while we stared at each other and talked about personal stuff. This way, half my attention was on other things, so I would be doing less blank staring and stuttering. Hopefully, that meant that I would also be embarrassing myself less.

Caleb finished making his sandwich and took a seat at the counter. "I'm going just to have you start from the beginning when you first met Evelyn. Even the smallest detail that seems insignificant can be important when you put it together with other information. I'm going to take notes while you talk, and I'll try to keep any questions I have until the end unless you need prompting."

"Okay." I felt awkward getting started but decided to jump right in. "I shifted into my wolf form for the first time one night when I was around 10. It was a stressful night…Evelyn thought that might have triggered my shift."

Caleb raised an eyebrow but didn't say anything; he just patiently waited for me to continue. I chewed on my lip. That probably sounded weird to him. I'm sure he was thinking, How could life be stressful for a 10-year-old?

I had no desire to explain my uncle or the fact that I lived most of my childhood buried in fear and anxiety. I was willing to let him think someone had stolen my Barbie or something and just continued with my story.

"I had no idea how to react to what happened to me when I changed. Obviously, I realized it wasn't normal, and a part of me wondered if I imagined the whole thing."

I paused, thinking back to that day.

"I'd seen Evelyn outside before, working in her garden but had never spoken to her; I was nervous around strangers. I changed back to human in her garden, and it was only after she came out that I realized later she must have seen through her window. She came out of her house in a fury, marched in front of me, and crossed her arms across her chest."

I laughed. "I'd huddled up with my knees up against my chest and my arms wrapped around myself, just staring up at Evelyn with wide eyes.

She glared at me and asked, 'What do you think you're doing in my garden?'

I was so scared and overwhelmed, I just burst into tears, hiding my face up against my knees and barely managed to stutter out, 'I don't know what's happening to me' in-between my sobs."

I paused for a moment to see if I could move a shelf in the fridge up a level to make some extra room. It took some wiggling, but I got it. I glanced back at Caleb; he was watching me with a small smile and waved at me to continue.

I told him how Evelyn had brought me inside and cleaned me up. I didn't mention that one of the reasons why she took pity on me was the bruises she found on my body. "She asked me a lot of questions about my adoption and my parents, but at that age, I didn't really know anything."

Caleb nodded. "She realized pretty quickly that I was a wolf adopted by humans. I asked her if she was a wolf, too, and she told me no, but she had family that was. I didn't understand genetics or anything like that at that age, so it seemed like a reasonable explanation."

I paused for a moment to critically eye the counters. I was pretty sure I'd gotten everything in the fridge that needed to go in.

"What did she tell you about her family?" Caleb prodded gently.

I told him every detail I could think of while I worked on the pantry. I decided it would be easiest to empty everything out and start over so that I could organize things a little better.

Almost everything I told Caleb about Evelyn's family was vague, but I knew Evelyn had lived with her father's pack. I explained their system to Caleb, how the pack kept females for breeding, and the way that the pack treated the females. I told him about Evelyn's daughter and the yearbook photos that Evelyn had shown me.

He looked interested when I described the photos that I'd seen her with, and the possible names of the high school Evelyn's daughter had gone to.

"From what you have told me so far, I'm surprised that the pack let the females go to school," Caleb said.

I nodded. "I told Evelyn the same thing. She said it was because the pack would send the females out to get jobs but keep the money 'for the good of the pack.' I asked her why they didn't just run away, but she told me about the punishments they would get if they were caught…" I swallowed, feeling nauseated by the memories.

"You're doing great," Caleb encouraged me. "Did she ever mention names for any of the other females?"

"No, she always referred to them as 'the other girls.' She didn't even tell me her daughter's name. She wanted to make sure that I wouldn't be put in danger by telling me pack secrets." I started to tear up. "Evelyn was always thinking about everyone other than herself. I loved her so much, she was like the grandmother that I never had." I had to stop to fight back my tears.

I shoved my emotions down as deep as I could but suddenly had an epiphany. Was I repressing these emotions just like I repressed my wolf? Is that why the emotions would come to the surface and seem almost uncontrollable? It seemed similar to when my wolf would come to the surface and how the emotions that I felt with her would seem unmanageable.

Caleb watched me carefully; I think he could tell that I had a revelation.

"What are you thinking?" he asked curiously.

I wasn't ready to talk about my inner feelings with him, so I tried to offer up another piece of interesting information. "I was just wondering if the school that Evelyn's daughter went to would have done mandatory fingerprinting. They do that at some schools up in New York."

Caleb considered it. "Is there anything in Evelyn's house that might have her daughter's fingerprints on it?"

"Evelyn had this little wooden box with a rose etched into the lid. She never said anything, but I just got the feeling it might have belonged to her daughter."

Caleb didn't look too hopeful. "We can check it out, but I don't know if any fingerprints would be left on it after all this time, especially if it was something that Evelyn had handled regularly."

135

I just nodded. Caleb drummed his fingers on the counter as he looked through the notes he had gathered on his iPad. "Is there anything else you can think of that she mentioned in passing that might help us?"

I told him about stories she told me about taking day trips to the mountains, snowstorms in the winter, and a waterfall that was in biking distance of her house. "She also mentioned penguins at a zoo she took her daughter to once."

"Let's change gears a little bit," Caleb suggested. "Did she ever talk about her captors? Any characteristics they might have had?"

"She never talked about anyone in particular except her father. She would just talk about wolves in general, but from meeting you guys, I have kind of seen that maybe she was wrong about some things."

"What were some of the things she told you about wolves?" he asked curiously.

I hesitated, unsure of what I should say.

"It might give us an idea of what to look for in a pack. If all of the wolves in the pack did certain activities or held certain beliefs, it could help us narrow things down."

I squirmed a little uncomfortably. I didn't want to repeat a lot of what she had said. "She said they were mean, abusive, barbarians who thrived on senseless violence." That was one of the nicer things she had said.

"Hmmm," Caleb responded. "Were there any activities or hobbies they engaged in?"

"They liked to fight and would hold matches like gladiators."

Caleb looked down at his iPad. "Did they have a specific venue?"

"Just outside. Evelyn said the loser would end up with their face in the dirt."

I couldn't tell what Caleb was thinking; his face was impassive. "What about the higher-ranking pack members? Was there anything they indulged in? Cars, motorcycles, maybe an expensive house?"

I shook my head slowly. "No, she never mentioned anything like that."

"What about jobs?"

"She told me that they would send the humans and lower-ranking wolves out to get jobs, but it seemed like all blue-collar stuff."

Caleb took notes on that. "Anything else?"

I shook my head no.

"Okay, this is a good start," he told me.

I looked at him doubtfully, but he smiled at me. "I promise we're going to figure this out. We already know she can't be from Florida with the snowstorms," he joked.

"Oh!" I said suddenly. "You can also rule out any states on the coast. She told me that she never saw the ocean until she left the pack because the closest beach was two states over."

"That's great! If anything else like that comes to mind, let me know." He smiled. "Let me look into some of this, and I'll come up with ideas of which packs this could be. Maybe if we examine the packs one by one, you might remember some other details to help narrow it down."

I looked at him hopefully. Maybe we could figure this out. Caleb gathered his iPad and a second sandwich to head back upstairs. He seemed deep in thought with the information I'd given him, so maybe I had given him something useful to work with.

"Hey, Caleb?"

He turned around, still lost in thought. "Yeah?"

"Will you be free around six tonight? I thought it might be fun for us to have a family-style dinner. You know, like they do on TV?" I asked shyly.

His eyes widened with surprise as they met mine.

Had I said something wrong? I backpedaled quickly. "I mean, it's okay if you're busy or have other plans-"

"No," he said quickly. "That sounds nice. The guys and I are used to just grabbing our food when we can, but I think that would be a good idea to sit down together. It'll be a nice break from work." He smiled at me. "I'll be here at six."

I smiled back. "Is Italian OK? I was thinking lasagna."

He nodded enthusiastically. "That sounds great."

"Okay, cool." I stood there awkwardly, not sure what to say next. He gave me a small wave with the hand that was holding his iPad and headed back upstairs, saving me from any further embarrassment.

When I lived with my uncle's family, dinner was a terrifying time. When he was working day shift, Uncle would be home at 5:30 and dinner would have to be served precisely at six. He had an armchair in the living room that I used to think of as his throne.

No one else was allowed to sit there or touch the chair except his wife, and she was only allowed to touch it to clean. He would sit in his armchair and be served dinner on top of a little rolling table that would slide right in front of his chair.

He would take his time eating while he watched the evening news and spewed angry political commentary. The rest of us were expected to be absolutely silent during this time and wait for him to finish; we were allowed to eat after he was done. After he rolled the table to the side as a cue for his wife to come to clean up after him, the rest of us would file back into the kitchen.

The kids lined up in the kitchen according to age, the oldest first, and myself last. Each of us was allowed to make a plate from the leftovers for our own dinner. The other kids took a perverse joy in making sure nothing was left by the time it was my turn. They would smirk mockingly at me as I gazed into the empty pot or pan with sadness.

Then to add insult to injury, it was my task to clean up after everyone else was done eating. As soon as they had shoveled what food they could into their mouths, the rest of the kids would run and hide in their rooms, staying as quiet as possible to avoid drawing attention.

Unfortunately, that left me alone in the kitchen, and while I tried to be as quiet as possible while I did the dishes, inevitably some small noise would always attract the ire of my uncle. I had nowhere to hide in the kitchen, so I was completely exposed to his rage. Part of me thought this was why I was left with kitchen duties; everyone else in the family used me as a sacrificial lamb to take on the brunt of rage from my uncle.

I loved the weeks he would be working the 3-11 shift. That meant there was no dinner time. My uncle's wife wouldn't even bother to cook; most days, she took her kids to her mother's house for dinner. I was never invited, but I loved the solitude that being alone in the house gave me.

Evelyn always made sure I had enough to eat and would have something waiting for me at her house after I was free from the agony of dinner time and the work of cleaning up after everyone.

I always wished I had a family similar to what I saw in the movies and on TV. They would all sit at the table and pass dishes around to each other, smiling and laughing. After spending time with the twins, I was hoping I could create something like that here. I knew I could get the twins to cooperate; they would be more than happy as long as food was involved. Caleb had seemed okay with it as well.

After I had everything put away, I stood in the kitchen. The silence around me seemed almost to echo, and I missed the twins. It would still be a couple of hours until they were back, and I could rope them into helping me prepare dinner.

I skipped up the stairs, remembering the large bath that was mine for this week. When I'd examined the tub earlier, it looked like there were jets that could be turned on as well. I figured it would be a good idea to make myself look more presentable if I wanted to convince the guys to make family dinners be 'a thing' here. I took my time soaking in the tub.

It had been a long time after I left my uncle's house before I was comfortable taking a bath, even in my own tub. He would fly into a rage anytime he heard the water running for more than five minutes, screaming about how we were using his hot water and costing him money. I got into the habit of taking showers only when I knew he was at work but still showered as quickly as possible, just in case he stopped home.

I made the mistake of taking a bath in the house once, he had stopped by the house on his lunch break unbeknownst to me. I was relaxing in the tub with music on, so I didn't hear his heavy footsteps approach. He had disabled all the locks on the doors inside the house, so there was no way to keep him or anyone else out.

The bathroom door had burst open, and my body jerked in shock. I tried to hide under what little coverage the water offered as he stood there and looked at my naked and exposed body. I shuddered in terror as I could see when his thoughts shifted from rage to something else.

I knew the only thing that had saved me that day was the sound of the car in the driveway; his wife had come home just in time. She took the brunt of his rage that day, as she hadn't been home and waiting to make him lunch in case he stopped by.

There were some occasions when I pitied his wife. She was treated almost like a slave and was expected to stay home and devote every waking moment to taking care of his needs. She didn't work so she could spend her days cleaning the house, doing the shopping, preparing his meals, etc.

As I got older, I pitied her less. She was an adult and could walk out whenever she wanted. I was a minor; if I left, I would just be dragged back here by the police. I wasn't stupid enough to attempt an escape. I knew that my life would only get worse if I 'embarrassed' my uncle by doing something like that. As the years went by, his wife became even more cruel to me, and there was no pity left in me for her.

I pushed those thoughts out of my mind and tried to relax in the tub. I'd gotten out of my uncle's house, put myself through school, had a great job, and lived a life that most people would label as 'successful.' To anyone on the outside looking in, I owned my house, a car, and even had a little bit of money in a savings account. I may have seemed independent and confident, but I had the deep ache of loneliness inside of me. I thought if I could make it to this point, I would've been happy, but instead, I just felt empty.

I worked for years to break myself of the constant, crippling fear and anxiety that had ruled my life for so long. I worked hard to appear 'normal' in my interactions with other people, and I no longer had crippling panic attacks when I would hear a man's deep voice or the sound of heavy footsteps coming closer to me.

I tried to appear confident and poised on the outside, but I mainly only succeeded at that when I was at work. I was hopeless at social interactions and just felt awkward and uncomfortable when trying to interact with people outside of work. I developed a self-imposed exile because I tended to try and avoid social interactions whenever possible.

Kelsey was the only person who made consistent and determined efforts to drag me out in public regularly. I think most people just gave up and assumed I didn't want to be friends with them because of how standoffish I could be. Kelsey was the only person who realized that I wasn't a snob; I was just scared and didn't know how to interact.

I relaxed in the tub and felt hopeful for the first time in a while. I was here with other wolves, so I could relax and open up to them in ways I would never be able to with a human. I just needed to overcome my innate fear and learn to trust them. I was the only person holding me back, and I didn't have to be afraid anymore. The twins had already done everything they could to make it clear they wanted me here. I just needed to relax and accept it.

I felt better after my bath and the pep-talk I gave myself. I dried my hair with the hairdryer and brush, so it fell straight and shiny down my back. I even dressed in cute skinny jeans and a light pink sweater to feel girly. I swiped some mascara over my eyelashes and put on some pink lip gloss. I felt ready to make my new start and headed downstairs to see if I could start getting some things ready for dinner while I waited for the twins to come back.

I bounced down the stairs and jumped down the last three. I quickly turned around the corner and collided into someone with an oomph.

Of course, it had to be James. I sighed as he took a step back from me. He glared at me, but it lacked his usual intensity.

"Oh, hey James," I said hesitantly, trying to be friendly. "I didn't realize you would be here."

"I live here," he said. I could hear the unspoken 'unlike you' that completed that sentence. I started to feel hurt but remembered this was James. He was mean to everyone on purpose, so I couldn't let myself take it personally.

I decided that being peppy and friendly toward him was my best option. It would show him that he couldn't intimidate me, and as a side benefit, it would probably annoy him.

I gave him a big smile. "I just didn't realize you were back from your trip. The twins and I are making lasagna tonight. Dinner is at six," I told him confidently.

He looked a little surprised and suspicious. "You cook?"

I fought as hard as I could not to roll my eyes or growl at him. "I guess you'll find out tonight," I told him brightly before I started to walk around him.

He touched my arm gently but dropped his hand when I glanced down in surprise. "I'll be there at six," he said quietly.

I nodded and continued to walk back to the kitchen. I could feel his eyes on me as I walked away but did my best to ignore him and not glance back. I was a little proud of myself with how I handled him, so when I reached the kitchen, I decided to reward myself with a snack.

I chopped up some fruit for a fruit salad in a big bowl and then scooped some out for myself. I put the rest in the fridge for snacking the next couple days and wandered to the living room area to eat my snack. I curled up on one of the couches with my iPad to entertain me. It was bizarre to have this much free time with nothing to do, but I found it relaxing.

It wasn't long before I heard the front door burst open. "Anna!" I heard the twins yell. I briefly considered hiding and making them look for me in an impromptu game of hide and seek but thought better of it when I thought back to their earlier confessions of being afraid that I would disappear on them.

"In here!" I yelled back. Jason came running in and flung his bag to the ground before jumping on the couch and wrapping me in a tight hug.

"I need to breathe, big guy," I teased him as I patted him on the back. He released me as Mason walked in and tossed his bag next to Jason's.

"How was class?" I asked them.

"Boring," Jason replied.

"What have you been doing without us?" Mason asked.

"Well, I invited Caleb and James to a family-style dinner that the three of us are going to make tonight."

"James is back already?" Mason asked with a frown.

"What makes a dinner family-style?" Jason asked curiously.

I nodded at Mason and turned to Jason. "You know, like how happy families eat dinner on TV."

They both looked at me with their mouths open in surprise.

"Like on TV?" Mason murmured as he shared an unreadable look with his brother.

I felt self-conscious as I blushed and chewed on my lip with a nod.

Jason jumped up. "We had better get started, I'm starving!"

I chuckled; it hadn't been that long since their sandwiches, but Jason was acting like he hadn't eaten yet today.

"After dinner, we should go on a pack run," Mason told me.

"Yeah!" Jason nodded enthusiastically. "It's fun, Anna, you'll love it."

I was nervous. "With James and Caleb? I don't think James likes me that much. What if his wolf attacks me?" I blurted out.

They both laughed. "James likes you," Mason told me. "He wasn't even that mad about the car and the mud last night."

I looked at him incredulously. That was James *not* being mad?

"And it's not James' wolf," Jason reminded me gently. "It's James. He would never hurt you."

Mason slung his arm around me as we made our way to the kitchen. "Besides, how could anyone not like you?"

I felt a little reassured, but still nervous. I tried to put it out of my mind as I directed the guys on what we needed to do to make dinner. I decided on lasagna with spicy Italian sausage, garlic bread, and a classic Caesar salad for dinner tonight. Simple, yet delicious.

The scent of lasagna filled the air as the twins and I waited for it to be done baking. The delicious smells must have made their way through the house because James and Caleb both showed up down in the kitchen a half-hour early.

"Damn, Anna. That smells good!" Caleb announced enthusiastically. Even James peered in the direction of the oven, looking interested.

"Where do you guys want to eat?" I asked them.

"I'll just take mine upstairs to my office-" James started out.

"No!" the other guys answered in unison.

They all looked at each other. "Anna wants to have a family dinner," Caleb told him seriously.

James looked at me in surprise. "A family dinner?"

"Yeah, you know, like they have on TV," Mason said significantly.

The other two guys nodded gravely, and James looked at me. "That's not a bad idea. I think it's good for the pack to gather and eat together."

The gathering tension in the room faded as the guys relaxed. "We have a formal dining room," Caleb said hesitantly, "but it's not set up for eating right now."

"We have been using it more as a command center," Mason added helpfully.

"What about on the patio?" I asked. "I saw a couple of tables out there that could fit all of us."

"That could work," James said thoughtfully. He turned to the twins. "You two, go clean one off and make sure it's ready for us to eat on. Preferably the one with the fire pit in the middle."

Surprisingly, neither of them argued or complained and just headed outside, maybe because there was the potential for a fire to be involved in their task.

James looked at Caleb. "Go find that dining set that Austin's mom left here. I think it's still in boxes in the dining room. We can use nice dishes for Anna."

Caleb nodded, and I was left staring at James. I guess it shouldn't have surprised me that he would want to take control, but it did surprise me that he was willing to play along with the family dinner concept.

I wanted to ask about Austin's mom since James had brought it up. Did she live around here? How did the mom of the pack-master fit into things here? Austin had told me that I was the only female in the pack. I guess it made sense that she would have her own pack since Austin had built this one himself. I wasn't comfortable asking James about any of this, so I started with an easier question while I opened the oven door to peek and see how the lasagna was doing. "How was your trip?"

"Not very productive," he answered with a sigh.

"Did your trip have anything to do with Evelyn?" I asked him, trying to pry some information out of him. I decided the lasagna looked almost ready, so I popped the garlic bread in there to heat up.

"Yes, I followed a lead that didn't pan out. On the bright side, we now can cross one pack off our suspect list."

"Hmmm." I chewed on my lip as I thought. I was hoping Caleb had been able to make some progress. I was feeling useless, just standing around and waiting to see what they came up with. I was used to doing everything on my own.

Caleb walked back into the kitchen hauling a heavy box. I blinked when James pulled a sharp knife out of a hiding place somewhere on his body and bent down to cut the tape. I peered over his shoulder into the box where thick and heavy plates were packed carefully.

"They look expensive. Are you sure we should take them outside?"

Caleb laughed. "Why have plates if we aren't going to use them?"

"Well, if they were a gift from Austin's mom..."

James grinned. "Don't worry, she knows better than to give a pack of wolves dainty and delicate things. I'm pretty sure she expected them to get broken at some point."

I chuckled. I could see that; she had to have met the twins.

I washed the plates and serving dishes we found in there as James and Caleb dried. They passed dishes, silverware, and cloth napkins over to the twins to set up the table outside.

I pulled the lasagna out of the oven and put the bread and salad in the pretty serving dishes that had also been in the box. I handed the salad to Caleb and picked up the bread. "James, I'm trusting you with the most important part of dinner." I pointed at the lasagna with my elbow.

"Good choice." Caleb chuckled. "I would have seriously questioned your judgment if you had assigned that to the twins."

I laughed, imagining what could go wrong in that scenario.

We were soon sitting at the table and filling our plates. The air outside was cool, and the sun was on its way down, but the fire in the middle of the table exuded warmth and provided plenty of light.

"I'm surprised you're not cold," Caleb told me as he blew on a forkful of piping hot lasagna.

"That's true," Jason said thoughtfully. "Girls are always cold and trying to steal my hoodie from me."

I just rolled my eyes. "Be careful not to burn your mouths with the first bite, or you won't be able to taste anything," I warned them.

Jason lowered the forkful of hot lasagna he was about to shovel in his mouth and decided to start with the salad first.

"Anna probably never gets cold," James added. "She's an arctic wolf."

The twins and Caleb all stared at me. I frowned. "How is that different from what you are?"

"Arctic wolves are smaller. They have shorter legs and smaller, more rounded ears, plus more white in their much thicker coats."

"Why shorter legs?" Jason asked.

"It helps with circulation to prevent frostbite, same with the smaller ears. If blood is too exposed when running through less insulated parts of the body, it can lower the body temperature."

"Huh," I said. "I guess that explains why I really do *not* like going outside in July and August."

The guys all laughed, and we ate in companionable silence for a few minutes.

"Anna, this is amazing," Caleb groaned out between bites.

"Hey! We made it, too," Jason added.

"I think we all know who is responsible for this, and it's not you guys," James joked.

Jason grumbled in reluctant agreement.

I was shocked to see the usually sour James acting pleasant and joking around. Maybe he wasn't so bad after all?

Since he was in a good mood, I thought now would be the time to remind him of his promises to me. "So, James, have you made any progress on getting Evelyn back?"

Caleb and the twins looked confused. James swallowed the bite of food he had just taken. "Anna, I have to move carefully here. No one knows about the relationship that you and Evelyn had. Austin and I decided it was best if we kept things that way."

I nodded. I could understand why he wouldn't want the pack that had brutally murdered Evelyn to have a reason to focus on me. "What's the plan, then?"

James cleared his throat. "I approached the subject delicately with the team that's handling the situation. It was difficult to explain why the pack would want the...why we would want Evelyn. But I made contact with someone earlier today who can help us."

I nodded. It seemed like James was doing the best he could, and I only had myself to blame for what had gone wrong in the first place. The rest of the group was quiet for a moment, and then we went back to casually chatting while we enjoyed dinner.

Our pleasant dinner was interrupted by the sound of a distant howl. James stood up abruptly. "Caleb, you have Anna. Jason front, Mason back." The twins started to strip quickly, and I just stared, not entirely understanding what was happening.

"I just sent an alert out to the pack, so our backup will be here in moments," Caleb said quietly, but on edge.

The twins bounded off in wolf form, one to the front of the house, and one to the back. "I texted Austin, he and Cody are heading back."

"Contract negotiations not go well?" Caleb asked.

"I don't think that's what this is," James stated as he pulled out a gun.

My eyebrows rose. Where did that even come from?

James glanced back at me, remembering I was there. "Take her inside. I want your eyes on everything," he told Caleb.

"What's going on?" I asked.

Caleb motioned to come with him, and James ignored me.

"I'm not going anywhere-" my voice cut off in a squeak when Caleb simply lifted me up and threw me over his shoulder.

"C'mon, Anna-banana, we have things to do."

I was too shocked even to struggle as he carried me inside. He patted the back of my thigh as we reached the stairs. "Can I trust you enough to set you down? We can move a lot quicker if I'm not carrying you."

I mumbled out an assent, and he set me down gently. "Let's go!"

He ran up the stairs, and I followed. What was going on? Were my guys in danger? I wasn't going to stand around and let them get hurt. I let out a small growl as I followed Caleb.

Caleb turned toward me as he opened the door to what I assumed was his room. "Don't worry, Anna, this is what we do best."

He grinned, and I followed him into the room. His room looked more like a fictional military command central than a bedroom. He had computer monitors covering an entire wall and all kinds of other electrical equipment scattered across the room. He flicked a switch, and the monitors lit up with images of the entire house and around the property. I looked through them, looking for signs of the guys.

Caleb sat down at his desk covered in computer equipment. He started typing, and I heard him making a call on speakerphone. A flicker of movement caught my eye on one of the outdoor monitors.

"Caleb!" I pointed to the monitor where I saw an unfamiliar wolf prowling. I hadn't met James in his wolf form yet, but since he had pulled out a human weapon earlier, I'm guessing that wasn't him.

"I see it," Caleb answered me grimly.

"Caleb, report!" a voice barked out from the speakerphone. It sounded like Austin.

"Quinn scented something at the border and warned us of a possible incoming."

"Multiple?"

"One that he saw, but I wouldn't discount the possibility of more. They could be coming in separately."

"Anna?"

"She's here with me, safe," Caleb assured him.

"Hi," I squeaked out nervously.

"Hey, Anna. Don't be worried, everything is fine." Austin had softened his voice a little when he was speaking to me but hardened up as he switched his attention back to Caleb.

"Cody and I are five minutes out."

"Trevor and a bunch of the guys just got here." Caleb gestured toward a monitor showing a couple of trucks pulling into the front gate.

"Excellent. James is directing from the ground?"

"He is."

The trucks stopped, and eight men piled out, stripping and tossing their clothes aside. These must be more of the pack I hadn't met yet. I was cautious not to look too closely as they changed into wolf form; I wouldn't want anyone spying on me while I was undressing.

I blushed when I realized just how much of the property was covered in cameras. The times I'd changed outside had definitely been caught on tape. I was going to have to ask Caleb who watched them and how long they kept the video footage.

"James is having them spread out and surround the house," Caleb informed Austin.

"I'm close enough to tap in now," Austin informed him.

I frowned. Tap into what? And how was James directing anyone? It didn't look like he had been speaking at all on camera. Could these wolves be psychic?

No way.

Could they hear my thoughts?

My eye caught on one of the cameras where a wolf fight came into view. Two wolves were savagely attacking a third. "We got one!" Caleb shouted. So that must be our wolves getting one of the intruders.

A chase appeared another one of the screens. A lone grey wolf was being chased by three brown wolves. The grey stumbled, and all three of the other wolves were on him.

"And we have two." Caleb pumped his fist in the air. "That's what you get when you attack Seaside Pack!"

"So, everyone in our pack is safe? No one got hurt?" I asked worriedly.

Caleb tilted his head to one side as if listening. "Robbie has a gash on his leg that might need stitches. They're bringing him in now."

I turned to the door, but he stopped me. "Not yet. Austin hasn't given the all-clear."

I fidgeted, wanting to see for myself that everyone was okay. I also had emergency medical training so I could help.

"I've worked as an EMT before, and I do rounds in the ED when a critical care patient comes in," I told Caleb. "If you don't have anyone else here, I can take a look at Robbie until we get him to the hospital."

Caleb looked surprised. "Let me check with Austin." He did another head tilt, and his eyes glazed over as if listening to a silent conversation. Yep, these wolves were definitely psychic.

Caleb nodded. "You can go downstairs. They're bringing him in the office now; that's where we keep medical supplies." He looked at me sternly. "But you can't leave the house until it's safe."

I nodded quickly and turned toward the door.

Caleb reached out and grabbed my hand. "Anna, I'm serious. We just found you; we can't lose you."

I looked into his worried eyes. "I promise that I won't leave the house. I also promise you that I'm not some helpless female that needs to be hidden away and protected."

He laughed. "I doubt we would be able to hide you away for long."

Caleb let go of my hand, and I rushed out the door and down the stairs. These wolves might be the best at fighting and protecting their territory, but I was at my best in a medical emergency. I turned the corner and caught up to two men carrying a third who was dripping blood. I followed them in the room as they laid him on the couch. He was groaning and clutching his leg.

"Medical supplies?" I asked them as I strode over to the couch.

A tall man with a beard nodded at a younger but still impressively large man to his right. The younger man ran to a cabinet against the wall and pulled out a large bag. I knelt to take a look at the injured man while he lugged the bag over to me.

"You're Anna?" the bearded man asked me.

"Yeah. Can you open the bag and look for clean gauze and sterile irrigation fluid?"

The younger man smiled at me before he dug through the bag and held up some sterile gauze pads. "This?"

I flicked a glance over to him and nodded while I worked on the injury. It looked deep enough to need stitches, but it didn't look like any major arteries or veins were nicked. The wound was filthy as if he had rolled around in the dirt right after being injured, but the bleeding was slowing and starting to clot. I was going to have to clean it thoroughly before stitching him up.

"Robbie?" I said softly to get his attention. Robbie looked over at me in pain. "I can stitch you up here, or I can have them take you to the hospital."

Without hesitation, all three men answered together, "Here."

"Okay, see what we have for pain meds in there," I directed my new assistant.

I cleaned the wound gently as he pulled meds out and read me their names. I was pleased with how well stocked the bag was; I was going to have everything I needed to treat the wound. I also had pain meds and antibiotics for my patient.

Once I identified what I needed, I asked my assistant, "What's your name?"

"Alex."

"Okay, Alex, I'm just going to need you to hand me the things I ask for as I need them. I might also need an extra pair of hands once I start stitching."

"I can do that," the bearded man told me. "I'm Tony, by the way," he said with a blush. I was surprised for a second to see such a large and intimidating man blush, but this was no time for idle thoughts.

Alex and Tony were excellent assistants, and I had the wound clean and almost stitched up when Austin walked in.

"How are we doing?" he asked.

Alex jumped to his feet immediately and stood straight. "Good, sir."

Tony, thankfully, didn't let go of where I needed his hands to stay to do the same. Tony gave Austin a respectful nod but stayed where he was, concentrating on the task I'd assigned him. My patient just moaned. The pain medication that I'd given him had kicked in, and he was limp and still the way I needed him to be.

Austin came a little closer to look at what we were doing. "Good work, Anna."

I grunted as I finished my last stitch and eyed my work critically. I was satisfied with the way the wound had come together and stopped bleeding, but I was still worried about infection because the wound had been deep and messy.

"They said it was okay to treat him here instead of bringing him to the hospital," I explained to Austin, a little defensively.

He nodded. "We stay away from hospitals whenever possible. I'm glad we have another person on the team that can help out with that."

He gently laid a hand on my shoulder. "Come upstairs to my office when you're finished."

I nodded, and Austin left the room. I finished cleaning the wound and bandaged Robbie's leg. I gave Alex and Tony instructions on how to use the pain meds and antibiotics and made them promise to keep Robbie here for a least a day, so I could keep an eye on the wound and monitor for infection.

After I was satisfied, I cleaned up my impromptu medical area and headed upstairs. I wanted to head straight to Austin's office so I could find out what was going on, but he probably wouldn't appreciate me getting blood on his stuff. I stopped in my room to wash up and change my clothes as quickly as I could.

I headed to Austin's office with a mix of anticipation, worry, and curiosity. I wanted to know what was going on and how I would be able to help, but I was also worried about the guys being in some serious trouble. Regardless of what was going on, I was sticking with them; these were the good guys.

I knocked on the closed door but decided to barge in without waiting for an answer. Austin was sitting behind his giant desk, with Cody and James sitting across from him. It looked like I'd interrupted a serious discussion, but Austin waved me toward them.

Cody stood up to offer me his seat. I tried to turn it down, but all three guys insisted. Cody stood behind me with his hands on the back of my chair.

Austin leaned forward as he started speaking. "Anna, I'm glad you're here. Thanks for your help earlier tonight."

I nodded. I didn't feel like I did anything useful, but I didn't want to waste time arguing. "So, what happened tonight?"

James cleared his throat. "We had a group of wolves attempt to gain access to the house tonight."

I frowned. "Why would they do that? Is this a territory issue? How often does this kind of thing happen?" I tried to stop myself from asking questions so that he could answer some of the ones I already asked. I was babbling again.

"Well, we think they were on a mission to get something from the house."

I nodded. That made sense; it looked like they had a lot of expensive things here. "How were the wolves planning to get it out, though?" I asked with a frown. "It's not like they could carry anything in their wolf forms."

"That's a good point, Anna," Cody added from behind me.

"James will have to look more into what they were planning and how they were planning to do it." Austin looked at James pointedly, and he nodded in response.

"Are you going to ask the wolves you took prisoner?" I asked, curious to know what was going on. It seemed odd that the three of them were sitting here when there were prisoners somewhere on the property that might have the answers that we needed.

Austin sighed. "We have laws among our kind that dictate what we can and can't do if we find members of another pack trespassing on our territory. We captured two, but it looks like there were a total of ten wolves on the property tonight. That's a significant number and leads us to believe it was the work of a pack, not the work of a few lone wolves."

I thought about that for a moment. "You think they were looking to attack our position here and not just steal something?"

"That's possible," Austin told me. He exchanged looks with James, and they seemed to have a silent conversation. James clenched his jaw and looked away while Austin continued. "We were aware that someone had our pack under surveillance, but we weren't sure why. Today, we set a trap. If they were interested in taking over the pack or my territory, they would have gone after Cody and myself while we were alone out in town today. They didn't."

Austin paused and looked as though he was considering his next words. I heard Cody shifting behind me, but I couldn't see his face to guess what he was thinking.

"Instead of coming after pack leadership, they came here. We had made it look like there were only a couple of wolves on guard duty on the perimeter and four wolves here in the house. The reality was that we had a lot more wolves on standby, just waiting for them to make a move."

Not that I didn't appreciate being kept in the loop, but I wondered why he was telling me all of this. I was a brand new wolf to the pack, just here on a trial basis. My heart dropped. Did he suspect me of being involved somehow?

As Austin shifted in his seat, my thoughts must have been all over my face. "Anna, the reason I'm telling you this is because we think those wolves were after you."

"Me?" I spluttered. "Do you think that's Evelyn's pack? That they know I had a relationship with her?"

"That's one possibility. At this point, we aren't sure. We're following protocol, which is to contact the council and have them act as a mediator between myself and the other pack-master."

Out of the corner of my eye, I saw James shift as he pulled out his vibrating phone. Austin gave him a wave, and James went outside of the room to take the call.

"Our next step is to have the pack-master identify himself and what he wants. If he wants our territory, he will have to declare war. If he wants you, it gets much more complicated."

Fear trickled down my spine. It seemed unreal that anyone would want to kidnap me, but Evelyn had warned me this could happen if wolves found out about my existence. She hadn't predicted there would be a pack of good wolves willing to protect me, though.

Or would they? Was Austin willing to negotiate something in return for me? Would he risk putting his pack in danger for a stray wolf he just met? He could hand me over, and all his troubles would be over.

"What are you going to do if they ask for me?" I whispered.

Austin sat back. "That depends on you. I need you to answer me honestly. Is there another pack that would have a claim on you?"

I was confused. "How would they do that?"

"Your father or a male that you had mated with could make a claim on you."

I just stared at him. "I don't know who my father is. And I haven't, uh, mated with any wolves."

"Are you sure?" Cody asked me quietly. "You couldn't tell I was a wolf until I told you."

I turned bright red. "I'm 100 percent sure. There was only one guy, and it was a long time ago." I closed my eyes in complete embarrassment. Oh my god, please let words stop coming out of my mouth. I slunk down on my chair, hoping to disappear into the floor.

"Huh," Austin said.

I peeked out of one eye to see if they were laughing at me for being a complete weirdo.

"I'm going to have to ask you to give James his info so we can check, just to make sure," Austin told me gently. "It would be better to find out now than to be surprised later."

"He's no longer alive," I told them awkwardly. "Even if he were a wolf, his pack wouldn't have any claim on me, right?"

"No, they wouldn't. But I still want to confirm the story," James announced as he strode back into the room.

Oh my god, now James was discussing this? How was he even a part of the conversation when he had just been out in the hall? If I could have sunk any lower in my chair, I would have. "Can't I just say I want to stay here?" I mumbled.

Austin looked at me with pity. "Unfortunately, wolf society has been very patriarchal over the centuries. Females are considered part of the pack they're born into unless they mate outside of the pack, while males are free to change packs and go where they want. Wolf society is behind on the modern times."

I shifted uncomfortably. "But I wasn't born into a pack, so I don't belong anywhere."

Austin shrugged. "That's what makes this a delicate situation, and why I decided to involve the council. They have the authority to name you as an official member of our pack so that other packs will respect that and back off. No one will risk the anger of the council to kidnap you after it's announced that you're one of us."

"But what if the council wants to give me to another pack?" I asked nervously.

"Austin's father and James' cousin are both on the council," Cody informed me.

"So it will be difficult, but not impossible, for us to have you named to our pack," Austin added with a smile.

"There's going to be opposition from the more well-established packs. They're going to argue that she should go to one of them," James voiced.

"We can argue about what may or may not happen all day. Right now, we need to plan for the things that we can control," Austin said firmly.

"I'm going contact the council members individually to try and get their ear before any official proceeding occurs. James, I need you on the investigation to see what we're dealing with. Cody, I need you in contact with the other local packs; see if they have had any problems with renegade wolves or another pack encroaching on their territory. I already have Caleb working this from a tech aspect."

Finally, Austin turned to me. "Anna, I need you to stay in the house and out of sight." I frowned. Everyone else got an assignment, but I was told to hide? Not fair.

"Can't I do something to help?" I asked. "I feel kind of useless just going to hide under my bed when all of this is kind of my fault." I chewed my lip nervously.

Cody chuckled, and James was hiding a grin. "None of this is your fault, Anna," Austin told me reassuringly. "We've been dealing with attacks on our territory a lot since we're a new pack. Having a female here now is just giving them extra motivation."

I nodded and tried not to worry. These guys were professionals, they knew exactly what they were doing and were the best at what they do. Everyone was going to be okay.

"I'm going to have you stick with the twins for now, so you can help them with all of their tasks," Austin told me.

"Okay," I agreed. That was going to be fine for now, at least until I was really a part of the pack.

James took that as a signal that the meeting was over and strode out. I stood up and headed to the door after him. I wanted to find the twins to check up on them and see what I could do to help.

# Chapter 12

Much later that night, I was snuggled into my bed. It had been organized chaos for most of the evening; almost all the pack members had shown up after the attempted attack on the house. I was able to meet everyone who came over. Some seemed more open to having a female in the pack, others wary. I was determined to win them over.

I was naturally shy and awkward, but Mason and Jason made me feel comfortable when I was around them. They kept the mood light as I was introduced to each new person. I tried my best to remember everyone, but all the new names and faces were a blur.

The twins and I had been responsible for assigning pack members to work details, coordinating the search efforts (from inside the house, of course), and keeping everyone fed and up to date. It was a lot of work, but I liked working as a team with my new pack.

I was worried about what was going to happen with the council, but I was filled with a warm, content feeling when I thought about being able to stay with the guys here. I was also grateful to have the rest of the week off from work; there was no way I could've managed all this in addition to my job.

I yawned and felt myself start to drift off to sleep. The sound of my doorknob twisting caused me to jolt out of my sleepy haze. My heart started to pound as I heard footsteps enter my room. I was extending all my senses to determine if this was a friend or foe before I let on that I was awake and gave up that small element of surprise.

The footsteps stopped a few feet from my bed. "Psssst, Anna."

"Jason!" I scolded him. "You almost scared me to death." I threw a pillow at him, but he just gave me a shit-eating grin. He hopped on my bed and tossed the pillow back at me. "Awww, the vicious arctic wolf was scared?"

I used the pillow to smack him. "What are you doing in my room at-" I glanced at my phone and groaned, "2:45 in the morning?"

"I was worried," he told me earnestly, scooting closer on the bed and lying down next to me. "You were almost kidnapped tonight, and I saw how nervous you were meeting all the new wolves. I thought you might be feeling overwhelmed."

My heart melted. "That's sweet of you, Jason. I know I shouldn't be worried because the house is full of our wolves-" a yawn interrupted my sentence before I could continue, "but I do feel better having you close."

It was true, having Jason next to me made a part of me relax that I hadn't even realized was tense. I closed my eyes, and just having his scent near me made me feel like I was home and safe.

I heard my doorknob twist again. I had a strong feeling that I knew who it was going to be this time. I saw that I was right as the light from the hallway illuminated Mason's face.

"Yo," Mason said as he saw I was awake and glanced toward Jason lying next to me. He padded over to the bed on my other side and lifted the covers. "Move over a little."

I rolled my eyes but scooted closer to Jason to make room. Mason reached for one of the extra pillows I'd tossed on the floor, and all three of us rearranged, so we were comfortable. I yawned again; there was no doubt in my mind I was safe now. There was nothing that could get past these two big wolves.

We lay there quietly, and I started to drift off again.

"Anna?" Mason murmured.

"Yeah?" I mumbled sleepily.

"You know you're not allowed to leave us now, right?" he asked quietly.

A small smile slowly spread across my face. "Yeah." I drifted off to sleep with a warm, happy glow, surrounded by my pack and wrapped in their scents.

# Chapter 13

I woke up with sunlight hitting my face and blinked as the events from yesterday came back to me. I snuggled deeper into the blankets; the bed was nice and toasty, as I still had a twin on each side of me. I pulled my pillow closer to me and snuggled with it. I was lying on my side and facing Mason. He was still fast asleep, with his hair adorably mussed and one arm thrown up haphazardly.

I was thinking of ways I could potentially prank the twins while they were vulnerable when I heard a knock on my door. I was more than a little surprised, I wasn't expecting anyone else to come looking for me.

The door opened, and I saw Austin peering into the room. "Ah, Anna. There they are. I was suspicious when neither of them were in bed this morning. There's no way they would wake up before me." He spoke quietly, so as not to wake them.

He walked closer to the bed, and I turned bright red. This was weird, right? I hadn't thought about it last night because it had just seemed right, but now that Austin was looking down at the three of us in the bed, I realized this was probably inappropriate.

He didn't seem to think anything was wrong with it because he just gestured at me. "Do you think you can manage to extract yourself without waking them?" he asked quietly.

I nodded and carefully scooted out from beneath the blankets and stood on the bed. I was probably going to have to jump over one of them or climb over the footboard to get to the ground. Austin saw the deliberation on my face and walked over to Mason's side of the bed.

He waved a hand at me to come closer and held up his arms to me. I moved as close as I could to Mason. Austin lifted me up, over Mason, and to the ground. My eyebrows rose. I was definitely not one of those ninety-pound girls; I was tall, athletic, and curvy, so I was amazed at his strength.

Jason mumbled something and turned over on his side. Mason grunted when he opened one eye halfway and saw Austin, but neither of the twins looked like they were going to get up anytime soon. They were both back asleep when I followed Austin to the door.

The house was chilly last night, so I'd worn sweatpants and a long-sleeved T-shirt over my cami to bed. The cami had a built-in shelf bra that didn't give as much support as one of my sport bras, but it was enough to make me feel comfortable with wandering around the house in pajamas.

Austin closed the bedroom door behind me and motioned for me to follow him. "Let's go down and get some coffee started for everyone."

I gave him a startled look. I wasn't expecting the pack master himself to be making coffee or cooking breakfast for his pack. Austin was showing me how wrong I'd been about every one of my preconceived notions of pack life.

Austin smiled at my surprise. "Normally, I drag the twins downstairs with me in the mornings. Otherwise, they'll sleep the morning away." Austin grinned at me. "They worked hard last night, so I can let them sleep. Plus, I wanted to have you to myself for a little while."

I was even more taken aback. "Oh?" I asked lamely.

Austin didn't seem to mind my lack of response and just smiled warmly at me as we walked down the stairs. I was glad I'd worn socks to bed last night, because I could feel the chill of the floor beneath my feet.

Austin gestured for me to have a seat at the counter when we walked in the kitchen. I sat and watched him as he busied himself with making a pot of coffee. He joined me at the counter when the coffeemaker started to do its thing. "I wanted to talk to you, one on one."

I swallowed nervously; this couldn't be good.

"I thought you handled yourself well last night," he started.

I was relieved; it didn't sound like I was in trouble.

He continued. "A lot of the pack members commented on how you were calm, collected, and helpful. Alex and Tony spent a good portion of the night talking you up to their pack mates."

I blinked. "I didn't do anything impressive…"

Austin smiled at me. "You weren't screaming in hysteria or trying to create drama to keep yourself at the center of attention, which is what most of us are used to seeing from females."

"You know, I've never met a female wolf before, but I'm starting to really not like them," I told him seriously.

Austin threw his head back and laughed. "I'm glad you're here," he told me and patted my hand. I think at this point I had a permanently surprised look on my face. He just chuckled at me. "Let's get coffee."

We made our cups, and I wrapped my hand around the mug that was radiating warmth. "Can we sit outside?" I asked hopefully.

"It's going to be cool out there," he warned.

I nodded. "I like being in the cooler air."

He smiled and waved me to go out ahead of him. I hesitated with my hand on the door. "It's safe, right?"

He nodded. "We're going to stay right under the alcove, plus the property is packed with our wolves right now." He looked at me sternly. "But I don't want you out here without me. Don't let the twins talk you into anything."

"Okay," I answered with a small smile. "Did you get in touch with any of the council members?" I asked as we sat. The cool air of the morning felt good as the breeze gently moved around my body. I was still warm from being in bed, surrounded by the body heat of two big guys, so it felt great.

The sun shone warmly on my face, and the lawn that stretched out in front of us sparked with tiny dew drops that caught the morning light. It was a beautiful morning.

Austin watched me take in the view. "I did," he answered before he took a sip of his coffee.

"So that's good news?" I tried to prompt him to tell me more.

"Yes and no. They want to meet you. Two of the council members want time to investigate your background further. They're convinced that your original pack would have never agreed to give you to humans to raise."

I wasn't sure how to respond to that. A part of me wanted all of this to just go away so I could stay here with this pack, but another part of me was curious about my past. What if I was stolen away from my parents at birth? What if they were out there looking for me, mourning the daughter they had lost?

I wanted to buy into the fantasy that I had a loving family out there, just waiting for me. But if life had taught me anything, it was that things like that didn't happen to me. With my luck, I would have an abusive alcoholic of a father and a mother who was eager to get rid of an unwanted baby. They'd probably thrown me in the trash and left me for dead.

I sighed sadly. Austin must have thought I was worrying about meeting the council, but that wasn't my concern - until he brought it back up.

"The council isn't that bad," he told me. "It's made up of some of the more powerful pack-masters in the country. They deal with major issues that might affect our community as a whole, and they also assist with disputes among packs. Their goal is to make sure the fighting doesn't get out of control or attract human attention."

I nodded. "How can I prepare for the meeting?" I asked.

"Be polite, be honest, and be respectful," he told me.

"That's it?" I questioned. There had to be something more to it.

He chuckled. "That's it. You're sweet and likable; I'm sure you'll charm them."

I looked at him doubtfully. No one had ever called me sweet and likable before. I was always, 'the nice one' when people described me. I always thought 'nice' was the word people used when they meant 'plain and boring' but didn't want to sound rude.

I observed Austin out of the corner of my eye. The morning sun was glinting off his tawny dark blond hair, and his face was peaceful and relaxed as he looked over the grounds.

He was tan, as if he spent a lot of time outdoors, and he was very well built. Most of the guys I met last night were. I wondered if that was one of the requirements for Austin's pack, or if all male wolves were like that.

"What kind of questions are the council members going to ask me?" I asked before he could catch me checking him out.

Austin brought his attention back to me. "They'll ask you questions about what you remember about your early childhood, if you've ever exposed yourself to humans, things like that. I've already provided them with all the information I have on you, so they'll mainly be asking questions to see if what I gave them is accurate. They'll also want to get a sense of who you are as a person."

I was starting to get more nervous as I pictured how this interview was going to go. I could see me sitting in a lone chair under a hot spotlight while a group of intimidating men sat on thrones up on a dais and glared down at me with disapproval.

I groaned as I thought about it. "When's the meeting going to take place?" I asked.

"In a few hours," he told me casually.

I almost spat out my coffee in shock, and my heart started to pound. "Hours?" I squeaked out.

"The council is already meeting nearby to discuss some other issues, so they decided to squeeze you in. Everyone is curious about you because females are rare. It's *extremely* rare to find an unknown female that's not part of a pack. You're the talk of the wolf community right now."

I sank down in my chair. "I just brought jeans and stuff. I didn't pack fancy clothes for meeting important people."

"I can have someone go out and get you some 'fancy clothes' while you're getting ready for the meeting," Austin told me with a glint of humor in his eye.

Great, I would be attending a meeting in clothing picked out by a random dude. With my luck, whatever he found for me wouldn't even fit correctly.

Austin picked up his phone and started texting. "What's your size?" he asked casually.

"Eight," I answered with a blush. I'm sure that the type of girls he usually dated were a size zero or two and looked like they belonged on the Victoria's Secret runway.

"Shoe size?"

"Eight."

He grinned at me. "That's easy to remember."

I nodded as he continued to text.

He looked over at me, and his eyes flicked down to my chest. "C cup?"

"Uh, yeah," I answered with my face turning an even deeper shade of red. "34C," I mumbled in embarrassment. I'd probably need to wear a bra that wasn't a sports bra if I were wearing nice clothes, so it was in my best interest to be forthcoming.

Austin nodded and set down his phone to finish his coffee. "If you want time alone to get ready, you can send the twins down to make breakfast." I grinned a little, thinking of them having to cook on their own.

I set down my mug to stand but hesitated. I had Austin alone; now was my time to ask him questions.

"So," I started hesitantly. "I'm slowly picking up on things about the pack as I spend time with you guys, but I'm not sure how the rank structure works."

Austin smiled and thought for a moment. "To put it in navy terms: you can think of me as the CO, James as the XO, and Cody as kind of a CMC."

I nodded. That made sense to me. James always seemed to be taking charge if Austin wasn't around. Cody seemed friendly with most of the guys but was definitely an authority figure within the pack. It was obvious that most of the pack members liked and respected him.

Austin tilted his head to the side. "Although Cody is more of an officer than enlisted, so maybe that isn't a perfect analogy. Think of Cody as my third in command but with the typical duties of the CMC."

That made sense. All three of them seemed close and made most of the decisions for the pack.

"The twins are like..." He paused and thought. "Lieutenants who just graduated and are learning the ropes, but still get stuck with a lot of shitty work details."

I laughed. The twins did get a lot of the odd jobs around here.

"Mason and Jason are responsible for making sure the household runs smoothly so the three of us can focus on pack responsibilities. I can honestly say that all of us are grateful to have you in the house right now. You've been a good influence on them."

I smiled. I can only imagine the shenanigans they usually caused daily.

"They've been helping me a lot," I confessed to Austin. "I've been struggling with melding my human side to my wolf side and adjusting to being around other wolves."

I struggled to put my thoughts into words, but I knew Austin wouldn't judge me. "I know I have a lot to learn, and the twins have helped me get to the root of some of the things I have been struggling with." I looked down at my coffee that was already halfway gone. "They have a way of coming up with unique solutions."

Austin nodded. "That's one reason I assigned you to them. You seemed nervous at the idea of being around the pack, and I thought those two would be a good introduction for you. They have a unique way of looking at the world and can always manage to find enjoyment in what they do. I thought that would help you relax and see that other wolves aren't that bad."

I smiled. "I'm glad you picked them, too," I said shyly. "If you had assigned me to James, I think I would have been afraid to come back after the first day."

Austin laughed. "James might seem intimidating, but he's loyal and protective of those he gives his affection to. He doesn't love easily, and he has a difficult time showing that he cares sometimes, but he has a big heart."

"Hmmm," I said. I doubted I would ever make the list of people he cared about, but I was hoping I could at least be moved up to neutral.

Austin continued, getting back to explaining the answer to my original question. "Of course, you've already met Caleb. He's our communications expert, technology guru, occasional hacker, and he handles the tech aspects of security. If it's electrical, he manages it."

Austin set his empty cup down. "That's everyone in the main core of the pack that lives here in the house. Trevor oversees the wolves that live in houses scattered around our pack lands. They live in small teams and work to keep our territory safe. We have interests in several businesses in the area as well."

I nodded. I'd heard about the various companies that the pack was involved in.

"We have wolves that work for our businesses but are more loosely affiliated with the pack. They live normal lives but still attend pack functions and respond if the pack needs them."

"Like reservists?"

"Exactly!" Austin gave me a surprised smile. "The last section of our pack is the wolves involved in the contracted government security jobs we take on. Most of those guys are currently on an overseas mission, but they also come back here to train."

"What kind of missions are they involved in?" I asked curiously.

Austin smiled mysteriously. "Let's get you integrated with the pack members here in the states before we start talking about that."

I sighed. I wasn't expecting him to go into detail about all the secret operations they may or may not be involved in, but I had to try.

"Where do I fit in here?" I asked Austin curiously. Even though I worked for the Navy, I had absolutely no military training or experience. My job was to be a healthcare provider for active-duty military members, their dependents, and some retirees who remained in the area. It seemed like Austin's pack was heavily weighted with wolves who had combat experience.

He thought for a moment. "I'm still tossing ideas around in my head. I want to give you some time to see how you fit in with everyone and where you fit naturally. So far, you're doing a great job." He smiled at me encouragingly.

Trevor walked out on the patio and gave me a friendly nod. "Hey, Anna. Hey, Boss, can I go over some things with you?"

"Sure," Austin told him before he turned to me. "Go get ready for the meeting, your clothes will be here soon," he told me with an affectionate smile.

I gave them both a small wave and brought my mug back inside. I got a refill and started another pot to brew for whomever was going to be needing coffee next. As I walked back upstairs, I gave friendly 'good mornings' to the couple of guys I passed on my way back to my room.

Everyone seemed friendly but tired, which wasn't surprising after last night's events. I understood how they felt; I would be more than happy to snuggle back in my bed with the twins and sleep for hours. I set my coffee down carefully before I pounced on the bed to wake them both up.

"Hey! Austin wants you guys to make breakfast!" I pestered them as I tried to tug the blanket away from them. Mason groaned and pulled a pillow over his head. Jason ignored me and pretended to snore loudly. I pulled the pillow off Mason and used it to smack Jason.

"Hey!" he said, laughing. He hit me back with his pillow, and then it was on. They ganged up on me, which wasn't fair at all in a pillow fight. I eventually decided retreat was my best option, and I ran to the bathroom and locked myself in there to start getting ready. The twins had given me a brief respite from my anxiety, but I needed to hurry to get ready to meet the council who would be deciding my fate.

# Chapter 14

I was glad I packed my hairdryer and some makeup so that I could make myself look presentable. I took my time and tried to make myself look pretty, like a real girl. I laughed at myself as I eyed the finished product in the mirror. That was the best I could do. I slipped my robe on and went out to investigate the status of my clothes.

I was just in time to walk out of the bathroom to hear a knock on my bedroom door. I walked over and opened it curiously, wondering who had drawn the short straw and had to go get the girl clothes.

Quinn was standing on the other side of the door. I'd met him very briefly last night, and my gay-dar had pinged, but I'd pushed it aside, as it was none of my business unless he wanted to open up and share with me.

"Let me in, girl!" he said jokingly as he pushed past me to set down a million different bags. He handed me a Victoria's Secret bag and pointed to the bathroom. "Go, we don't have much time."

Jeez, this guy was bossy. I went back to the bathroom and pulled everything out of the bag. It had bras, panties, and a couple of skimpy thongs. I set those aside and picked out some of the more modest bras and panties to put on. I slipped my robe back on and went out to the bedroom.

Quinn was laying out all my outfit choices, along with shoes and handbags. This was a lot of stuff for just one meeting. I sighed; this was the kind of thing Kelsey was good at. If she were here, I would just have her pick something out for me to wear. I reminded myself to text Kelsey after the meeting. She was probably still mad, but it wouldn't hurt to reach out.

Quinn turned back to me after laying out the last dress. He eyed me up and down.

"Your hair looks pretty down, but we're going to have to style it a little more. Conservative makeup, well done, very appropriate." He had a running commentary going as he examined me with a clinical eye.

"We should probably neaten up those eyebrows a little," he told me thoughtfully. My hand drifted up to my face. I didn't remember the last time I'd done anything more than casually pluck some stray hairs.

"Um, okay," I answered. It seemed like Quinn knew what he was doing. He probably would do a better job than I would.

He clapped his hands together. "Okay, off with the robe."

I just looked at him and thought, *Nope*.

He saw the 'nope' on my face because he chuckled. "Honey, believe me, I'm not interested in anything you have under there. I'm interested in getting you properly dressed for an important day today."

I guess my gay-dar had been right, but I hadn't wanted to stereotype. I just shrugged my robe off and set it on the bed. He started handing me items of clothing to put on. The first was a pair of dress pants and a blouse. "No, too short," he mumbled to himself as he motioned for me to take it off. I just sighed. This was a common occurrence. I could never find clothes that fit me in the stores and frequently had to special order tall sizes online.

We finally settled on an outfit both of us agreed on; a fitted black skirt that came to just above my knee, a pale pink blouse, and pearl accessories. I had to hand it to Quinn, he had somehow made me look poised and sophisticated.

He pointed to a pair of heels.

"Nope," I told him.

"Honey," he started in on me. I was starting to enjoy his sassy commentary. He didn't pull any punches and was blunt. "You're wearing the heels," he told me firmly.

"I'm *not* wearing the heels," I told him steadfastly. We stared at each other.

He eventually sighed. "Why not?"

"In case you haven't noticed, I'm already freakishly tall. If I wear heels, I'm going to be put in a circus, and I'll never make it to the meeting."

Quinn snorted. "In case you haven't noticed, wolves are taller than humans. I'm a runt at 5'11"."

I thought about what he said. It did seem odd that all the guys I met so far had been taller than me. It had felt strange last night, not being the tallest person in the room.

"Wolves like their females to be tall, statuesque, and strong," he informed me. "You need to get over any insecurities that spending too much time with humans gave you and embrace your heritage."

I blinked. He was right. I shouldn't try to make myself smaller; I should stand tall and proud. This was the way I was born, and I had nothing to be ashamed of.

I was grateful for this time I'd spent with Quinn - he was awesome. I let him put the heels on me as I sat on the bed and stood up carefully. I took one step, and then another.

Quinn started laughing at me. "You look like a baby deer that was just born and is trying to learn how to walk." I just glared at him and tried to practice walking without twisting an ankle. He gave me some tips and then walked me over to the mirror.

"You're good, Quinn," I told him as I looked at the final product in the mirror.

"I know," he told me confidently. We both laughed.

"You know, I was upset when the guys told me that Austin had moved some bitch in the house," Quinn disclosed to me.

I gave him a hurt look.

"My word, not theirs. They all assured me you were kind and lovely, but I didn't believe it at all," he stated.

"I came in here expecting to find a blonde bimbo with huge tits that had all the men wrapped around her little finger." I just gaped at him, not sure how to react. "I'm relieved to find that you're the exact opposite," he told me. "I came in here plotting about how to run you out of here, but instead, I want you to stay."

"Awww, Quinn."

"Don't get sentimental," he sniffed. "I've just always wanted a giant blonde Barbie to dress." He gave me a smirk, and I laughed.

"Seriously, though, Austin has something good going on here. This probably won't come as a shock to you, but most wolves aren't accepting of a gay wolf who wants to be a stylist. Austin welcomed me here with open arms when every other pack had thrown me out or wanted nothing to do with me. He invested in my business and has encouraged me to be myself." He hesitated and then gave me a mischievous grin. "I just need him to find me a hot, gay mate."

The more I heard about Austin, the more I liked him. I was glad it was his pack who had found me, and I genuinely wanted to stay. "So, are all wolves outrageously good looking, or is that just Austin's pack?" I asked him curiously.

"Austin knows how to pick them, right?" Quinn gave me a conspiratory look. "I heard you've been getting close with the twins. Oh, to be the man-meat in that twin sandwich..." He sighed, and I giggled. "Dish, girl. I want to live vicariously through you."

"Oh, it's not like that between us. I wouldn't go out on a date with either one. I would be worried about the other being hurt."

Quinn let out a loud laugh. "Haven't you ever heard of #whychoose?"

I shook my head no.

"Those boys share everything in their lives. Do you think they would draw the line at a female?"

"Uh, yeah?" I was starting to get uncomfortable with Quinn's bantering, so I tried to change the subject. "I'm sorry you had to get all of this when I only needed one outfit for today," I told him as I motioned to the bed covered in rejected outfits.

"No worries, girl," he said and winked. "I'll just put the rest of this in your closet. Well, except those pants; we'll never be able to make those work." He shuddered and flung my closet door open.

"Ahhh!" he let out a dramatic scream.

"What?" I asked and tried to rush over in a panic. I tripped and almost fell flat on my face but managed to make it to the doorway. When I looked in the closet, I was expecting to see a dead body, or maybe a giant spider waiting to devour us; instead, I just saw one of my hoodies opposite two pairs of my shoes in the closet.

He turned to me with his hand over his heart. "You've been robbed!"

I started to laugh. An empty closet was his worst nightmare? "No, I just have everything else in the drawers."

He went through them dramatically. "Ahhh!" he let out another dismayed, high-pitched scream. "Honey, no one told me that you were like…a…a refugee."

I just stared at him with my mouth open. "You have *nothing!*" he told me emphatically.

"Well, I still have some of my things at home, but this is most of it. I don't need a lot because I wear hospital-provided scrubs to work every day."

"Ahhh!" This time the scream was more horrified but still just as high-pitched.

He held out his hands to grasp mine. "Don't worry, honey. We can fix this," he told me, holding my hands tightly.

"Umm…" I started out, very embarrassed at this point. "I don't have a lot of money to spend on clothes right now. I just bought a house, and I still have student loans -"

"Don't worry, I have one of Austin's credit cards. It's my job to make sure the pack stays well-dressed," he assured me.

"Well, maybe you should check with Austin before you do anything…" I told him uncomfortably. I didn't need a bunch of new clothes, and I definitely didn't want to make it look like I was taking advantage of Austin's generosity.

Quinn walked over to pick up his phone. "Let's talk basics."

"Ummm -"

I have never been so happy to hear a knock on my door. "We're busy!" Quinn yelled.

"We're not!" I tried to hobble to the door as quickly as I could before the interruption changed their mind and left. I flung open the door to see Cody.

"Cody! I'm so excited you're here!" I said enthusiastically.

"Anna, wow, you look amazing," Cody told me. "Not that you don't always look amazing," he added cautiously.

"Cody!" Quinn yelled from behind me. "Were you aware this poor girl does not own any clothing?"

"Umm…" Cody looked at me uneasily. "She's been wearing clothing every time I've seen her."

"Well, that's just unfortunate for you," Quinn said snarkily. I turned even redder.

"Did you need me for something?" I asked Cody, hoping he would say yes.

"Yeah, I came up to see if you were ready for the meeting. We need to leave in a few minutes."

*Thank god*, I thought to myself. I turned to Quinn. "Do you think we could work on this another day?"

He nodded and seemed to have calmed down a little. "I'll just put the rest of these clothes in your closet and be on my way."

"Thank you," I told him, extremely relieved.

I stepped closer to Cody. With my three-inch heels on, I was only a few inches shorter than him. It was strange to look at him from this angle.

I held out my arm for him. "Would you mind? I haven't had much practice in these shoes, and I don't think falling down the stairs would make a good impression on the pack."

He chuckled. "Yeah, that would cause a lot of problems if you showed up to the meeting covered in bruises with broken bones."

We left Quinn, and I managed to make it down the stairs and into the waiting limo without incident.

"This is fancy," I told Cody as he followed me into the limo.

He smiled. "We need to arrive in style and make a good impression."

I agreed. "Is Austin coming?"

"Yeah, he should be here in a minute."

We sat in awkward silence. "Soooo…" I asked. "Do you have any advice for me? What can I expect?"

He looked more worried than Austin had. "Just be honest, you don't know anything about your birth family. That's going to be their major concern."

"What about what James said? That they're going to want to put me in a well-established pack?" I twisted my hands in my lap nervously.

Cody ran his hand through his hair. "We were waiting to talk to you about this until we were on our way, because we didn't want to give you too much time to worry." He paused, and the suspense was killing me.

"Tell me what?" I demanded.

"Let's wait until Austin gets here."

I groaned to myself. I couldn't wait any longer. It was killing me already. I was just about to open my mouth and tell him that when the limo door opened, and Austin climbed in.

I was practically bouncing in my seat, waiting for him to get situated. Finally, I decided I'd waited long enough. "What's the secret plan that I needed to wait for you to get here to find out about?" I burst out.

Austin gave Cody a dirty look. Cody just shrugged. "She asks a lot of questions."

"It's not a secret plan," Austin told me and sighed.

I couldn't handle the suspense. I just wanted to scream out, TELL ME!!!! But I managed to hold it in and say, "What's the non-secret plan, then?"

Austin and Cody both chuckled. Austin must have realized that I was going to jump across the seat and strangle him if he didn't just tell me, because he took a deep breath.

"We wanted to give you an easy option. I think that if you told them that you were going to be mated to someone in our pack, it would be accepted easily by the council. It would give you a legitimate reason to stay in our pack."

My jaw dropped. "But wouldn't I need to follow through with that? I can't just lie to the council; they'll know. And who would get stuck with me?"

Austin and Cody looked at each other and then Cody motioned for Austin to continue. Austin tapped his fingers on his thigh. "It would be the most binding if you chose me. I'm the pack master, so it would make the most sense to them."

"Wouldn't that prevent you from being able to get a real mate, though?" I asked, confused. "I couldn't let you sacrifice your future for me."

Austin gazed at me sadly. "You're a rare white wolf. My father would support my claim on you if I told him you were my future mate."

I just stared at him in complete shock. "Do you think he would believe it, though?"

"Is it really that outlandish for the two of us to have something together?" Austin asked quietly.

"No," I said slowly. "It's just that I'm-" I gestured at myself at a complete loss of words. "Weird? Wouldn't he be upset that you picked me out of everyone? Plus, I guess I just assumed that I was going to be single the rest of my life, so you're throwing me for a loop here."

Cody looked uncomfortable to be in the middle of the conversation, but he spoke up anyway. "You don't have to agree if you aren't ready, or if you aren't sure."

I nodded in relief. "This is a huge decision, and I wouldn't want to make it while I'm under duress. I'd rather choose a mate because I want to, not because I have to."

I watched Austin carefully. I couldn't tell if he made the offer because he was interested in me or felt obligated to 'save me'. He was a smart guy, so I'm sure that he realized by now that I was damaged and felt bad about handing me over to another pack to be abused again.

Sudden darkness came over me. If I was going to be sent to a pack like Evelyn had told me about, I wouldn't go. I would do whatever it took to prevent that, even if it cost me my life. I looked at Austin again. If I was given a choice of being in a loveless relationship because the man felt obligated to be with me versus death, what would I choose?

I'm not sure that I'd choose death if I had another way out. I liked Austin's pack, and I liked being here. Maybe this was my only option. How would he feel about that? Knowing that I chose him because he was my only option? He might not care if he didn't want to be with me either. What kind of relationship would we have? Helpless tears filled my eyes, and I stared out the window to try and hide them before they fell.

I decided I would try to reason with the council first. If they didn't listen, I would take Austin up on his offer. He may not ever love me, but he would care for me as a friend.

Austin was texting, and Cody was pretending to read something on his phone but watching me out of the corner of his eye with concern.

"What are you thinking?" he asked me quietly.

Austin looked up at me to hear my answer to Cody's question. "I just..." I swallowed. "There's a part of me that just wants to go back to my old life and pretend none of this happened. But another part of me recognizes that I feel like I belong with your pack. I've never felt like a part of something before. I've always been alone, and I've always been on the outside."

My voice broke, and I stopped speaking to touch the corner of my eyes to prevent any tears from falling.

Cody reached out to hold my hand, and Austin reached in his inner suit pocket to hand me a cloth handkerchief. I didn't even know modern men carried cloth handkerchiefs; it made me smile a little.

"I'm just not sure that I can be a mate to anyone. I'm not..." I didn't know how to communicate what I wanted to say. "It's difficult for me to let people touch me. I'm working on it, but -" I shrugged, not sure what else to say.

I don't think Austin or Cody knew how to respond to what I said. I highly doubt they understood what I was trying to tell them. I was too afraid to look in either of their eyes. I just wanted to hide. I didn't want them to know that something was seriously wrong with me, but I didn't want Austin to make a commitment he would regret later. It was only a matter of time before he figured out how messed up I was.

I dabbed a little at my eyes, trying not to smear my makeup or get anything on the handkerchief. I attempted to hand it back to Austin, but he pressed it back in my hand.

"Keep it. It's going to be a rough day." He gave me a gentle smile. "Let's talk about the council members you're going to meet today."

During the rest of the car ride, all three of us pretended that our earlier conversation had never happened. The guys told me about the council members who were going to be interviewing me, and I tried to take in as much as I could, but I was feeling scared and overwhelmed.

# Chapter 15

We arrived at our destination sooner than I would have liked; never would have been preferable. I was surprised when the location for the meeting was a hotel. I looked at Cody with a question in my eyes.

He answered with a smile, "Wolves don't like to meet in another wolf's seat of power. The council wouldn't want to meet on Austin's home base or a council member's territory because it would be too much under someone else's control."

Austin nodded. "It's better for the pack as well. Having strange wolves on our land and trying to assert their authority over us while in our home can cause a lot of tension and aggression that's better avoided."

I nodded. I wouldn't want the council in our house either. Well, technically, it was Austin's house, I reminded myself. I was just a guest there, and I could only stay as long as he wanted me there. I tried to push that thought away because I needed to be strong and confident, not sad and depressed.

We were met at the entrance by several men who gave off a 'bodyguard' vibe. They ushered us into a comfortable meeting room with refreshments on a table in the back corner of the room.

I stared at the selection of fruit and pastries. My stomach was churning, but I didn't want to show weakness in front of these guys. I'm certain that if they heard my stomach growling, it would ruin the strong and confident vibe I was going for.

Austin noticed me eying the snacks and gave me an encouraging nod. "Better get something to hold you over until we get back home."

I sighed and walked over to pick up a pastry. I hoped I had enough time to digest it; having it come back up mid-interview would be even worse than my stomach growling. Austin and Cody remained standing, but my shoes were uncomfortable, so I sat and nibbled on my pastry. The guys were both casually working on their phones. I hoped I was pulling off a similar look, but I doubted it.

I finished my pastry and started eyeing the drinks next. I'd was too anxious to be able to handle any coffee right now, but a bottle of water would be a good choice.

I could sip on the water if the interview got too intense, and I needed a second to gather my thoughts. I'd just made it back to my chair with a bottle when the door opened, and a man entered.

Right away, I could tell he was related to Austin. They looked so much alike, but upon closer inspection, I realized that he didn't look old enough to be Austin's father. Maybe a brother?

Austin shook his hand and greeted him warmly. "Father, good to see you."

So, this *was* Austin's father? I was confused. This man only looked a few years older than Austin; he was certainly not in his forties or fifties.

"I wish it was under better circumstances. Cody, good to see you." He shook Cody's hand as well and then turned to me. "And this must be Anna."

I stood and smoothed my skirt down before stepping over to them. I walked carefully so I wouldn't trip and fall; that was the last thing I needed right now. I tried to hold my chin up and shoulders back so I wouldn't slouch and attempted to appear graceful.

Hopefully, I came off as being confident and not creepy. I beamed at him. "It's nice to meet you, Mr. Zilker."

"Likewise. I have to admit, I'm curious about you. You're the talk of the community right now. Austin hadn't mentioned how stunning you were, though."

I turned bright red and looked down at the floor. "Thanks." I wasn't sure how I was supposed to react to comments like that; they just made me feel uncomfortable. It didn't seem possible that he meant it genuinely, unless wolves had different beauty standards than humans did.

"And she's modest." He turned to Austin. "You've found a unicorn."

All of us were saved from replying as three more men entered the room. None of them was as friendly as Austin's father, but they all greeted us politely.

I was introduced to Mr. Phillips, who was in control of the territory which bordered ours on the North Carolina border and extended to Georgia. He looked to be in his mid-thirties and stern with dark hair and a beard.

Mr. Richardson had a huge chunk of territory that included a large part of the Midwest. He looked about forty, had a red face, and I got a whiff of alcohol on his breath when he insisted on pulling me close to air kiss both my cheeks.

Mr. Morgan had a territory that included California and Oregon. He was only here because he had been in negotiations with Mr. Zilker when the news of me had reached both of them. He was young and looked to be around his mid-twenties with highlighted blond hair and a surfer vibe. He made me feel uncomfortable when he looked me over, but Austin quickly directed his attention elsewhere by asking how the negotiations were going.

I was grateful to have both Cody and Austin by my side. We were still waiting for one more person to round out the council I was going to be questioned by today.

A man with dark hair and similar coloring to James entered the room. This had to be James' cousin, Mr. Reed. I was hoping he had a more pleasant disposition than James did, but my hopes were quickly dashed when he looked at me derisively and said. "Are we ready to get this over with?"

The council members all took seats on one side of a conference table. I guess that meant we were supposed to sit on the other side. I followed Austin and Cody to that side of the table, but Mr. Reed stopped them. "We just need Anna for this, thank you."

I looked at Austin in a panic. Austin's attention was on his father. "She'd like the support of her pack during this event."

"Sorry, Austin," Mr. Zilker said. "We haven't decided if she's going to be part of your pack. Right now, she's a lone wolf without representation."

Austin and Cody frowned. This didn't look like it was going well, and my interview hadn't even started yet. My heart started to beat faster with apprehension.

"She'll be fine," Mr. Morgan told them. "You can wait right outside, and we'll return her to you in the same condition she is in now."

Austin and Cody exchanged glances. It didn't look like they had any choice but to leave me here by myself without disobeying the council. From what they told me earlier, that would be a huge faux pas and could negatively affect the council's judgment.

Austin reached out and squeezed my hands. Cody gave me a supportive smile, and then they both headed out the door and left me alone with the five big bad wolves sitting at the table in front of me.

"Please have a seat, Anna," Mr. Zilker said.

I pulled out a chair and tried to sit gracefully while trying to hide my shaking hands.

"I believe all of us should have had enough time to look through the information that the Seaside pack submitted on Anna?" Mr. Morgan asked the rest of the council.

Everyone nodded, except Mr. Reed. "I had a few questions about the material that was submitted on Anna," he said with a raised hand.

Of course, it had to be James' cousin who was going to be giving me a hard time.

Mr. Zilker waved at him to continue. It appeared that he was going to be playing mediator today.

Mr. Reed gave me a hard look. "How did you escape the notice of any packs while you were growing up?"

"I grew up in Western New York in a small town in the suburbs of Buffalo. It was my understanding that's an undesirable area for most wolves because of the large amounts of snow that cover the ground for months at a time."

"But it wasn't a problem for you?" asked Mr. Morgan curiously.

"Even if it was a problem for me, I wouldn't have been able to leave," I told him. "As a minor, it was the decision of my human family as to where we would live."

Mr. Morgan nodded. "And they were completely unaware of what you were?"

"Yes," I told him. "I was adopted, so I was afraid that if they found out what I was, they would have thrown me out of the house."

"It never occurred to you to try to find your own kind?" Mr. Reed asked incredulously.

I looked at him, trying to hide my annoyance. "I tried finding my birth parents through the resources that I had available to me through the Internet, but I didn't know of the wolf community as a child."

Mr. Zilker and Mr. Morgan nodded in understanding. Mr. Reed wouldn't let it go. "But didn't you try to find anyone else who was like you?"

"I was too afraid of exposing what I was to humans," I told him.

That seemed to satisfy him because he nodded. I sighed in relief.

"How did you learn to shift without any guidance?" Mr. Morgan asked gently.

"I accidentally changed once when I was around ten. I realized what had happened and practiced while I was alone so that I could control the change."

Mr. Phillips raised an eyebrow. "That must have taken a lot of dedication and discipline. Would you consider yourself to be a disciplined person?"

I took a deep breath. "Yes, I would. I put myself through college and spent my nights and weekends working or studying when most of my classmates would be partying. I've always been hard-working and dedicated to my goals."

Mr. Phillips nodded in approval, so I guess I'd said something right.

"Where did you get the money to go to school?" Mr. Reed asked suspiciously.

I was irritated at what he was implying but tried to keep a pleasant demeanor. "I was ineligible for financial assistance because of my adopted family's income. However, I was able to get work-study funds and student loans. I worked full-time in the summer, sometimes with more than one job if I was able to find enough work, and part-time in the school year. I also had several scholarships that were based solely on academic achievements when I could find one that didn't have restrictions based on income."

"Your adopted parents didn't give you any assistance?" Mr. Reed asked.

I tried to keep a pleasant expression on my face and sound sympathetic to them. "They had three children of their own to take care of."

"Why would they adopt *you*, then, if they had children of their own?" Mr. Reed asked callously.

I narrowed my eyes at him, but kept my voice steady. "The couple who originally adopted me passed away when I was a child. They had named my adopted aunt and uncle as my guardians in case of their death."

"Hmmm," was Mr. Reed's only response. "I'm satisfied with the explanation of her childhood," he announced.

"Anyone else need clarification?" Mr. Zilker asked.

All the council members shook their heads no. I let out a breath I hadn't realized I was holding; it seemed like we were moving in the right direction.

"Let's move on to her current pack status," Mr. Zilker suggested.

Several of the council members tried to speak at the same time. "Why don't we start at the right and work our way to the left?" Mr. Zilker suggested. "We have a second round if anyone still has questions after their initial turn passes."

Everyone seemed satisfied, except Mr. Reed. He scowled but didn't argue, surprisingly.

"Mr. Richardson, would you like to start?" Mr. Zilker prompted.

Mr. Richardson looked like he was falling asleep and was propping his head up on one hand. "Do you want to stay with the Seaside Pack?" he asked.

"Yes," I answered simply.

"That's all I need," he stated. "I vote we end the meeting and leave her to her pack."

I was shocked but hopeful. Could it be that easy? Mr. Reed raised a hand to speak. I held back an eye roll; of course not.

"I object," Mr. Reed stated.

I just sighed. I would have been surprised if he'd agreed to settle in my favor.

"Mr. Phillips, do you have any questions?" Mr. Zilker prompted the next council member.

"Do you understand that Austin's pack is not well established, Anna?" Mr. Phillips asked gruffly.

I nodded. "I understand that they're a new pack and that Austin is still working on making it better," I replied.

"But do you understand the potential consequences?" Mr. Phillips asked shortly.

I swallowed. "I'm not sure of what consequences you mean, sir," I stated politely.

"If another pack master manages to take over the pack, or if the Seaside pack is absorbed into a larger pack, you can lose your status as the pack master's mate and any pups you may have had with him may no longer be permitted in the pack."

My jaw dropped. I hadn't realized that was a possible consequence, but I didn't want to admit that in front of these men. "I have every confidence in Austin and the rest of the pack to keep me, and any children I might have, safe."

Mr. Phillips nodded. "Don't say we didn't warn you."

"Anything else, Mr. Phillips?" Mr. Zilker asked.

"No. I'm going to support Anna's decision to stay with the Seaside pack, but I would like to have my reservations documented. I would also like the council to put a plan in place to protect Anna's interests if the pack falls."

"That's highly unusual." Mr. Reed frowned. "Why would we care to do that?"

"I believe we should protect our future generations, and Anna is one of the few purebred wolves left who are even capable of providing us with a future."

"We shouldn't allow her to breed with wolves who aren't deserving of her," Mr. Reed stated angrily. "I don't see how putting a plan in place for the eventual collapse of her pack is more efficient than simply putting her with an appropriate pack to begin with."

It took everything I had in me to keep from shouting at them. Austin hadn't been kidding when he said that the wolves were patriarchal. How could they possibly think that they had the right to tell me who I could and couldn't fall in love with. And to refer to me as something they needed to breed to produce the next generation of wolves? That was one of the most ridiculous things I'd ever heard. I'd never felt so insulted before.

"I'm going to note your reservations, Mr. Phillips. I suggest working out a contingency plan for Anna at a later date, when we decide where we wish to place her. Do you find that acceptable?"

"I do," Mr. Phillips replied and sat back in his chair, apparently satisfied with that resolution.

I was still nervous but hopeful. So far, I had two votes for me to stay with the Seaside pack. I was fairly confident that Mr. Zilker would also agree to let me stay. That meant I would have three votes to overrule Mr. Reed. If the rest of the wolves in this world were like these council members, then I had absolutely no desire to meet any of them.

"That makes it my turn, Anna." Mr. Zilker smiled at me.

I smiled back at him. I didn't know what to say, so I just stayed quiet and waited for his questions to start.

"What is your plan if we let you stay with the Seaside pack?" Mr. Zilker asked.

I'd been dreading this question, but I remembered Austin's words. If Mr. Zilker thought that I was going to mate with Austin, he would probably approve of me staying with the pack.

"Austin and I have talked about mating," I told him honestly. Technically, we had talked about it on the way here. I had to be careful with what I said, though.

"I was hesitant to make definite plans with him, though, because I was afraid of how this meeting would go," I told him sadly. "I didn't want to get my hopes up and plan for my future if I wasn't going to be able to make it happen. It makes me nervous that my whole future is up in the air."

Mr. Zilker nodded in understanding. "But if we gave you a choice?"

"I would definitely stay with Austin and the Seaside pack," I told him confidently.

"Very well. Mr. Reed, I withhold my statement of my intent until after you're finished with your questions."

Mr. Reed snorted. "I think we all know how you're leaning, but I will continue with the meeting regardless," he said arrogantly.

"Anna, have you ever met with a pack other than the Seaside Pack?"

I frowned. "No -"

"Had you ever met any other wolves before the Seaside Pack?"

"Well, no -"

"We're the first wolves you have met outside the Seaside Pack?"

"Yes -"

"So, how do you know that the Seaside pack is your best option?"

I saw the point he was trying to make, and I thought about how to counter it. "I have found that I can rely on my instincts. When I was welcomed into the Seaside pack, I felt as though I was coming home."

"But that was the first time you met any wolves at all. How do you know that wasn't just a reaction to meeting your own kind? After all, you've only interacted with humans before."

My jaw dropped, and I hesitated, trying to think of a response. I glanced down the table, and to my horror, I found the other council members thoughtfully considering what Mr. Reed was saying.

"I trust my instincts," I replied lamely. I had a feeling my answer wasn't going to be sufficient, and Mr. Reed's smug face confirmed that feeling.

Mr. Zilker looked like he was deep in contemplation. "Mr. Reed has a point."

"I agree," Mr. Phillips stated. "I think it would be a reasonable request to ask that Anna meet other wolves outside of the Seaside Pack before she makes a final decision."

"Anna, are you agreeable?" Mr. Zilker asked.

"I'd really prefer not to," I replied.

Mr. Reed chuckled. "I'm sure the Seaside Pack has you quite convinced that they're your only option, but you need to realize that we're doing this for your own good."

I couldn't help it. I glared at him for a moment before I remembered that I needed to keep a pleasant look on my face.

Mr. Phillips chuckled. "I would like to change my vote to require that Anna meets with a minimum of three other packs that meet this council's requirements before we have a follow-up meeting with Anna to determine our next steps."

"Does anyone disagree?" Mr. Zilker asked.

All the council members shook their heads. Mr. Reed looked at me smugly, and I wanted to wipe that look off his face, preferably with my claws.

I was dismissed and asked to send Cody and Austin in. I didn't have time to do anything other than give them a sad look as they passed by me into the conference room. I was left outside with the bodyguards.

Time passed, and I agonized over every answer I gave to the council. The worst was my final statement, "I trust my instincts," which had sealed my fate. I thought of everything else I could have said instead, everything I should have said.

Aaaahhhhhh! Why did my brain have to freeze up during the most pivotal moments of my life? I thought about everything that I had to lose. I'd finally found somewhere I could belong, and now I was at risk of losing it all. I spent the next hour just replaying everything that had happened in the room.

After what seemed like an eternity, Austin and Cody came out of the conference room and herded me back to the limo. None of us said anything until we were well on our way. "So, how badly did I mess up?" I asked them nervously.

"You did nothing wrong," Austin assured me.

"They had probably already made up their minds before you stepped in the door," Cody added.

"I don't think so." I told them everything that had happened in the meeting, how everything had been going my way until Mr. Reed started talking.

"Hmmm," Austin said thoughtfully.

Cody frowned. "They might be right."

I looked at him in shock. *They were most definitely not right*, I thought to myself. "What makes you say that, Cody?" I asked him with narrowed eyes.

"You haven't ever met any wolves outside of us. I don't want you to look back years from now and regret throwing your lot in with us."

My jaw dropped, surprised that he would think something like that. "There's no way that's going to happen," I told him firmly.

Austin gave me a smile. "That's good to hear. I'm glad that you still want to stay with us."

"Of course I do," I told him.

I got warm smiles from both guys.

I chewed on my lip worriedly. "But how is this going to work? With them having me meet other packs? I was worried they weren't going to let me leave with you."

"At first, they weren't," Austin told me.

Cody chimed in, "But we made them see reason."

Austin snorted. "It was more like none of them trusted the others with you."

"Great," I groaned.

"They still haven't decided which packs are going to get time with you or how it's going to work. They were tossing ideas around about having packs gather on neutral territory or having you visit another pack's lands." Austin paused. "The problem with that is that no one is going to trust the pack to give you back at the end of your time with them."

"They will probably argue amongst themselves for months, honestly," Cody told me.

That made me brighten up considerably. "They might even forget about me?" I asked hopefully.

Austin gave me a wry smile. "Not likely."

"Nope." Cody chuckled.

"The good news is that we officially have custody of you right now. That should make any other pack that is trying to get a hold of you back off," Austin told me.

Cody nodded. "It also means that any pack interested in you is going to be harassing the council, instead of us. They're all going to want to be one of the three packs chosen to spend time with you."

I nodded. All of this was sounding good; I would be left alone in my quiet life with Austin's pack for a while. That would give me time to get to know all of them better, and for me to learn how to manage my wolf-side.

I settled down in my seat and gazed out of the window contently. I also had the opportunity to prove to Austin's pack that I could be a valuable asset. My stomach growled, and both of the guys looked up from their phones with grins of amusement.

"What? I was too nervous to eat anything substantial today," I told them defensively.

Cody laughed. "I know a great place not too far from here that has amazing food. How would you feel about a black and blue burger?"

"Oh, yum!" I said enthusiastically.

"So, the thought of new clothes gives you anxiety, but a burger gets you excited?" Austin asked curiously.

"Pretty much," I responded with embarrassment. I decided to try and change the subject. "Oh! That reminds me, Austin. You're probably going to have to talk to Quinn. He's convinced that I need a new wardrobe."

Austin laughed. "He's convinced everyone needs an entire new wardrobe."

"He's going to end up maxing out your credit card if you don't talk to him," I cautioned him.

Austin grinned and cocked his head at me. "I don't know, Anna, I kind of like you wearing 'fancy clothes'." He made air quotes with his hands, and Cody laughed at me.

I shook my head at Austin. "And here I was telling people you were a nice guy."

"Oh, Anna," Austin said with a grin. "We can't have you ruining my reputation."

The guys stopped teasing me long enough to ask the driver to stop at the restaurant Cody suggested. We had a great time there, and I got to know Austin and Cody better. Time flew by, and eventually Austin announced regretfully that it was time for us to head back.

The guys worked on their phones on the way back while I napped. I was tired after all the anxiety earlier today, and then having a full belly. I hadn't gotten much sleep the night before either. I was dozing off when I realized just how much had changed in the short time I'd know these wolves. A couple of weeks ago, I would have been terrified to be in the presence of a male wolf. But here I was, feeling safe and content as I drifted off to sleep with them.

Finding Somewhere to Belong

# Chapter 16

I woke to Austin gently stroking my hair. "Hey, Anna. We made it home," he said softly.

I yawned and sat up. "Since everything seems good now, is it okay if I go on a run?" I asked him hopefully.

He chuckled. "You just woke up, and you're ready to go already?"

"Yup," I told him. "After all the stress of the last few days, I just need to run wild and free."

He frowned. "It's not safe just yet. Let's give the council time to get the word out about their decision. We can re-evaluate the situation tomorrow."

I pouted, and he looked at me affectionately. "We do have an indoor gym. Running on the treadmill isn't the same, but it would let you get some of that pent-up energy out. Have the twins show it to you this afternoon. They need to work out and stop causing so much trouble in the house."

I laughed and followed him out of the limo. He escorted me into the house but then left to find James for an update. I drifted through the house in search of the twins. I found them in the kitchen, looking miserable.

Jason saw me first. "Anna!" He ran and scooped me up, giving me a hug that left my feet dangling. I tensed up nervously but forced myself to relax; this was Jason, not a stranger. I closed my eyes and took in his scent and the warmth of his body, focusing on the fact that this was Jason.

Mason didn't want to miss out on hug-time, so he stood behind me and wrapped his arms around both of us as much as he could. I was being smushed, so I squeaked out, "Guys!"

Mason stepped back, and Jason let me go, setting me back down on my feet.

"Anna, we missed you!" Jason told me.

"So, what happened?" Mason asked.

"Are you ours forever?" Jason added.

I helped them clean up the post-lunch mess and load the dishwasher while I explained everything that happened. They were both disappointed that a final decision hadn't been made yet, but hopeful that it was just a matter of time. I wasn't as sure as they were, but I appreciated their optimism.

I asked them about Robbie and how his leg was doing. They told me that it was almost healed and that they had an Army medic looking after him. That reassured me, but I still wanted to check on him later.

After we were done cleaning and they were caught up with the day's events, I asked them to show me the indoor gym Austin told me about.

"Oh, yeah," Jason said. "Cody told us that we still weren't supposed to bring you outside."

Mason nodded. "A good workout can sometimes help if you can't go on a run."

I agreed. I needed some kind of outlet, because I had a lot of pent-up energy that needed to be let out.

"Oh, hey! Don't you guys have class today?" I suddenly realized it was midday, and they were at home instead of school.

"Yeah," Mason told me and rolled his shoulders back.

"We wanted to stay here and wait for you," Jason told me with sad eyes.

"But then James realized we were still in bed-"

"And assigned us to make lunch for all twenty of the pack members who were still here." Jason had finished the sentence that Mason had started.

"You poor guys." I laughed at the vision of them scrambling around the kitchen, but my heart melted when I thought about them here, waiting to see if I was going to be allowed to come back.

I wasn't brave enough yet to reach out and hug either one of them, but I gave Jason a gentle shove on the shoulder and reached for Mason's hair. I wanted to muss his like he was so fond of doing to me.

He saw what I was going for and quickly had one arm around my waist, holding both of my arms pinned down and unable to reach for his hair. He used his other hand to muss my perfectly coiffed hair that Quinn had managed to put into place this morning.

"Hey!" I yelled, trying to squirm away from him.

Jason laughed, and Mason let go. I tried to smooth my hair back into place and threw one of my heels at him. They had been lying on the kitchen floor, where I'd discarded them when I first came into the kitchen. I decided to throw the second one at Jason since he had laughed at Mason tormenting me.

They both just caught the shoes I threw at them. "You know girls usually wear heels on their feet, not use them as weapons, right?" Jason asked me as he laughed.

"Weren't you guys the ones who told me not to start wearing dresses and heels?" I laughed.

"We didn't realize how pretty you would look," Mason told me, tilting his head to the side with a grin.

"We're going to change the rule to say you're only allowed to wear dresses and heels for approved events."

I just laughed and shook my head. "Let go get changed and go to the gym," I told them as I headed out of the kitchen.

My skirt was too snug for me to run up the stairs after them unless I wanted to hike it up to my waist, so I lagged behind them. I made it back to my room and noticed my phone lying on the bed, where I left it this morning.

*Now would be a good time to text Kelsey*, I thought to myself.

When I picked up the phone, I realized I missed multiple calls from her and a text that just said: **Call me!**

I was worried. I hadn't expected to hear from her unless I apologized first. I called her back, and all kinds of thoughts ran through my head as her line rang. She didn't pick up, so I sent her a quick text.

**Hey Kelsey! I tried to call you but got your voicemail, is everything okay?**

She didn't respond right away, so I decided to keep my phone on me in case she called again. If I didn't hear from her soon, I'd try again.

Before I even made it to my closet to look for clothes, I heard banging on my door. "Anna, are you naked?"

That was definitely Jason. "No!" I yelled back.

"Well, why not?" he asked me with a grin as he strode into my room. I tossed the phone on my bed and walked to the closet as Jason flung himself on the bed.

"One of my friends was trying to get a hold of me," I told him worriedly. I chewed on my lip as I pulled out yoga pants and a tank top for working out. I shut my closet door part of the way so I could change in privacy but still chat. The closet was bigger than my dorm room had been my freshman year in college, so it wasn't like I didn't have the space.

I heard Mason enter the room. "Less talking, more changing," he called out to me.

I just rolled my eyes as I laid my new outfit down on one of the shelves in my closet after I took it off. I was going to investigate if it needed dry cleaning or washing later. I pulled on underwear appropriate for working out and slipped into my gym clothes but brought my shoes and socks out with me so I could sit on my bed to put them on.

"I'm worried about my friend Kelsey," I told them as I put my shoes on. "I have a bunch of missed calls from her, and she's not answering her phone."

"She's probably just busy. It's the middle of the day. Aren't most people at work?" Mason asked.

I nodded. That could be it; she had probably meetings during the day.

After I tied my shoes, the boys jumped up. "Let's go!" Jason shouted.

I grabbed my phone and headphones and followed them to the gym. Like everything else in this house, the workout room was insane. There was a large area with multiple weight benches and barbells. There were racks upon racks of hand weights, pull up bars, and a variety of weight machines. There was also a mini-fridge filled with water bottles. I took one of those for myself.

I was interested in the treadmills lined up on the right-hand side of the gym. They faced the wall, but all the walls were lined with mirrors.

So even though my back was to the room, I would still be able to see everything going on behind me. I hopped on one of the treadmills and straddled the belt so I could familiarize myself with the controls. Mason headed for the weights, but Jason chose the treadmill next to mine.

I rolled my shoulders and flipped through my phone to find my running playlist as the belt slowly started up.

I settled into a comfortable warmup pace, and Jason eyed the speed I was running at competitively. I reached over to try and grab his emergency stop cord, but he smacked my hand away before I could reach it. Ugh, fine. I did my best to ignore him and ramped up my speed once I was warmed up.

I lost myself in my music and in my run. Running has always been therapeutic for me; it had served as an outlet for all the helpless frustration and anger that built up inside me while I was living in my uncle's house.

Even after I moved out, it had taken years for my anger to fade. While I was living there, fear was my primary emotion. It was only after I moved out and had a taste of freedom that I realized just how much he had polluted and warped my childhood into something ugly.

I spent years trying to repress and forget about my childhood, to no avail. After I was out of the nightmare and realized what life could be like without a constant haze of threat and oppression looming over me, I became angry.

I was angry about what I'd lost. I was angry at the way I'd been treated. I was angry that no one had stood up for me or stopped him. I was angry that no one had recognized the signs of abuse and tried to investigate. I thought about all the signs that should have been obvious to doctors and teachers. But most of all, I was angry at myself.

I'd allowed him to treat me that way. I'd never stood up to him, I never threatened to tell anyone what he was doing. I just kept my head down like a little mouse and hid. I was a wolf, not a mouse! Why had I allowed it?

Because at the time, I thought there were no other options, I finally admitted to myself. I didn't know what life could be like without his torment because I'd never experienced it.

While I was running, I could lose myself in the emotion of certain songs. I could listen to Linkin Park or System of a Down screaming out their frustrations and internally scream out my own. Running helped me release all that emotion and energy in a physical form. After a run, I would feel more relaxed, and the physical aches and pains I felt in my body matched my internal pain in a satisfying way.

I felt a lot of that anger enveloping me now. Anger that I'd missed out on having a pack my entire life. Fury that someone was now trying to take my new pack away from me before I even settled in with them. Hatred for the person who had taken Evelyn away from me. Sadness that Evelyn would never get to experience having a pack who loved her. Outrage that she never had the opportunity to have safety and peace in her life, and now she never would.

I let my anger fuel my run, and I kept turning the speed up until I reached a pace that could satisfactorily burn the anger out of my body.

Finally, exhaustion started to set in after seven miles, and I turned my speed down for a cool-down. I wiped my face with the bottom hem of my tank top, exposing a little bit of my tummy but not caring if anyone saw.

I slowed to a walk and opened my water bottle. I tried not to gulp it too quickly because I didn't want a stomachache. While I'd been running, the guys had been lifting weights. Now that I was paying attention to my surroundings instead of my internal pain, I saw that more of the pack members had come to the gym to work out.

I was a little embarrassed because my clothing was soaked in sweat and my face was bright red, but I told myself not to care.

I hopped off the treadmill with a lot less energy than when I'd hopped onto it before my run. I went over to the back of the gym area where mats were laid out for stretching and gave a wave to the guys as I passed. Most of them gave me polite nods or small waves in return.

I started stretching out after my run so my muscles wouldn't tighten up and tried to ignore that I was the only girl in here. I felt self-conscious when I caught some of the guys looking at my butt out of the corner of their eyes when I bent over to stretch.

I put my headphones back on and changed to happy pop music. That should be enough to keep me distracted and put me back in a positive mood after my run.

Jason came over to where I was stretching and plopped down on the mat next to me. He didn't even pretend to stretch; he just laid back and laced his hands behind his head with his eyes closed, as if he were there to take a nap. If I had anything to throw at him, I would have.

Mason wandered over and tossed another cold water bottle at me. I smiled in thanks and took a few gulps. "You almost done tormenting us guys?" he asked in a teasing tone.

I just stared at him quizzically, and Jason laughed. "Dude, she has no idea what you're talking about."

Mason smiled. "I know. That's part of what makes her so awesome."

I frowned at both of them. "Care to let me in on the secret?"

"Mason's just teasing you because you look hot in your workout clothes," Jason told me seriously.

I looked at him incredulously; I was hot, sweaty, and disgusting. Instead of replying, I just shrugged and said, "You guys done?"

"Yeah-" Mason started to say before my phone rang. I hurriedly glanced down; it was Kelsey. I picked up and headed for the door, so I didn't interrupt anyone else's workout with my chatter.

"Kelsey!" I exclaimed. "I was worried about you when I saw your message."

"Well, I was worried about you," she replied. "What have you gotten yourself into with these shady guys?"

"What shady guys?"

"There were these guys that came by Sunday night after you left," she told me. "They looked rough, like bikers or something."

I gasped, but Kelsey continued without pausing. "When I opened the door to see who was ringing my doorbell, they leaned close to smell me! Isn't that weird and creepy? Then they pushed past me into my house and sniffed around like bloodhounds or something. I was so weirded out, I threatened to call the police."

My heart was pounding. Those had to be wolves she was talking about. Austin or James never said anything to me about sending someone to Kelsey's house. Could it have been Evelyn's old pack? Could they have been looking for me? I felt fear creep down my spine and turned to face the twins.

They had followed me out of the gym and were listening to my conversation curiously. "Did they leave?" I asked Kelsey. "After you threatened to call the police?"

"No!" she said. "They kept asking me questions about 'another female that lived here'. I told them that there wasn't anyone else here, but that a friend visited over the weekend."

A cold hand squeezed my heart. "Are you okay, Kelsey? They didn't hurt you, did they?" I asked, concerned for her safety.

"No, I'm fine," she answered. "They just took your info and left."

"What info did you give them?" I asked her as I chewed on my lip.

"Don't be mad, Anna. I had to give them something! I was scared, and they wouldn't leave!"

"I'm not mad," I told her. "I just need to know what you told them, so I know if I'm safe or not."

She paused. "I gave them your address." My heart dropped. "And I told them where you work."

Jason grabbed the phone out of my hand. "Are you insane?! You told a bunch of men, who you were afraid of, where Anna lives and works back on *Sunday*, and you're just now telling her about it?!"

"Who are you?" Kelsey shouted back at him. "You have no idea what I've been through this week!"

I snatched the phone out of his hand before he could answer. "Sorry, Kels, that was a friend of mine."

"Well, I don't appreciate the way your *friend* just spoke to me, and since when do you have guy friends?" she said snidely. I'm sure she could hear Mason and Jason standing right next to me, cursing about her.

"I'm sorry Kelsey," I said soothingly. "I'm sure you had a good reason for not calling before now. Is everything okay?"

"No! I was stressed out and pissed off at you! First, you ditch me on Sunday, then it's your fault I have a biker gang threaten me!" she yelled.

"I'm sorry," I told her.

"Are you fucking kidding me?!" Mason yelled. He reached for the phone, and I smacked his hand and walked away from him, holding the phone close to my ear.

"Anyway," Kelsey continued. "Because of what you put me through, I asked my boss for an out of town assignment."

I suddenly realized why she was calling. She confirmed my suspicions when she continued. "I'm going to be out of the country for the next three weeks or more. I need you to take the puppies."

Even though I'd worked through most of my emotions while running, I felt a tiny thread of anger rise in me. I pushed it away quickly. Kelsey was just scared; she didn't mean to be hurtful. "Okay, Kelsey, when are you leaving?"

"In a few hours."

"Seriously?" I heard Mason yell from behind me.

"Um, Kelsey, I can't come to your house right now." Austin had specifically told me not to leave the property.

"Oh, I know," she told me. "I figured you would be at work, so I was just going to drop them off at your house."

"No!" I raised my voice at her without realizing it. I tried to calm down before I continued more quietly. "I don't think it's safe at my house, Kelsey. Let me see if they can stay at my friend's house with me. Give me a sec."

"Not the rude one, I hope," she sniffed.

I ignored her and covered the phone with my hand. "Do you think Austin would mind having two additional house guests?" I asked.

They both looked at me as if I were completely insane. "Anna, this chick just deliberately put you in danger, didn't even warn you about it, and now the only reason she's calling you is because she wants something?" Mason growled.

"Fuck her," Jason added.

"I understand how you feel about her," I told them, "but we're talking about two sweet, innocent puppies right now."

"Fuck," Jason said.

"Your heart is too big, Anna," Mason told me with sad eyes.

"But do you think Austin would be okay with it if I told her to drop them off here?"

They looked at each other and communicated silently. They were quiet for a little too long, and I started to fidget. "Well?"

"James said yeah, have her come over," Mason told me, with a tone I couldn't identify.

I ignored his comment about James for the moment and held the phone back up. "Hey, Kels?"

"Yeah," she answered.

"They said it's okay. Can I text you the address?"

"Yeah, just hurry up, I have a plane to catch."

I rolled my eyes when she just hung up; she was still determined to be a bitch even though she needed my help. I texted her Austin's address and hoped there wouldn't be a confrontation when she got here.

I could tell that Jason and Mason were still angry, but I decided to ignore that for the moment. "What's up with the psychic thing you do?" I asked. "Were you just talking to James?"

Mason looked embarrassed. "Um yeah, sometimes I forget you don't know stuff that everyone just knows."

"So, tell me," I said impatiently.

Jason chuckled, the wrath fading off his face. "I don't know, Anna. We're kinda mad at you right now. Maybe we shouldn't tell you anything."

"I'll wipe my stinky sweat on you," I threatened.

"Oh, Anna, I'd love to have your sweat all over me," Jason teased.

My jaw dropped, and I turned red, not sure where he was going with that. Mason punched him on the arm and glared.

Jason rubbed his arm. "Sorry," he muttered.

Mason started to explain. "When you join a pack, you...bond with the other wolves. I don't know if there is a human word to describe the process. You just become one with the pack."

"How does that work?" I asked him doubtfully.

"So, you can magically change into a wolf anytime you want, but you find it difficult we can communicate by thought?" Jason pointed out.

"I didn't say I didn't believe you; I just don't understand how it would work. I mean, are you sending out brain waves, or…" My voice trailed off as Jason snorted in amusement.

"How do you change into a wolf?" Mason prodded gently. "It's not a physical change, your bones don't break, your tendons don't snap, your blood doesn't spray everywhere. If your body had to physically rearrange itself to a wolf form, you would bleed to death before you got very far in the change."

I thought about that for a moment. He was right; one moment I was human, and the next I was a wolf. It was a seamless, painless transition.

"It's magic," Jason told me seriously.

"Magic is just science we don't fully understand yet," I told them stubbornly.

"That's what I said. It's magic," Jason insisted.

I didn't have a better explanation, so I just nodded.

"How does it work?" I asked curiously. "Can you just hear each other's thoughts?"

Mason laughed. "No, you have to project your thoughts to someone, and they have to let you in. It's a little bit different for Jason and I," he continued. "We've been able to share our thoughts since we were born."

"Austin thinks it's because we shared blood in the womb, like in the bonding ritual."

Mason nodded, agreeing with his brother. "For everyone else, it takes a conscious effort. You have to reach out and make contact with who you want to speak with and then try to project a clear, concise thought or emotion."

"It can be challenging for some wolves who didn't grow up in a pack that used those abilities," Jason told me sympathetically.

"But it's useful to be able to speak to each other while in wolf form," Mason added.

"So, what's the bonding ritual?" I asked.

"It's a ceremony," Mason started.

Jason nodded. "You exchange blood with each of the other pack members, and the pack master draws you into a bond together."

"So, when do I do that?" I questioned.

The twins looked at each other.

Jason looked uncomfortable, and Mason shrugged. "Whenever Austin thinks you're ready and the pack is ready to accept you."

"He might just have you bond with a few people first," Jason told me.

Mason nodded. "That way, it won't be too overwhelming for you, and you can practice with the people you feel comfortable with."

"That makes sense," I said thoughtfully.

"If he asks, make sure to tell him you want to bond with us first," Jason kidded.

Mason's eyes lit up. "Yeah! We should definitely be first since we're your designated wolf tutors," he said enthusiastically.

I laughed. "I'll ask him about this pack-bonding thing next time I see him. I want to be psychic with the rest of you."

Kelsey texted me back: **Be there in an hour.**

"I'll race you upstairs!" I shouted, taking advantage of the twin's surprise at my sudden announcement to get a head start. While I was in the shower, I was going to have to figure out a way to keep the twins distracted while I got the pups from Kelsey. Even though I knew Kelsey was just using me as a babysitter, I was excited to have my two sweet little babies back. I loved those little dogs like they were my own, and I hated having to leave them behind with Kelsey whenever she returned.

# Chapter 17

After my shower, I got dressed in yoga pants and a hoodie because I was done dressing nice for today. I put my hair up in a ponytail, and I was ready for whatever happened next.

I bounced downstairs to spy out the front and wait for Kelsey to bring my little pups. I needed some puppy kisses and affection after the last couple days. I glanced at my phone; it hadn't been a half-hour yet, and there was no sign of her outside, so I headed to the kitchen for some more water and a snack.

It looked like some of the other pack members had finished off the fruit salad I made the other day, so I opted for an apple. I surveyed what was left of the food that I'd thought would last the rest of the week. All the sandwich meats and cheeses were gone, the chicken and ground beef were gone. The meat I bought for the pot roast was still there, probably because it would have taken too long for the boys to cook.

I smirked; it looked like we were going to have pot roast for dinner tonight. It also looked like I was going to have to send the twins out for another grocery stop tonight if we wanted breakfast tomorrow. Having twenty to thirty grown wolves traipsing through the house really took a toll on the food stores. I idly wondered just how much Austin spent feeding his pack.

I sat at the counter and started working on another food order while I crunched on my apple.

"Hey, Anna," Caleb gave me a friendly smile as he headed to the fridge. He peered inside to see what was left and seemed almost as disappointed as I was with the selection.

"I'm ordering some more groceries now," I told Caleb. "Any special requests?"

"Pop-Tarts?" he asked hopefully.

I gave him an amused smile.

"What?" he asked. "Pop-Tarts are good."

"Oh, I agree," I told him. "It's just not what I expected from a fierce wolf."

Caleb blushed and sat at the counter next to me, peering over my shoulder as I searched for pop tarts.

"Oh, get s'mores," he told me bashfully.

I chuckled. "Okay, but the frosted cherry with sprinkles are the best."

"No way! The chocolate fudge ones are the best of all time!" Caleb exclaimed.

I laughed, but I ordered him some chocolate fudge Pop-Tarts, along with the s'mores. "Don't forget to hide them somewhere for me," he said seriously. "Otherwise, the twins will eat the entire box and leave the wrappers in the box on the shelf just to taunt me." I couldn't help but laugh; that seemed like exactly something they would do.

"Tell you what, I'll plant some decoy Pop-Tarts in the pantry and give you yours to hide."

Caleb laughed and leaned in close to me. "You're devious; I like it." His low voice got the butterflies in my tummy moving. I gazed into his warm brown eyes to see a mischievous glint there.

"What kind of dinner foods do you like?" I asked him.

We talked about food for a while, and I managed to get a lot of his likes and dislikes down for future meal planning. I suddenly realized it had been a while since I heard a peep from the twins. I had the feeling that wasn't a good thing. Caleb had already gone back upstairs, so I went to look for the two troublemakers.

I headed for the front door to see if Kelsey had gotten here. I expected an '*I'm here*' text from her, but that never came, and it had been well over an hour now.

I was lucky that I'd checked. I peeked through the front door to see that Kelsey was already here and outside in the driveway. She was currently facing off with the twins, and James was heading toward the group from around the back of the house. I hurried outside to try and smooth over what was sure to be an awkward and tense situation.

When I got closer, I heard the pups barking their 'Hey, did you forget me?' barks from inside Kelsey's car.

"Kelsey!" I shouted in welcome.

She didn't take her eyes off the twins. "You need to call off your guard dogs," she told me.

I tried not to laugh out loud. *If she only knew*, I thought to myself.

"I was worried about you. I'm so glad you're here!" I exclaimed. She looked mollified as she turned towards me.

James walked up to the group. "Anna, go inside. I need to talk to your friend."

I simply raised an eyebrow, but Jason snorted. Mason mumbled under his breath.

I ignored James. "I can get the puppies, Kelsey. Do you have a bunch of their stuff with you?"

Kelsey nodded. "I brought their bed and food and stuff. I already know you wouldn't use the kennel, though."

"You keep your dogs in a cage?" Jason asked, horrified.

"They like their kennel," Kelsey told him defensively.

Jason looked like he was going to explode. I stepped in quickly. "Kelsey keeps their kennel door open most of the time, so they can go in and out when they please. They usually go in there when they want to nap because it's quiet and private, like a den."

Jason seemed soothed by that. Mason was still glaring at Kelsey.

"I need to ask you some questions," James told Kelsey.

This wasn't going well. James was acting like his usual irritable self.

The front door opened, and Austin stepped out. I groaned internally; this was about to get even worse. As Austin walked over, Kelsey primped her hair a little bit. "I could use some help getting everything out of my car."

"Okay," I said and started to walk over to the car.

"Not you, Anna," Kelsey told me as she smiled at James.

Was she flirting with James? I stared in disbelief. I guess he would be good looking if he weren't a complete ass, but this was *James* we were talking about.

Kelsey's smile got even brighter as Austin reached our group, and she tossed her hair. I groaned out loud this time, and the guys glanced at me before all turning their attention back to Kelsey.

Austin smiled at her. "You must be Anna's friend. I'm Austin."

"Ohhh," she purred. "The two over there mentioned you're the one who owns the house." She waved a hand toward the twins.

I blinked. It hadn't occurred to me before, but Austin was exactly Kelsey's usual type. He was wealthy and even better looking than any of the other guys I'd seen Kelsey with. I sighed. I'm not sure how I would feel about that, Kelsey dating my pack master.

I felt a little twinge of jealousy and was surprised by it; did I have a crush on Austin? Sure, he was insanely hot, but he was my pack-master. *He had offered to be your pretend mate*, a little voice whispered from inside me.

I pushed the voice away. Any tiny chance of Austin being interested in me would have quickly disappeared when he met Kelsey. I was invisible to men when I was next to her.

To my complete shock, Austin turned away from her to take my hand in his. He turned back to her as he ran his thumb gently over my wrist. "Anna mentioned you needed her to babysit?" Austin asked.

Kelsey looked down at our clasped hands and frowned before taking a step closer to him. She turned the wattage of her smile up and twirled a finger in her hair. "Oh yes, Anna is a good friend of mine. I can always count on her to watch my dogs or help with my housework. Isn't that right, Anna?"

I didn't know what point she was trying to make, so I just agreed. "Um, yeah."

I tried to pull my hand away from Austin, but he held on a little tighter. "Would it be okay if James and I asked you some questions?" he asked Kelsey. "We're worried about you after what Anna said happened at your house."

"Oh, yeah," Kelsey said. "Anna totally set me up and then went into hiding."

I opened my mouth to disagree, but Austin squeezed my hand. "Don't worry," he told Kelsey. "We'll take care of Anna."

"Anna," he turned to me, "why don't you see if you can get the pups settled in?"

I nodded and walked over to get them out of the car. They barked excitedly as I approached and wagged their little tails full-force, so that I couldn't help but smile at how ridiculously cute they were. I opened the car door and let them jump down to the ground on their own. They both danced happily at my feet, so I knelt to give them pets and attention.

My two pups responded to me affectionately with kisses. "Oh, my sweet babies, I missed you so much!" I told them in the high voice I reserved just for them. I heard snickering behind me and glanced back to see all the guys laughing at me. Even James had a smile on his face. Kelsey had an irritated frown.

"Mason, Jason, why don't you help Anna get the things from inside from the car?" Austin suggested.

"You two have rhyming names?" Kelsey asked. "Isn't that a bit too much?" she asked mockingly.

"Hey-" I started to say with a growl.

"Anna," Austin interrupted me with a smile. "Why don't you go show the twins where you want the stuff?"

I fumed, but I trusted that Austin had a reason behind his request. "All right." I grumbled, but I stood and called for the puppies to follow me. They ran after me without even a glance at Kelsey – not that she noticed; she was much too busy gearing up for a major flirt session. The twins grabbed all the puppy accessories out of the car, and we walked back inside.

As soon as the door closed behind us, I whirled around to face them. "Why did Austin call me off like that?" I asked angrily.

Mason shifted the dog bed under the same arm he was using to carry a bag so he could wrap his now free arm around me. "Awwww, Anna, are you defending our honor?"

"Maybe," I grumbled prickly.

Jason laughed at me. "Awww, Anna, it's okay. We know you're a fearsome little wolf who would have ripped that mean girl to shreds for us."

I punched him in the arm, and he just laughed harder. Mason mussed my hair. "We love you, too."

I gave him a pretend glare, but a sense of warmth and belonging filled me. They loved me? A dopey grin spread over my face. The pups were dancing around the twins, trying to get some attention. "Be careful of the pups, guys," I warned the twins. I didn't want anyone to get trampled or tripped.

We set down the stuff in the living room, and when Jason got down on the floor to play with the puppies, they were overjoyed. I dug through the bag Kelsey had packed; she had food and treats and their brushes, but none of their toys. "Your mom forgot to pack your toys," I told them sadly. They watched me and tilted their heads. I know they recognized the word toy, but my sad tone of voice was throwing them off.

Jason jumped up. "I have tennis balls!" He ran out to the garage. Tennis balls were going to be way too big for them to fit in their little mouths, but Jason was too quick for me to stop him. It warmed my heart to see how sweet he was with them.

Eeyore starting sniffing around the floor, looking for a good spot, so I hurriedly scooped him up and ran outside. I sat him down in the grass, and he happily started sniffing there before taking a leak. Mason followed me with Tigger and set him down in the grass next to his brother, chuckling.

I looked at Mason curiously. "So, what was with Jason's reaction to the cage? It seemed like more than just not liking the idea."

Mason cleared his throat. "Yeah, I should probably tell you...make sure you never, ever cage an animal around him."

"Can I ask why?" I said softly.

Mason looked uncomfortable. "When we were kids, we were kind of...a lot for our mom to handle."

I nodded. I could see that.

"When we just got to be too much, she would put us in a cage and leave us there. Sometimes it was for the rest of the day and through the night. No food, no water, no bathroom breaks."

My jaw dropped. "What?"

"Yeah. Jason would panic because when you're a young pup, that length of time seems like an eternity. We never knew when we were going to be let out. I think sometimes he was afraid no one would ever come for us."

"Oh my God..." I was horrified. Who would do that to their children?

I gave his hand a squeeze. "I can't believe anyone would do that to you. Wasn't she at least afraid of someone calling the police?" My uncle had done a lot to me, but he had been limited by the fear that someone would find out.

Mason shook his head no. "She would leave us in our wolf form. No one would even blink at her keeping two puppies in a kennel."

"In your wolf form?" I frowned. "How old were you?"

"Oh, ever since I could remember," he told me.

"How could you change that young? I didn't change until I was ten."

Jason picked that moment to run out of the house with a handful of tennis balls. Mason shot me a warning look, and the meaning was clear: *don't tell Jason that I told you.* I nodded and gave his hand another squeeze.

The puppies ran after Jason and the balls, but the balls were way too big for them to do anything but nudge them with their little noses. I laughed, but Jason looked disappointed. He trotted over to where Mason and I were standing.

"What are you guys talking about?" he asked.

"Mason was just telling me about wolf puppies," I told him. Jason looked at Mason in shock, but Mason just shrugged. "She might decide to have pups one day."

"Huh." Jason looked too surprised for words, so I turned back to Mason. "So, when can kids start turning into a wolf?" I asked curiously.

"Oh, kids can't turn themselves back and forth." Jason laughed. "Can you imagine the chaos? How would you keep them from changing in preschool?"

I just looked at him. "So...?" I asked him with a raised eyebrow.

"A parent or a high-ranking member in the pack can help with the change or even force the change on you if you're injured or unconscious," Mason told me.

"That makes sense, I guess."

"Eventually, kids can change on their own once they're old enough and understand how it works."

"I changed without knowing what I was," I told them slowly. "How could I have done that?"

They looked at each other. "I've heard the first independent change can be triggered by fear," Mason told me.

"Yeah, like you want to escape something so badly that your body responds by changing," Jason added.

I nodded, deep in thought. That definitely made sense. The night I changed, I was afraid for my life and desperate to get away.

The twins were watching me expectantly. I think it was because they wanted me to share the whole story with them. I wasn't ready to share all of my deep, dark secrets, so I tried to change the topic.

"Most of our food is gone," I told them. "I started another order, but I wanted to check with you guys to see if you could pick it up before I placed it." Both guys groaned in response.

"I put bacon, chips, and sandwich stuff on there. Plus, we can get the puppies some toys," I tried to entice them.

"We just have to pick it up, right?" Jason asked.

"Yeah, I'll even start making dinner without you." I was trying bribery now. "And brownies for dessert," I added.

"Deal!" Jason yelled out.

I rolled my eyes, but with a smile on my face. I was starting to relax and enjoy my time with the twins here. A twinge of guilt hit me when I realized I was losing myself in these daily tasks. Had I forgotten why I was here? Evelyn's killer was still out there, and we'd just been attacked by rival wolves. My struggle was far from over.

# Chapter 18

A little bit later that day, I was left alone in the kitchen. I'd sent the guys off to get the groceries and corralled the puppies into one area of the kitchen where I could keep an eye on them. I hummed as I prepared the pot roast. I needed to hurry up and get this in the oven ASAP if we wanted to eat at a decent time tonight. It was going to take about three and a half hours to cook.

When I had the roast in the oven and the timer set, I decided to get started on the brownies. It was way too soon to make them, but I could measure out all my dry ingredients, so later I just had to add the eggs, oil, and water.

Today had gone on forever; the meeting with the council this morning felt so long ago, it could have been yesterday. I reflected on the outcome. I was still a little upset about my failures in the meeting, but I was relieved that nothing would come from it until several months down the road. Anything could change in that time. I might not even have to go through with meeting the other packs. I decided to let myself believe that for now so I could have a good night tonight.

I'd already tried questioning Austin and James about what they spoke to Kelsey about, but they were both tight-lipped. I was hoping to get some more out of them at our late dinner tonight. They'd already been through the kitchen to make themselves protein shakes but had promised to be back for dinner later tonight.

The twins had been gone for longer than they should have needed for a quick grocery stop, so I started to get worried. I texted Mason: **Hey! Did you guys get lost?**

Mason texted me back a picture of Jason holding up a plaid dog sweater and grimacing. I could see a rack of clothing for dogs behind them - they were obviously in the pet store.

My heart melted at these two sweet guys. I had no idea how I'd been so lucky as to get them in my life. I hadn't found anything for the two pups at the grocery store when I submitted my order, the only toys they carried were for much larger dogs. The two guys must have decided to take a ride further into Seaside to go to a pet store with a more extensive selection.

I decided the twins would probably be a half-hour or longer, so I took the pups out for a potty break and contemplated what I should do next. I decided I would go visit Caleb; I'd forgotten to invite him for dinner earlier.

I ran up the stairs and giggled as my two puppy shadows chased after me.

I hesitated for a second before knocking on Caleb's door. Would he be upset with me for bothering him while he was working? I did have a legit excuse: I wanted to invite him to dinner.

I hurried and knocked on his door before I lost my nerve. I quickly regretted it when I heard, "What!?" angrily shouted out.

"Um, sorry to bother you, Caleb, but I was just-" I'd heard some movement when I first started speaking but was startled when the door burst open, and Caleb stood in front of me.

"Sorry, Anna, I thought you were James again," he said abashedly. "He's been bugging me and impatient about some information he wants. I told him that the more he interrupts me, the longer it's going to take for me to get it."

I blushed. "I'm sorry, I should have realized you would be busy working-"

"No!" he interrupted. "I'm working, but you're not an interruption," he assured me. "Please, come in." He stepped away from the door and motioned for me to enter.

"If you're sure it's okay?" I asked him, unsure.

He nodded enthusiastically. "Yeah, absolutely. I could use a break."

I smiled at him and stepped into the room. The two puppies ran ahead of me and jumped up and down at his feet to try and get his attention. He blinked in surprise, just noticing them. "What's this?"

"Oh, sorry. I should have asked if it was okay to bring them in here." I turned bright red. "I'm babysitting my friend's puppies. Austin said it was okay."

"Huh." He looked surprised but bent down to give them some attention. He smiled as they enthusiastically tried to get him to play with them.

"That's Eeyore, and that's Tigger," I said helpfully as I pointed them both out. He gave an amused chuckle and looked up at me.

"I know," I groaned. "I wasn't the one who named them."

Caleb cleared some computer equipment off a chair for me to sit, and then he sat on the floor to play with the pups. I ignored the chair and sat on the floor opposite him with the pups in between us. I touched Eeyore's tail gently to get his attention and then rubbed his head when he barreled my way. Tigger was more than happy to keep playing with Caleb.

"What brings you to my door, Anna?" Caleb asked curiously.

I blushed. "I wanted to see if you wanted to come to dinner. There's going to be pot roast."

He looked surprised, then pleased. "I love pot roast. Sorry your family dinner didn't go to plan last night." He grimaced. "I spoke with Austin earlier today, and he thought it would be a good idea to have more family dinners here at the house."

"Really?" I asked with a huge grin.

He smiled back at me. "Yeah, it's nice to have something other than pizza and wings for dinner. Plus, it was nice, all of us sitting there together..." He trailed off and blushed.

"It was nice," I said softly. "I'd like it if we could do it more - minus the home invasion and drama."

"Oh, of course," he agreed with a grin.

"Soooo..." I said when a slightly awkward silence settled over us. "Whatcha working on?"

Caleb laughed. "I have a bunch of projects. I'm working on getting some satellite images for one of our overseas teams, running the fingerprints, and doing background checks for the two wolves we captured last night. Plus, I'm working on putting some specs together for tech that one of our teams might need for a job coming up. And that's in addition to my usual maintenance and monitoring duties."

"Oh, wow," I said, genuinely impressed.

"Can I ask you something, Anna?" Caleb asked hesitantly.

"Sure," I answered curiously.

He hesitated. "Is your friend male or female?"

Caleb clarified when he saw the confused look on my face, "The friend you're babysitting for?"

"Oh, Kelsey!" I exclaimed in sudden understanding. "She's a girl. Austin, James, and the twins met her earlier. Why do you ask?"

He looked a little embarrassed. "Well, I was just wondering if you had a human boyfriend? You know, because you didn't know any wolves?"

I stared at him for a second in surprise. "Nooo...no boyfriend," I said slowly. "I don't really date."

My thoughts swirled. Was Caleb interested in me? Why else would he ask if I had a boyfriend? He seemed like a nice guy, and he was super cute and sweet. But I was afraid for him to find out just how weird I was. There's no way I could pull off pretending to be a normal girl for any length of time.

I sighed. He was probably just asking because he found it difficult to believe a human guy would ever date me, and he was curious about how the wolf/human dating thing worked.

I was delusional. Why would I ever think a guy like Caleb would be interested in a girl like me? I was so stupid. I finished beating myself up and went back to playing with Eeyore. He had started to look interested in one of the cords that ran across the floor.

"Annaaaaaaa!" I faintly heard a voice calling me from downstairs.

That must be the twins, back from their errands.

"Can you tell them I'm up here with you?" I asked Caleb.

I could tell he used his pack bond when his eyes glazed over, and he stared off into space. Not even a minute later, I heard footsteps pounding down the hall a moment before Caleb's door burst open. Both the twins ran in, and the puppies abandoned me and Caleb for the twins.

Mason and Jason were both carrying a multitude of pet store bags that looked full. I got up to peer curiously in the bags to see what they had gotten. This was more than just a chew toy or two.

They were both excitedly talking over each other to explain all the stuff they had found when Caleb interrupted.

"Can you guys do this somewhere else?" He looked apologetically at me. "There's a bunch of stuff I need to get done so I can come to Anna's dinner."

The guys both nodded. "Anna's making pot roast," Jason told him enthusiastically.

"I heard." Caleb looked at me with a smile.

"I should probably check on it," I admitted. The last thing I wanted was to build up hype for a meal that failed to impress.

"And make sure the twins bring in all the groceries," Caleb warned me.

The twins both grinned, and I held out my hands for Mason to pull me up off the ground. He rolled his eyes but pulled me up and nudged me to the door.

"See you later, Caleb!" Jason waved over his shoulder.

"Make sure you help Anna put those groceries away this time!" Caleb told them.

They groaned again but headed down the stairs with all the pet store items. I tried to steal the bags so I could peek inside, but the guys kept them away.

"Sorry, Anna, we can't let you play until the work is done," Mason teased me and then tossed the bags in the kitchen.

"Yeah, Anna, stop trying to distract us from our chores," Jason added.

I gave Jason a poke in the side but followed them out to the car to help with the groceries. The puppies bounded after us, thinking it was a great game.

We managed to get the groceries put away and have some time to play with the pups while the pot roast cooked. The guys had bought a huge selection of balls, chew toys, and treats for the pups. The guys seemed to have almost as much fun as the puppies did, and I couldn't remember the last time I'd laughed so much.

When dinner was close to being done, I whipped up the brownies to bake in the second oven. Yes, this house had a second oven. Insanity.

The other guys started drifting downstairs as the smell of dinner drifted through the house. I put them to work, setting the table and pouring drinks. Soon, Austin, James, Caleb, the twins, and I were settled around the table outside, ready to try and have a successful family dinner this time. I yawned as I sat down, I hadn't had much sleep last night, and it was getting late. Chances were that I was going to pass out right after dinner.

"This is nice," Austin said with a smile. "It's going to be getting too cold outside for this soon, so Cody is going to get a dining area set up inside."

I glowed with happiness. It was starting to get chilly outside for Virginians. Right now, it was around sixty degrees but would be getting cooler as November set in.

"The guys mentioned you had a dining room you weren't using?" I asked.

"Oh, we're using it. Just not for its intended purpose." James smirked.

"Cody and I were going to make a dining area in the open space next to the kitchen."

I thought about that. There was a 20x20 empty space where the kitchen flowed into the living room. There would be more than enough space there for a dining table, and it would be convenient to have it that close to the kitchen.

"That sounds awesome," I told them, and the other guys made mumbles of agreement. I sliced into my portion of the pot roast; it had turned out perfectly tender and moist.

Caleb made a motion to throw a piece to the puppies, who were happily napping over in the corner. "No-" I tried to yell, but I was too late. The puppies were now aware that not only did we have delicious food up here, but also that we were willing to share.

They gobbled down the first piece Caleb threw and started barking insistently at Caleb for more. I groaned.

"Caleb, I know this is going to sound mean, but we can't feed them anything until we're done eating."

The guys all looked at me in confusion. "Trust me, Shih Tzus are notoriously stubborn. If you teach them to wait quietly until we're done, then they will happily wait their turn to eat. But if you teach them they can have food on demand," I waved my hand at the incessantly barking pups, "then they think they're the bosses and can demand food anytime they want it."

Caleb blushed. "Sorry, Anna. They're just so cute."

"I know." I smiled at him to let him know I wasn't upset.

James wasn't so kind. "Can you make them stop?" he asked impatiently. "Or can you just kennel them somewhere in the house?"

"No!" Jason and I both yelled out. Jason was starting to look agitated, so I hurriedly got down on my knees and called the puppies to me. "Okay guys, I need you to be quiet. I know you know the word 'quiet'." They were quiet for about three seconds before Caleb made some kind of noise, and they ran over to bark at him some more.

Jason was glaring at James, who was glaring at the noisy little pups, Caleb looked embarrassed and was trying to shush them, Mason was watching Jason with concern, and Austin was looking at me with an eyebrow raised. I needed to take care of this quick.

I called the pups back over to me and repeated my commands. They listened for a little longer this time, but when I saw Tigger take a deep breath to start up again, I reminded him, "Quiet," in a soft and soothing voice.

Both the pups watched, and after they were quiet for about a minute, I praised them. "Good quiet! That was a very good quiet!" They got excited at the praise, and I gave them each a dream bone as a treat. They ran off to the corner to gnaw on their treats in peace, so I sat back down at the table. All the guys seemed to relax again.

"We can save them a little bit of the roast for after dinner," I told Caleb with a smile. He nodded at me.

"So, Austin," I started, wanting to change the topic of conversation. "You hadn't mentioned how the chat with Kelsey went earlier. Did you manage to figure out who the guys were that harassed her?"

Austin grimaced. "Your friend is certainly…something." It made me chuckle that he wasn't quite sure what to think of Kelsey. Most guys were just instantly in love with her because she was beautiful.

"Yeah, Anna. Why are you friends with that chick?" Jason chimed in.

I wasn't about to let Jason get me off track from questioning Austin, so I just shrugged.

"What do you think, Austin?" I prodded him. "Who were they?"

Austin gave a nod to James, who sighed. "The wolves we turned over to the council weren't part of a pack," James told me. "They were either paid to try and kidnap you or offered some kind of a reward."

"A reward?" I asked.

"Yes," James replied. "I have some feelers out now, but our concern is that a bounty was put on your head. That could bring all kinds of lone wolves out of the woodwork here to try and attack."

My jaw dropped. "What could be worth it, though? They have to know they would be caught."

"A lot of the lone wolves are desperate," Austin told me quietly. "If there's a pack out there that's offering admittance if they bring you in, it could be tempting. The life of a lone wolf is challenging, and not many packs are willing to accept anyone who has been given the label of lone wolf."

"We don't know that's the case," James interjected. "They may just be offering money."

"Well, that's reassuring," I told him with a little bit of snark in my tone.

Jason laughed, and Mason nudged him to be quiet.

"Do you think it was them who questioned Kelsey?"

James nodded. "We found video surveillance of them at a gas station near Kelsey's house that night."

"Do you think they could have...been involved with what happened to Evelyn?" I asked James quietly.

I was afraid of his answer. What if Evelyn hadn't been murdered by her old pack? What if it had been because of me? Guilt threatened to consume me, and I looked down at the rest of my dinner. I felt nauseous and had completely lost my appetite.

"Hey," James said softly, shocking me with his gentle tone. "As far as we could tell, they weren't involved with that. And I need you to remember, what happened to Evelyn isn't your fault. We're going to find whoever is responsible and make them pay." He was adamant at the end, and I was surprised again. It almost seemed like he cared.

Austin smiled and nodded at me reassuringly. "Don't worry, your entire pack is standing behind you now."

Mason took my left hand, and Jason my right. They each squeezed my hand; they had insisted on sitting on either side of me earlier tonight, and I was glad for that now.

"We're all here for you," Caleb added quietly.

These guys were too sweet; I was about to burst into tears. I squeezed both the twins' hands back and gave the other guys a grateful smile.

James looked uncomfortable. "Don't look so pleased," he told me. "There were also other wolves here last night. Most of the ones we've found so far have been lone wolves, and we're still not any closer to identifying the pack we're looking for."

"Do you think Evelyn's pack is the one that put out a reward for information on me?"

"It's possible." James shrugged. "It seems highly likely that the wolves tracked you from Evelyn's house."

"But it's also likely that more packs will be interested in you now that everyone knows about you. You have some protection now that the council is aware of you, but some of the lone wolves might think that coming after you is a ticket into the pack of their choice. We need to give it time for word to circulate that anyone caught with you will be severely punished."

I sighed. "What about next week when I go home and go back to work?"

The twins looked at me sharply. "I'm not leaving you guys," I assured them. "I just can't abandon my house and disappear from my job suddenly."

Jason stilled eyed me suspiciously, but Mason nodded slowly. "Yeah, you'll probably need to put in two weeks' notice, and we can help you pack up your house."

"Um…well, Austin said you have pack members who have jobs outside of the pack, and you guys go to school all day," I pointed out. "And I would be quitting my job to do what, exactly? I didn't get a doctorate degree so I could sit around all day  and make you dinner every night."

"We don't have to talk about this now," Caleb tried to save me as he looked down and pushed food around on his plate.

"Yes, we do!" the twins said in unison.

James rolled his eyes. "She's not even officially in the pack yet," he told them. "And Austin never said she could live here permanently."

Austin cleared his throat. "Anna is here on a trial basis," he added. "But I was hoping that she would want to stay," he gave the twins a hard look, "without anyone here pressuring her into it."

Mason looked a little guilty, but Jason just looked down at his plate sullenly.

"Whether or not Anna wants to quit her job is up to her," he said, looking at me. "That's something I'll discuss with Anna, and it's not something I want anyone forcing on her."

Everyone at the table nodded, even James.

"But Anna, I'm concerned because I don't think we'll have enough time to take care of everything by next week. Do you have any more leave you can use?"

I shook my head. "I'm covering for LT Sullivan in the NICU next week so she can take her kids to Disney. The only other pharmacist who can cover for her is on medical leave."

"NICU?" Jason asked.

"The neonatal intensive care unit. It's for babies who are born prematurely and need extra special care. Some of the babies born there are only twenty-four weeks gestational age and half a kilogram."

Some of the guys looked confused. "Babies are usually born at thirty-seven weeks or later and are three to five kilograms," I explained. "They need doctors, nurses, and pharmacists who are specially trained and qualified to care for them. There isn't a lot of data on how their bodies will react to treatment, so it can be nerve-wracking to dose antibiotics and other medications to get their bodies functioning correctly."

"Why don't their bodies function correctly?" Jason asked curiously.

"Babies that young aren't just smaller than normal; they didn't have enough time for them to develop fully functional organs. Sometimes they need surgeries to create a gastrointestinal tract or to correct anatomy that didn't develop completely because they came out of the womb too early. Premature babies are especially prone to infection because their immune systems are even less functional than a full-term infant. When you see them in person, their skin is so thin you have to be very careful handling them."

James looked surprised. "I didn't realize what you did at the hospital was important," he told me. "I thought pharmacists just put pills in a bottle."

I rolled my eyes, but I wasn't offended. That's what most people thought; James was just more blunt than most.

Jason looked mollified now, and I sighed with relief. It was becoming more and more apparent that he had some issues with abandonment. I wanted to help him through that, not make it worse. It made me feel even closer to the twins, knowing that they also didn't have a normal childhood. I was feeling hopeful that the three of us would be able to work through some of our issues together. They were already helping me, so I wanted to return the favor.

I was more than ready to change the topic of conversation now. "So, how's the pot roast?"

Most of the guys mumbled, "Good", or something to that effect, and we all went back to eating.

I went deep into thought as I ate. Obviously, my assumption that wolves wouldn't go on my military base was completely incorrect. Cody had gotten on quite easily to track me down. Maybe I could stay in the pharmacy while I was there?

You had to have badge access to get into the pharmacy, and admittance was tightly controlled. I sighed. As long as no one waylaid me on my way in from the parking garage and I didn't go into any public areas, I should be safe. I pushed those thoughts away for now. I had plenty of time to worry about all that before I was expected back at work.

The guys looked like they were finishing up, so I went back into the kitchen to retrieve the still-warm brownies. I developed a fantastic recipe over the last few years. My brownies were fudgy and thick, not like the cake-like brownies that were out of the box.

Every time I brought them to work, my co-workers went insane over them. I was hoping these guys would like the brownies just as much. I liked the idea of being able to do something for them since they had already done so much for me. The guys did enjoy the brownies. I know that feeding them was something small, but it made me feel better inside to know that I could give them a tiny bit of happiness.

After dessert, James and Austin excused themselves to work. I don't think those two took any time off at all. Caleb asked me if he could take the rest of the brownies up with him, which set off a playful fight with the twins. They eventually gave up the brownies when I assured them I was perfectly capable of making more at a later time.

The twins stayed and helped me to clean up. I claimed the little bit of what remained of the pot roast for the puppies and cut it up into tiny bite-sized pieces for them. I was exhausted and ready for sleep. The twins were disappointed when I told them I was taking the pups out for a potty break and then up to bed, but I promised them that we could have another movie night tomorrow.

Exhausted, I was finally able to drag myself up the stairs and to my room. I took a quick shower and collapsed on my bed, snuggling up to the puppies. They settled right down with a couple of wide yawns that matched my own.

Even though my body was exhausted, my mind was still working overtime. I knew the twins wanted me here. I also knew James did NOT want me here. Where did the rest of the guys fall on that spectrum? Would I be overstaying my welcome by hanging out here too often? James had made it clear that the house was for full time, high-ranking members of the pack, and I wasn't one of them. I didn't have anything to offer the pack at all.

I was worried about the rest of the pack viewing me as a useless female who was just taking advantage of the pack and living here for free. From looking at this house, there's no way I could afford to pay anything meaningful towards the mortgage. I doubted I could even afford to keep up with the grocery bill here; I had some pretty hefty student loans I was still paying off every month.

I chewed on my lip. How would I explain to the twins I was leaving, though? I would genuinely miss them. Now that I was accustomed to having them around all the time, their absence left me feeling empty.

I thought about going back home, to my old life. I hadn't realized just how lonely and sad it had been. Tears filled my eyes as I realized how empty it would be now that I no longer had Evelyn. My only friend was Kelsey, and yes, I was aware she wasn't that great of a friend. But who am I to judge? I had social and emotional issues, so I doubt I was that great of a friend to have either.

I thought about Cody, my gentle giant; about Austin, the charismatic leader who wanted to change the world; about Caleb, the brilliant but sweet techie. And James; the more I got to know James, the more I realized there was more to him that appeared on the surface. He acted like an asshole, but deep down, I think there was a good guy. He acted annoyed with the twins most of the time, but when he thought no one else was looking, I saw glimpses of affection. He acted like he hated me most of the time, but he had been gentle with me at one point tonight when he forgot he was supposed to be acting like the tough guy.

I fell asleep with thoughts of all the guys running through my head.

# Finding Somewhere to Belong

# Chapter 19

I woke up when Jason pounced on my bed to shout, "Anna!"

I groaned but then bolted up to make sure he hadn't crushed the puppies. He hadn't; they were on my opposite side and promptly climbed over me to happily greet him. He rubbed both of their heads affectionately. "Mace and I have class all day today," he pouted. "We're going to be gone from nine to four."

I groaned and lay back down. "What time is it?" I asked him groggily.

"About eight," he answered brightly. "Come downstairs. Mason's making coffee."

I groaned again. I didn't want to get up, but now that the puppies were awake, they were going to need to go out.

I gave a huge sigh and heaved myself out of bed as Jason grinned at me. "C'mon, Anna, you got a good nine hours of sleep last night." I gave him a dirty look but lifted the two puppies down to the floor, so that they could race Jason downstairs. I threw a hoodie over my cami and sweats and took a quick bathroom break before I followed them down. Hopefully, Jason realized puppies needed to go outside when they first woke up.

I found Mason alone in the kitchen, so I guess that Jason had taken the pups outside.

"Hey, Anna," Mason greeted me. "You just missed Austin and Cody."

"Oh, I wanted to say hi to Cody before he left." I frowned in disappointment. Cody had been busy last night when the rest of us had dinner. I hadn't seen him since yesterday during lunch.

"Yeah, they both told us to let you sleep. Jason ran upstairs as soon as they left, though." I couldn't help but laugh a little.

"Jason said you guys have class all day today?" I asked him.

"Yeah." He frowned. "Austin and Cody are going to be out all day, and James is going to do whatever it is that he usually does all day. But Caleb is here, and Trevor has a bunch of the guys patrolling the grounds."

I poured a mug of coffee for myself and looked in the fridge for some creamer to make it sweet and delicious. "You think anyone else will be here for dinner tonight? Or will it be just us and Caleb?" I asked him.

He smiled. "This was supposed to be a surprise, but Cody's having a dining room table delivered here today."

I gave him a happy smile, and walked over to where we would be putting it, envisioning all of us sitting there as I sipped my coffee.

"Cody promised he would be here for dinner tonight. He was disappointed that he missed the last two," Mason teased me.

"I should probably make him some brownies," I teased him right back.

"Just him?" Mason asked sadly.

I laughed. "If you guys are nice, he might share some."

Jason ran back in with the puppies chasing him. They ran over to their food dishes and started licking the empty bowls aggressively. "That means they're hungry," I informed the two guys as they laughed.

"Jase, we need to leave in, like, fifteen minutes. I need you to get dressed," Mason told him.

Jason scowled at him. "Does it matter if we're late? Mr. Roberts probably wouldn't even notice."

"If Austin asks, we'd have to admit we were late," Mason told him seriously.

Jason sighed but headed back upstairs.

"Do you guys want some sandwiches to take with you, or do you usually buy lunch?" I asked Mason.

"We would love some Anna sandwiches," he said with a huge grin. I rolled my eyes but turned back to the fridge to see what I could make for them. "You had better get ready, too, Mason."

He laughed. "I'm packed and ready to go. I even have our breakfast protein shakes already made." He motioned to the counter, and I was impressed.

Mason and I put some sandwiches together as he told me about the classes they were taking. "I should start packing you guys lunch bags, like kids get in middle school," I teased him. "I can pack you drinks, a sandwich, and some snacks to bring with you." I nudged his shoulder with a grin.

He looked at me sadly. "We never had lunch boxes or lunches packed for us before."

I immediately felt bad for teasing him. My uncle's wife had never packed anything for me, but she made her own children lunches every day. I used to enviously look at the lunch boxes lined up on the kitchen counter in the morning for them to grab on their way out to the bus.

I guess I'd just assumed that the twins would have also had lunches packed for them. I probably shouldn't have, given what they had already told me about their childhood, but how could anyone not love these two guys? They were probably even more adorable as kids.

Mason looked down at the sandwiches in longing before putting a grin on his face and giving me a nudge back. It was at that moment I decided to get them both some lunch boxes. They made manly lunch bags for men to take to work with them these days; I'm sure I could find something that would work for them.

The guys ran out the door with their bags and sandwiches until I shouted at them that they forgot their protein shakes. Jason ran back out from the car and met me at the garage door to grab them from me. He gave me a peck on the cheek and a grin before running back in the car.

I sighed when I headed back into the kitchen on my own; the house was a lot emptier without them. I rinsed out my mug and put it in the dishwasher for later. The pups needed to go outside for their after-breakfast-potty-time, and then I think I was going to head back to the gym that the twins had shown me yesterday.

# Chapter 20

After the gym and a hot shower, I sat back down on my bed and watched the puppies play with one of their new toys. They had a million different toys that the twins had found for them, but of course, they both wanted the same one. I laughed and played with them for a little while before I decided to go find Caleb and see if he wanted a lunch break.

Caleb opened the door with a grin this time when I knocked. "Hey, Caleb!" I greeted him. The puppies jumped up and down to get his attention until he crouched down to give them some affection. He looked up at me with a smile. "What have you been up to today?"

"Nothing much," I told him. "I was just checking on you to see if I could interest you in some lunch?" Caleb grinned enthusiastically. "Absolutely!"

I laughed and led the way downstairs. "What are you in the mood for?" I asked him.

"Oh no, Anna," he told me with a sweet smile. "You've already cooked for me multiple times, and now it's my turn to return the favor."

I was surprised but sat at the kitchen counter and watched him with curiosity.

"Is there anything you won't eat?" Caleb asked me as he gazed into the fridge.

"Mushrooms and Brussels sprouts," I told him seriously.

"Mushrooms, huh?" he asked teasingly.

"What are you thinking of making?" I asked. The suspense was killing me.

"Someone's impatient." He smirked. "How do you feel about soup and grilled cheese?"

"I love it!" I told him with a huge smile.

Caleb turned to me. "I do have to warn you that the only soup I know how to make comes out of a can."

I giggled. "Totally fine with me."

"I love your laugh," he told me with a grin.

I blushed, embarrassed. I didn't know how to respond, so I changed the subject. "So how does one become a tech expert for a pack of wolves?" I asked.

"Why, do you have your eye on my job?" he teased me.

"No way!" I laughed.

He told me about his past as he cooked on the stove with dramatic flourishes and kept me laughing.

He had grown up in a pack that didn't buy in too much to modern technology. Growing up, he had spent what little money he could earn on his own on tech equipment. "My pack master thought the computer was a passing phase," he told me with a laugh.

I grinned. I couldn't imagine the computer or technology going out of style. So much of what we did was so dependent on technology, and it was tightly woven into our lives. "So, what does he think now that the world is so dependent on tech?" I asked Caleb.

"Oh, he still thinks people will one day decide they want to go back to life before cell phones."

"I have a difficult time imagining that."

"Yeah, I was more than happy to get out of the pack when I joined the Air Force."

"Weren't you worried that you'd be exposed as a wolf?" I asked him.

"Nah." He plated both the grill cheeses before presenting mine with a bow and a flourish.

"Why, thank you, sir," I said with a giggle.

"I've never had a problem keeping the wolf side of myself under wraps," Caleb explained.

"But what about blood testing? Or deployments?" I asked as he placed a bowl of soup in front of me. I enthusiastically picked up my spoon and took a bite.

"They just type your blood. Plus, we have people to keep anyone from getting curious or asking questions like that. The council has an entire team dedicated to keeping our kind a secret. It's not fun to stay in human form for long periods of time, but you can get through it as long as you have other outlets."

"Huh." I thought about that. "So, did you meet Austin in the military?"

"No, I got out after my first four years and used my GI bill to go to college. When I was in my senior year here at Northern Peninsula University, Austin recruited me to the pack."

"We must have been students there at the same time," I told him. "I wonder if we ever crossed paths and didn't realize it."

"Definitely not. I would have remembered you if I'd passed by you at a party or something."

I blushed. I hadn't used my college years to party. I focused on studying, working, and keeping my scholarships. I was a huge dork and had only been to one party in my life. It hadn't gone well at all, but I didn't want to ruin my good mood by thinking back to that mistake.

Caleb kept me entertained by telling me stories about his awkward days in college and trying to fit in at parties. I wished I'd known him back then; my college years would have been much better than the years of isolation and loneliness I felt as an outsider.

I finished up the last bite of my lunch as Caleb told me about a frat that had tried to hire him to hack into the university system to change their grades so they could keep their charter.

I just shook my head. "I'm glad you were smart enough to turn them down. I can see how the money would be tempting for a college student."

He nodded. "If I'd gone to college right out of high school, I might have been desperate enough to fit in that I would've done it. My years in the Air Force gave me discipline and the self-confidence to always do what's right, regardless of peer pressure."

I smiled. Caleb was an awesome guy. "It seems like Austin knows how to find good pack members. Everyone I've met so far is one of the good guys."

Caleb agreed. "He's pretty selective. Austin has gathered people from all different parts of the country and all different walks of life, but everyone must have honesty, integrity, and loyalty."

I nodded. I could definitely see those characteristics in everyone that I'd met so far. Even James, I smirked to myself.

"What's so funny?" Caleb asked.

"I just thought that it must be difficult to get anyone approved by James. I can't imagine him approving fifty different people."

"James is definitely a hard-ass, but he trusts Austin's judgment. If Austin approves of someone, James lets them in with a warning and a plan of supervision."

"He hasn't said anything to me about a plan of supervision," I said thoughtfully.

"He also hasn't let you leave the house," Caleb pointed out.

I nodded. "So, what's going to happen once I have to start living my life again?"

"Do you think you can go back to how things were before?" Caleb asked before taking a bite of soup.

I sighed and paused a moment to reflect. "No, I don't think I can," I said slowly. "I didn't realize how much of life I was missing out on. When I look at going back to my life the way it was before, it just seems…empty."

Caleb nodded. "I felt the same. I'd always been on my own and had always been an outsider. Then Austin let me into the pack on a trial basis, and my life changed. I suddenly had other people to support me and care about me. If I didn't leave my room for a day, I had someone knocking and asking if I was okay or bringing me food."

He smiled at me. "You might not realize it, but you fit in here."

"I don't feel like I have anything to offer," I told him sadly.

"You're the heart. You bring us all together and turn us from a group of guys doing the best they can into a family," Caleb told me with a smile.

"I don't know," I said hesitantly. "You guys already seem like a family without me."

"Do you think any of us would have insisted on 'family dinners?' I think that was something that all of us craved deep down, but no one could put into words. We all want to belong and be part of something larger than ourselves."

Caleb was smart. I wondered if he were right. Could I contribute something valuable to the pack?

"What about pack meetings? Don't you guys have male bonding time?"

He laughed. "No, it's more like a cross between a business meeting and, hmmm, what do you call it in the Navy?"

"Quarters?"

"Yeah, exactly."

An idea suddenly struck me. "How would Austin feel about a weekend barbecue, with the whole pack invited? Not like a 'mandatory fun day'; just a casual 'if you're free, you should come by'."

"I think that's an awesome idea," Caleb told me encouragingly. "I know a lot of guys would come because they want to meet you."

I was starting to get more excited. "We could make it like a pot luck. We could have guys bring meat they want to grill, or some chips or drinks and just hang out here in the house or around the pool." I took a moment to envision that and had a smile slide over my face.

Caleb looked pleased. "I think Austin would like that. I think he wants the pack to be more like a family but doesn't know how to get the guys to buy into that. We have a lot of wolves that were once lone wolves and are nervous about gatherings."

"Aren't lone wolves joining a pack rare?" I asked curiously.

Caleb nodded. "Yeah, Austin takes it on a case-by-case basis."

He hesitated. "Have you met Alex and Tony?"

"Yeah, what's their story?" I asked him. I was curious, Alex and Tony had both helped with the medical treatment I'd given to Robbie, and they both seemed like good guys. Austin had also mentioned that they had spoken well about me to other pack members, so it seemed like they liked me, too.

Caleb cleared his throat and looked down at his empty plate. "Tony had Alex with a human woman."

My jaw dropped. Alex was only half-wolf?

He was just like Evelyn, with one foot in both worlds.

Caleb continued. "The pack-master wanted Alex put out of the pack when it became obvious he would never change into a wolf. Tony refused - he took his wife and son and left the pack."

"Oh, wow. That must have been difficult for them."

Caleb sat his soup bowl on top of his plate and reached out for my empty dishes. "The pack-master didn't take it well. He retaliated by killing Tony's wife."

I was horrified. "That's awful!"

Caleb looked sad. "Tony and Alex have been on their own for the last ten years. They were reluctant to be a part of a pack, but Austin promised Alex a safe place to live. I think Tony only agreed because he was tired of hiding and worried he couldn't protect Alex on his own."

My heart warmed, thinking of how Austin was giving good people fresh starts. "I like Alex and Tony. I'm glad they're here," I told Caleb.

Caleb smiled back at me and then stood to take our dishes to the sink. "Me, too. Alex is a cool kid. He wants to go to school to be a nurse."

"That's awesome!"

"Yeah, Austin offered to pay his tuition if he gets into nursing school and keeps his GPA up. He does the same for the twins when their GI Bill doesn't cover everything."

I was surprised. Austin seemed like he went above and beyond what the usual pack master did to take care of his pack.

"How did Austin meet the twins?" I asked curiously. There was so much that I didn't know about them, and I wanted to know their story.

"They came with Cody," Caleb told me. "Cody was in the Marines with their father; they were like brothers. Cody and Mark spent most of their time together on deployments in Iraq and Afghanistan. Mark had no idea what the twin's mother was doing to them."

"Wow."

"Yeah," Caleb responded.

"So, where is their father?"

"He committed suicide. He came back from Afghanistan pretty messed up. He found out his wife had been sleeping with their pack-master and other males in the pack the entire time they were married. She told him the twins weren't his and that she wanted him out of the house and out of the pack."

"Oh my god. I can't imagine." No wonder the twins had issues with trusting females.

Caleb nodded empathetically. "It was just too much for him. He shot himself."

"Shit." I stared down at my plate.

"Yeah." Caleb sighed heavily. "They were lucky Cody took them in."

"So how did Cody get the twins?" I asked nosily.

"They were angry with their mother and tried to run away. Their mom wouldn't take them back, so Cody kept the twins with him when he could and got out of the military to take care of them. They joined the Marines once they were old enough. Austin recruited Cody to Seaside, but Cody made the twins a package deal."

Caleb cleared his throat uneasily. He probably didn't like telling other people's secrets. "The twins just got out of the Marines a year and a half ago when they were offered different assignments for their next duty stations. They didn't want to be separated."

I could understand that. They definitely had separation issues and were never far apart.

"How did they manage to stay together in the first place?" I asked inquisitively. I always assumed that the military sent you where they wanted you, regardless of where you want to go.

"The Marines offer a 'buddy program'. You can join up with someone, and they guarantee that you'll go to basic training and your first duty station together. After that, there are no guarantees."

"I noticed they don't like to be separated."

Caleb nodded. "Yeah, I've never even seen them agree to sit separately until you came along. They put you right in the middle of both of them. All of us were shocked. I think having you here has been good for them. They've never had an interest in getting attached to anyone but each other before."

"I wonder why?"

"You're sweet, and I think it appeals to them to have someone who needs their protection. But I think they need you even more than you need them."

I couldn't argue, I did need them. But I didn't see how they would need me. "That's why Austin has been okay with them staying close to me?"

"Yeah, I think he and Cody have been glad that you've been keeping their trouble-making and shenanigans to a minimum. They're dangerous when they get bored."

"Well, they are Marines."

Caleb laughed in appreciation. "I could tell you some stories about Marines..."

Caleb and I traded funny stories for a while. I told him how the different branches of the military had been explained to me when I first started working for the Navy. "When the Navy hears the phrase 'secure the building', they turn off the lights and go home; the Marines kill everything inside and set up a base for their operations; the Air Force takes out a five-year lease with the option to buy."

Caleb laughed. "I haven't heard it explained that way before, but it sounds accurate to me," he joked.

Caleb glanced down at his phone in regret. "I'm having so much fun, I hate to say this, but I do need to get back to work."

I glanced at the time; we had spent almost two hours together. "Hey, before you go, can I ask you something as the communications expert?"

I could see him wavering. "What do you need?"

"Can you hook me up with everyone's number?"

He laughed. "I can definitely do that."

He forwarded his contacts for Austin, Cody, the twins, James, and himself. I also asked him for the group message he had for the pack as a whole. I was going to check with Austin first, but I thought it would be a good idea for me to contact the pack for a weekend barbecue.

I wanted to make it clear to everyone that I wanted to get to know them. I thought that offering them beer and grilled meat would make a good first impression.

Caleb was back upstairs, and I was trying to organize all the new contacts in my phone when I heard Cody yell out, "Yo, anybody here?"

I jumped up and skipped to the front door. "Cody!" I said brightly.

"Hey, Anna." He grinned happily at me. "These must be the puppies," he said. He leaned down to give each of their heads a scratch.

"I missed you at dinner last night," I told him.

"Me, too. Sorry I had to miss it."

"No worries. The twins are already jealous that I told them I was making you brownies tonight."

He laughed.

"You do like brownies?" I asked cautiously.

"Oh, yes. I especially like to eat my brownies in front of the twins and tell them how delicious they are."

"I told them you would probably share if they were nice," I teased him.

"We'll see." Cody winked. He walked to the fridge and stared into it for a moment before grabbing a bottle of water.

"The guys delivering the table just called and said they'll be here in the next thirty minutes. I wanted to be here to inspect it," Cody explained after taking a sip of water.

"I'm so excited!" I told him. "Austin said there would be space for us to have family dinners inside now."

He chuckled. "I heard about the family dinners."

"Are you not a fan?" I asked worriedly, taking a seat at the counter with my own bottle of water.

"I am. I just haven't gotten to go to one yet," he sulked with a sparkle in his eye that told me he was joking.

I grinned happily, glad that Cody was going to play along with the family dinners. "I'm sorry, but as a consolation prize, you can pick what we have for dinner tonight."

"Oh, man. I need to think about this." Cody took a seat at the counter, deep in thought.

I tried not to giggle at how serious he was taking this. "I can give you options, based on what we have here."

"Okay." He focused on me, waiting to hear his choices.

I listed what we had and gave some suggestions.

"You know, ever since I moved here, I've become a big fan of southern comfort food," Cody told me contemplatively.

"Ah, I think I have some attractive options I can offer you," I joked.

Cody gave me a suggestive grin. "I'm sure you can."

I blushed but kept my focus on the food. "Bacon mac and cheese, chili, cornbread, and brownies for dessert?"

"Girl, add some fried chicken, and I will be yours forever."

"Deal, but can you handle both fried chicken and chili?" I asked flippantly.

He nodded seriously. "Yes. Without a doubt." He paused. "I don't want to miss an opportunity to taunt the twins, but how do you feel about apple pie instead of brownies?"

I smiled. "Lucky for you, I have vanilla ice cream on hand for such an occasion."

He groaned. "I'm definitely in love with you now."

I giggled. "The feeling might be mutual when I see this table you've promised me." I was surprised at how easily I could flirt back with him.

The doorbell rang in time to save me from further flirting. It was the furniture delivery team. Cody had them bring in a large table and had them set it up with the optional inserts for more room.

I sighed with pleasure when I saw it set up with plenty of room for everyone. Thanksgiving was still a month away, but I had some ideas of what I wanted to do. Hopefully, Austin was agreeable to letting me plan a Thanksgiving dinner here.

I started to get excited. And Christmas? I bet the twins would go along with me planning a real Christmas. When I was growing up, my uncle and his wife would have Christmas celebrations every year. I'd be assigned to cook breakfast while they all opened their presents for each other. They would all laugh and take pictures of each other opening presents while I looked on from the kitchen.

My uncle would be in one of his good moods on those occasions because Christmas meant he could show off on how generous he was. He made sure his wife got their kids all kinds of presents so they could post the pictures on social media and pretend they were a perfect family.

I used to dream about being in a family with who I could have a real Christmas with. I know the twins would cooperate with me, and probably Cody. Austin would probably agree; maybe he would even let me decorate the house for the pack!

I was ready to start dancing around the house in joy at the thought, but I had to force myself to calm down. I didn't know what the pack did for the holidays; maybe they all went elsewhere to celebrate with their families back home?

They were from all parts of the country. Would Cody bring the twins with him wherever he went to spend the holidays? My heart started to sink when I thought of spending the holidays here alone. This would be the first year without Evelyn.

Cody walked over as I tried to push back my tears.

"Is it that bad?" he asked me with concern.

"No!" I said adamantly. "It's that awesome. I was just thinking about the holidays…"

"Oh, yeah." Cody reached an arm around my shoulder and squeezed. I tried to relax. I was starting to be okay with the twins touching me, but Cody was still new to me.

Luckily, Cody didn't seem to notice my discomfort, lost in his thoughts. "Austin will probably go all out for this year's holidays. Our pack is pretty much complete, now that we have you." He smiled at me warmly.

I felt a sense of warmth filling me. It felt like Cody wanted me here just like the twins did. The head delivery man interrupted the moment and asked Cody to sign some paperwork. Cody examined the table for damage before signing for it.

I was starting to get excited about dinner tonight and having everyone there. "Hey Cody?" I asked as he walked back inside from escorting the delivery team out.

"Yeah?"

"Is it usually just you guys for dinner, or do you have some of the other pack members join in sometimes?" I asked thoughtfully.

"If anyone is here working on something, they stay for dinner, but usually it's just us. Why do you ask?"

"I just wasn't sure how much food we would need for dinner," I told him with a shy smile. "You male wolves eat so much, I'm paranoid about running out of food."

He laughed. "Yeah, it's horrifying if you look at how much we spend on food every month. It takes a lot to feed us." He flexed a muscle and grinned. "But it's worth it, right?"

I turned bright red. Um, yeah. It was totally worth it; these guys were seriously built, but there's no way I was going to admit that to Cody.

I just shrugged and started pulling things out of the fridge to plan for dinner. I had a lot of time, but I at least wanted to start the chili simmering in the Crock-Pot. Plus, I kind of needed something to do until the twins came back.

Cody took a seat at the kitchen counter. "I heard you're an expert cook?"

"Oh, no," I told him. "I'm the head chef, but I utilize multiple sous chefs." I pulled out the Crock-Pot and started lining up my ingredients.

"Is that right?" He laughed.

"Yep, what are you doing now?" I asked facetiously.

He grinned ruefully. "Um, helping you prepare dinner?"

"Excellent answer," I told him assertively.

I set him to work peeling apples after I assured him there was no way possible that he could mess it up. He watched me dance around and sing to the puppies as I measured out ingredients for the chili into the crockpot.

"You know, I was a little nervous about you joining the pack, but now I'm glad you did," Cody told me thoughtfully.

"Really?" I asked, a little hurt. He hadn't wanted me in the pack?

"I didn't think you liked me the first couple times we met," Cody told me honestly, watching for my response.

I cleared my throat. "I was nervous about meeting another wolf. You were my first." I blushed at how that came out and turned to mess with the dial on the Crock-Pot to hide.

He chuckled. "Well, as your first, I hope I didn't disappoint."

I turned even redder. "Um…" I tried to think of something to say. "You're kind of a big guy. I was a little intimidated."

He burst into laughter, and I realized a second later how bad that sounded. "Um…I mean-" I couldn't even think of one thing to say to make this less awkward.

"I meant that you're tall…" I tried to explain self-consciously.

"I know what you meant," he told me reassuringly. "Austin filled me in later about your past. I think if we had known more about that, we would have approached you differently."

"Uh–" Now I *really* didn't know what to say. Exactly how much did they know about my past?

"I meant about your fear of being found by wolves," he clarified.

I nodded as if I hadn't come close to having a panic attack. "Yeah, I realize now that everything I heard about wolves might not be true, but I'm still learning."

"You're handling all of this quite well. I think all of us were expecting you to have a mental breakdown," he told me bluntly.

"Well, the twins have helped me a lot," I told him honestly.

He smiled at me. "I'm glad. I was worried about how they would react to you, and about how they would react to a female wolf in general."

"Yeah, I understand they may not have had great experiences with female wolves in the past," I said absentmindedly, measuring out spices for the apples that Cody was almost finished cutting.

"That's putting it mildly. They blamed their mother for a lot of things that went wrong in their lives." He set down the paring knife and started to gather up all his apple scraps to toss in the trash.

"I don't know exactly what happened, but it sounded like she *was* to blame for a lot," I told him pointedly.

He shrugged uncomfortably. "I blame myself for not being there enough. I'm not sure exactly what happened, and they aren't exactly open about it. I was here for the last time Austin tried to bring a female into the pack, though."

"Really? I haven't heard that story," I prompted him curiously. I knew these guys didn't have great experiences with females, but I didn't realize that I was the second attempt to bring a female into the fold. That was going to make things even more difficult for me to fit in.

"Yeah, she was nothing like you," Cody assured me. "She was more of a typical wolf. She thought that as the only female wolf, she could come in here and run things."

"I hope you guys don't feel the same way about me," I said anxiously, sprinkling my sugar and spices over the bowl of apples that Cody had cut.

I was worried. Wasn't that what I was doing, though? I was trying to make them have family dinners, monopolizing the twins' time, and spending Austin's money. Not to mention, my mere presence was causing other packs to attack them. I was essentially causing them to risk their lives to protect me.

I chewed on my lip. Was it actually a good thing I was here? Maybe James had a legit reason to hate me.

"I promise you're the day to her night," he told me confidently. "You have nothing to worry about."

I looked at him doubtfully.

"She treated the twins as if they were her personal servants and complained to Austin when they rebelled against her. She wanted them kicked out of the house, and possibly out of the pack. I told Austin that if they go, then I go."

"I'm glad that Austin chose you guys over her," I told him genuinely. "I would rather have you guys over a chick like that, any day."

He smiled at me. "Glad to hear it. The twins can be a lot to handle sometimes, but they're good guys."

"I know," I told him seriously. "They've already helped me so much, and I can't imagine my life without them now. I honestly feel sad when they leave for classes."

Cody gave me an affectionate smile. "I hate to tell you this, but you're in the minority. Most people can't handle them for long periods of time."

"I think they're sweet, and kind, and funny," I told him honestly.

"They've definitely shown you a side of themselves that they don't show to everyone. They don't give you a hard time at all?" he teased me with a glint in his eye.

"Sometimes, but I know they do it out of affection, not because they wish me harm. Besides, I can always just punch them in the arm if they get out of line."

He let out a loud belly laugh. "I do see why they like you."

"Should I be worried that they offered to play paintball with me?" I asked apprehensively.

He smirked. "Only if they team up against you."

I grinned. "Then I need to make sure one of them is on my team, or it's every man for himself."

Cody laughed. "I highly doubt they'll agree to be on opposite teams or that they'll be able to resist teaming up, even if it is every man for themselves."

I laughed. "So, I'm screwed."

"Yep," Cody sniggered.

I was done making the chili and had set it to cook in the Crock-Pot, so I decided to make the crust for the pie. Cody walked over to the sink to wash his hands. He decided to be funny and flick some water at me. I waited until he started to walk away from the sink and grabbed the hose to spray him.

"Hey!" he shouted, trying to block the water from his face.

"You started it!" I yelled back at him.

Jason ran in. "Water fight! We got back just in time!"

I was giggling as Cody tried to wrestle the sink hose away from me.

"I got him, Anna!" Jason shouted as he tried to put Cody in a headlock. Cody somehow ended up having Jason in the headlock instead.

"You're going to side with Anna? I see how it is!" Cody rubbed Jason's hair into a mess as he howled.

Mason walked into absolute chaos but took it all in stride. He merely rolled his eyes. "This is what happens when we leave you alone for the day, Anna?"

I just giggled more as Mason got in on the wrestling match. It wasn't long before Cody admitted defeat and went upstairs to change out of his soaked clothes.

"Whatcha making, Anna?" Jason investigated the contents of the Crock-Pot carefully. "Is this chili?" he asked excitedly.

"Yep, Cody picked dinner tonight since he got us a table." I gestured toward the table now in the space connected to the kitchen.

"Awesome!" Mason said. "Now we can have family dinners inside!"

I shared a grin with him, pleased that he shared my enthusiasm.

"What are we having with the chili, though?" Jason asked, his voice sounding concerned.

I had to laugh at how concerned he was over the menu for dinner. "We're having bacon mac n' cheese, cornbread, chili, and apple pie with ice cream."

"What!" Mason exclaimed in excitement.

"I'm guessing the menu is approved by you guys?" I asked dryly.

"Oh, yeah," Jason told me. "I'm not even upset that brownies were taken off the menu. I love apple pie. We had one for Thanksgiving last year!"

I felt better about my situation here, knowing that doing something as simple as making them a homemade meal could make them so happy. But I didn't want them to get used to me doing everything for them. I wasn't going to set myself up to be their housekeeper and maid.

I didn't mind doing extra when I was off from work, and they needed to go to school, but once I went back to my job, I wasn't going to have this much time. "You guys know I'm going to make you help me set the table and do some prep, though, right?"

Mason groaned, but he had a grin on his face, wide enough to match Jason's. Jason wasn't phased at all by that proclamation. "Do the pups need to go outside before we do that?"

The puppies both got excited when they heard the word 'outside'.

"I think that's a yes," Mason said wryly.

"Let's go!" Jason told the puppies and ran so that they would follow him outside. I laughed at how cute it was to watch them fall all over each other in an attempt to be the first to reach Jason.

Mason gave a chuckle and stood next to me. He bumped his hip into mine. "How was your day?"

"Good," I told him. "How was class?"

He made a face. "Boring, but we liked your sandwiches."

I smiled. "So, let's just say that Amazon showed up with some lunch boxes one day. Would you guys use them?"

Mason looked delighted. "If they were packed by a pretty wolf named Anna, I would use mine and make sure that Jason used his."

I gave him a secret smile. "Good to know."

I walked over to the fridge and got out a couple of blocks of cheese. "I need you to grate." He pretended to look upset, but I could tell that he was still pleased with the idea of having his lunches packed. "Do you want to grate by hand or use the automatic?" I asked him.

"Automatic?" he said, obviously not sure what he was getting into. I showed him how to use the food processor attachment to grate cheese, and he seemed pleased with how easy the task was.

Jason wandered back in as he was finishing up. I didn't trust either of them with anything other than raw material prep yet, so I asked if they had any assignments for class. They admitted they had a paper due the next day.

"Write your papers while I finish up dinner, and I'll proofread for you," I told them both.

Jason eyed me dubiously, and I rolled my eyes. "Out of the three of us, I'm pretty sure that I'm the only person here who has had papers published in peer-reviewed journals." They both raised their eyebrows.

"Sorry, Anna," Mason said. "I can't get used to the fact that you're super-smart and well-educated."

I threw a piece of sliced apple at him. He just grabbed it out of the air and ate it with a grin. "Love you, too."

"You guys are lucky you're so cute," I told them both.

They looked pleased but pulled laptops out of their backpacks and started to work.

I slid the apple pie in the oven to bake and started mixing up the mac and cheese. Cream cheese was my secret ingredient; it made it super creamy and delicious. I used the food processor to blend all the ingredients perfectly. Once I was satisfied, I mixed in the pasta and set it aside to bake once the apple pie was done. I started to fry up some bacon to add to the mac and cheese before I baked it.

The twins looked like they were still working, so I started on the cornbread while the bacon fried. I was going to make it a sweet cornbread to go with the spicy chili and the salty bacon flavor of the mac and cheese.

The smell of bacon had the twins distracted, so I let them steal a couple of pieces before sending them back to work. I crumbled the bacon into the mac and cheese and stirred it all together before it was time to take out the apple pie.

I set the pie down on top of the stove to cool down and thicken up. It was time to put in the mac and cheese. I set the timer so that I could add the cornbread to the oven when it was about halfway done; that way, both would be done at the same time.

With my tasks done for the moment, I took a seat next to Jason and peered over his shoulder. "I have almost two pages done," he told me defensively.

"What is the assignment?" I asked.

"We need to write a three to five-page paper on how we would handle a product recall situation," Mason explained.

"Oh, lucky for you, product recalls happen a lot in pharmacy," I told them both.

"Really?" Jason asked. "How do you usually disclose that to patients?"

I explained to both of them how the product recall situation worked in a pharmacy and how it's handled differently in a retail versus hospital setting.

I also explained the public relations difficulties that were involved. There was a lot more involved when I was interning with an independent pharmacy who manufactured their own medications in comparison with a chain pharmacy that simply distributed them.

They both asked a couple of relevant questions and went back to working on their papers with renewed vigor, so hopefully, my opinions had been helpful.

I jumped up when the timer when off to tell me it was time to add the cornbread to the oven. I checked on the mac and cheese while I was in there; it smelled amazing. The apple pie also smelled delish and looked like it was cooling perfectly.

I heard the front door slam and footsteps head in our direction. The puppies ran to greet whomever it was, and I was worried when I just heard only silence in reply. I started to head in that direction when James appeared in the kitchen doorway. He was eying the puppies, who were jumping up and down in front of him to try and get his attention, but he didn't respond to them.

"What's for dinner?" he asked gruffly.

I looked at him, and then I looked at the puppies begging for his attention with a raised eyebrow. He got the message and bent down to pet the pups with such a faint smile that I almost missed it. I tried to hide my own smile. He liked them; he was just afraid to show it.

After he greeted my sweet little babies, I answered his question. "Per Cody's request, we're having bacon mac and cheese, chili, fried chicken, cornbread, and apple pie."

James looked interested. "Do we have ice cream?"

"Of course, we have ice cream," Jason answered absentmindedly as he worked on his laptop. "Anna was in charge of shopping. She never misses anything."

I rolled my eyes. I was sure that he was still just trying to get all the shopping duties assigned to me. Deep down, I was still a little flattered, though. I was useful, even if it was just to make sure we had ice cream.

I sighed to myself; I needed to start small. It might just be ice cream today, but one day, I would be an integral part of the pack.

"Why does Cody get to pick what we're having for dinner?" James asked. Was that a hint of jealousy I heard in his voice?

I hid my smile. "Cody missed the last two family dinners, and he got us a new table to eat at." I motioned to the new addition.

James walked over and ran his hand over it. "This is nice."

I nodded. "Could you set the table while I work on the fried chicken? The twins are busy with homework that I need them to finish before dinner, so I have time to review it."

James' jaw dropped. He looked at me, then he looked over to the twins working, and then back to me.

Cody came back into the kitchen before James had a chance to respond. "Anna, that smells amazing! Austin won't be back for another half-hour or so. Can dinner wait?"

"Yeah," I told him. "I haven't started on the chicken yet, and everything else can stay in the oven until we're ready to eat. "

"Cool," Cody said. "Trevor might come by with some of the guys. Is that okay?"

"Of course," I answered enthusiastically. "Can you help James set the table while I finish this and the twins finish their homework so we can eat on time?"

Cody gave James an amused look. "I'll get the dishes, if you get the silverware."

James sighed in resignation but walked over to the silverware drawer. I was proud of myself for how successfully I was able to hide my smile.

Caleb was the next person to make his way to the kitchen. He eyed Cody and James setting the table incredulously. "How did you manage that?" he whispered to me.

"I think it was more the tantalizing scent of food than anything that I said," I told him sincerely.

He chuckled. "What can I do to help?"

"Can you fry while I bread?" I asked him.

He looked at me doubtfully.

"You just have to make sure the chicken stays in the oil, and nothing catches on fire," I told him reassuringly.

He chuckled. "I guess I can handle that, but if anything catches on fire, I'm blaming you."

"Deal," I grinned at him.

The twins started to hover over both of us once we had some of the fried chicken ready for eating. I kept smacking their hands away until Austin came in.

"Time to eat!" I shouted loudly.

"Finally!" James groused.

"Yeah!" Jason leapt over to the table with enthusiasm.

"Jason!" I scolded him. "Take the mac and cheese to the table. Mason, you're in charge of the cornbread." I carefully handed them each a dish to carry over to our new table.

"James, I need you to help with the chili." He came over to the Crock-Pot without a word of protest, and I handed him the ceramic dish out of the Crock-Pot carefully wrapped with a hot pad on each of the handles.

"I think the last pieces of chicken are ready!" Caleb called. I walked over to check on them and add them to the serving dish that I asked Caleb to carry over.

Austin walked over to me and chuckled. "You put them all to work, huh?"

"You'd be surprised what hungry wolves will do for food," I joked.

He laughed but walked over to the table with me. "This table looks great, Cody. Thank you for getting it for us."

"Yes, thank you, Cody!" I added enthusiastically. The rest of the guys added in their thanks.

"And thank you, Anna, for coordinating this delicious meal."

I smiled. "Thank you to everyone who helped."

James groaned. "Do we have to keep thanking everyone or can we eat?"

"We don't have to thank anyone else, just pass the food around!" I told him.

Everyone laughed but started making their plates. I grabbed some sour cream and cheese out of the fridge for the guys to add to their chili.

"Austin?" I asked.

"Yeah?"

"Are we having more guests? Cody mentioned Trevor might stop by with some other guys."

"Oh, yeah." He glanced at his watch. "He'll probably be here any _"

I heard the front door open and a shout, "Yo!"

"We should start using Marco Polo," I told Austin seriously.

Jason snorted, and Mason laughed. James looked confused, and I think Cody was just so happy to be eating, he didn't hear a word that was said.

Austin smiled and shook his head at me. "In here!" he shouted back.

I stood up to grab some extra plates out of the cupboard and hand them out to the three guys as they walked into where we were sitting. They each greeted me with a 'Hey' or a nod and took a plate.

Austin stood up. "Anna, I don't remember if you've met Trevor, Rich, and Davis."

I nodded. I had, but I appreciated the reminder of everyone's names. The three latest additions to the dinner party helped themselves to food while I grabbed them some silverware.

"Did you cook this?" Trevor asked.

"Oh, everyone helped," I told him.

All three guys eyed me and then the food dubiously. "Who helped?" Davis asked.

"Relax," Caleb assured them. "Anna supervised everything. She just had the rest of us grate cheese or do the easy tasks."

The guys all relaxed and continued to help themselves.

"I feel like there must be a story behind you guys being nervous about eating food that was prepared by the group here?" I asked Rich, since he was the only one who was still waiting for food to be passed to him.

Rich chuckled. "Does anyone else here remember the Thanksgiving of 2018?"

A couple of the guys groaned. "Everyone got sick," Caleb told me.

"What happened?"

"No one will admit to anything going wrong, but we all blame the twins."

"Hey!" Jason said defensively.

Mason shrugged. "We're infantry Marines, not cooks. The only cooking I've ever done is heating up an MRE."

Everyone at the table laughed.

"Well, if Anna's cooking, then I'll be more than happy to come this year," Davis announced enthusiastically as he shoveled a helping of chili into a bowl. The rest of the guys seemed to agree.

I smiled. It looked like I might get a family Thanksgiving this year. "Do you guys celebrate Christmas, too?" I asked hopefully.

"Oh, yeah," Jason said enthusiastically.

Mason nodded. "Austin let us have a tree last year!"

"We tried to make eggnog..." Jason started.

"Let's not talk about that." Mason interrupted, to the amusement of everyone else.

I just giggled. "Can we have a tree this year?" I asked Austin hopefully.

"Of course," he told me with a smile.

I settled back in my chair as the guys shared stories of past Christmases here with the pack. This was going to be so awesome.

The food quickly disappeared. When I saw Davis sadly scraping the chili pot in an attempt to get the last of it, I jumped up. "Who's ready for apple pie?"

The twins volunteered to clear everyone's plates and put them in the sink to wash later. I went to get some dessert plates out of the cupboard, where I'd decided to store them yesterday. I handed the plates to Jason and asked Mason to get the silverware while I grabbed the pie. I asked Caleb to go back for the ice cream.

The pie was still warm when I cut into it, but no one complained, as it was a perfect combination with the cold ice cream.

Davis leaned back in his chair. "Is it okay if I show up here every night for dinner from now on?" he asked Austin jokingly.

"Yeah," Rich added. "I'm fine with extra guard duty if I get dinner."

"I'll remember that when I make the schedule," Trevor said gruffly as everyone laughed.

The whole group was leaning back with full bellies, so I decided to call tonight a success.

"I need to see you three in my office before you go," Austin told Trevor, Davis, and Rich. The three of them nodded and made a move to get up. Austin also stood. "Cody?"

"Coming," he groaned before heaving himself up to his feet. I couldn't help but giggle.

"It's not my fault you make such delicious food, Anna," he told me as he gave me a kiss on the forehead. I pressed my hand up to where he had given me a kiss with a dopey grin on my face.

James looked at the twins sternly. "Anna cooked, so you two can clean up while she looks at your homework."

Neither of them groaned or complained; they just nodded. James stood and headed out of the room. Caleb looked at me. "What are you doing after that, Anna?"

"We get Anna tonight!" Jason interrupted.

Mason gave him an exasperated look but added, "Anna already agreed to movie night with us."

"Is movie night just for Anna?" Caleb asked.

"Do you want to come, too?" Jason asked. "Tonight is Thor."

Caleb nodded. "I love that movie."

"Me, too!" I said enthusiastically. I stood up and headed to the twin's laptops. "The sooner we get our work done, the sooner we can play," I told them both with a cheeky grin.

They both laughed at me but cleaned up after dinner. Caleb helped them with the dishes while I reviewed the final copy of their papers.

"Do you guys need to email or print them?" I asked.

Jason just shrugged, and we both looked at Mason. "Email is fine," he told us. They emailed their papers into the professor, and it was movie time!

We all settled down to watch Thor, and despite my long-time crush on Chris Hemsworth, I didn't even make it halfway through the movie before I passed out. At the end of the movie, I woke up groggily in time for Mason to scoop me up with a murmured, "Come here, pretty girl."

He carried me upstairs and to my bed. I yawned and crawled under the covers. Jason got in the bed on my right, and Mason on my left.

I should probably feel self-conscious that I was in bed with two men right now, but honestly, it just felt right. I nuzzled my pillow, and Mason absentmindedly rubbed my back, as if to soothe me back to sleep.

Not too long ago, I would have been a bundle of nerves and anxiety at the thought on being this close to two men. Having even one guy in my bed would have probably caused me to have a panic attack. But now, having the twins here with me just made me feel safe and protected.

Being here with the pack gave me a sense of belonging that I hadn't realized I was missing in my life. I'd thought that there was nothing more that I could want in life after achieving my goal of being a pharmacist and being able to provide for myself.

I'd always prided myself of being self-sufficient and never wanted to put myself in the position of needing anyone. I wanted to be able to exist completely on my own. Now that I was here with the pack, I realized that I may have been off-base in my goals. Yes, it was important to be able to take care of myself, but what about everything that I'd been missing out on while I was alone?

I'd never truly let go and tried to enjoy life before. Being with the twins and joining in on their shenanigans made me realize that life was a lot more fun when you had people to share it with. Having people in my life could make it better, not everyone was out to take something from me.

I drifted back off to sleep with the scents of the twins mingling with my own in my bed. My last thought for the day was how glad I was that I finally found somewhere to belong.

NOTE FROM THE AUTHOR

Everyone has dark moments in their life that we sometimes wish we could erase or forget. But sometimes it's the pain and struggle that we have gone through that gave us our inner strength.

For me, writing started as a way to confront some of the demons of my past so that I could put them behind me forever. Most of my characters have a dark or troubled past and my books follow their progress as they emerge from the darkness that has held them down for so long.

As the darkness fades, hope for a better future starts to emerge (like the sun after a storm). A piece of my soul goes into each one of my books, and my hope and faith in a brighter tomorrow is reflected in each one of my characters.

Books have always been a source of escape and enjoyment for me, so I hope that my work can help others in the same way☺

-C.C. Masters

# ABOUT THE AUTHOR

C.C. Masters lives in Virginia Beach with her two furbabies, the inspirations for Tigger and Eeyore. She enjoys long walks on the beach and loves to run through the forest under the light of the full moon☺

SeasideWolfPack.com

## Books by C.C. Masters

### Seaside Wolf Pack Series
Book 1: Finding Somewhere to Belong
Book 1.5: Finding Anna
Book 2: Finding the Fire Within
Book 3: Finding the Power Within
Book 4: Finding Truth Beneath the Lies
Book 5: Finding My Breaking Point
Sam's Book: Finding Buried Treasure
Book 6: Finding Hope

### Hollow Crest Wolf Pack Trilogy
Book 1: New Beginnings
Book 2: The Struggle
Book 3: A Place to Call Home

Made in the USA
Columbia, SC
26 September 2022